The Gathering

The Watchers Series: Book 4

Eilidh Miller

Copyright © 2021 Eilidh Miller

All rights reserved.

Eilidh Miller has asserted her rights under the Copyright Designs and Patents Act 1988 to be identified as the author of this work. This book is sold subject to the condition that it shall not, by way of trade or otherwise, be lent, resold, hired out, or otherwise circulated without the publisher's prior consent in any form of binding or cover other than that in which it is published and without a similar condition, being imposed on the subsequent purchaser.

This is a work of fiction and any resemblance of the fictional characters to real persons is purely coincidental and non-intentional.

Cover Design by Matthew Weatherston

Griffith Cameron Publishing

ISBN - 978-1-955212-04-5

THE GATHERING

CHAPTER 1

Grace walked through the halls of Council headquarters, looking for all the world like a young woman with a singular focus, someone whose way one would be smart not to be in. It wouldn't be an incorrect assumption by any means, but the assumption as to just what that focus was on would be harder for anyone outside of her head to guess. She'd decided to take some time to come here while Euan was busy training. It was something he liked to do, something that kept him agile and in practice, and he'd pulled her in to teach her so that he'd have someone else to work with. There were times, however, like today, where he'd decided to go through some of the exercises alone. Normally when he did that, she liked to sit and watch him, amazed by how fluidly he moved from one guard to another or one strike to another. It seemed like it should be impossible for someone his size to move the way he did, and it was easy to get lost in simply watching.

Today, however, she'd made excuses to skip that and come here instead because something was weighing on her mind. There were so many questions, and she knew she needed answers, or she'd never be able to get around it. Ever since Euan had revealed to her and the rest of The Council that his skill set for war was far beyond what they'd known or imagined it to be, something had been nagging her. Euan was a warrior, one who'd survived every battle he'd fought in due to his skill with a blade, but he'd served other purposes, too. Tactics, strategy, movements, lines. He'd been heavily involved in the strategic decisions for both Prestonpans and Falkirk, and both had resulted in massive losses for the Hanoverian army because of his involvement.

More than that, he was skilled at intelligence gathering, at psychological and guerilla warfare, though it hadn't been called that then. It wasn't that she hadn't known, or at least suspected because of the parts he played in their missions, but it was the *depth* of his skill in those arts. It was this detail that ate at Grace and was why she'd come here: she had a suspicion and needed to confirm it. She hoped she was wrong, *prayed* she was wrong, and the archives were the only place to find what she was looking for.

As Grace stepped into the massive space that housed the Council Archives, she smiled at the woman sitting at the front desk. "Good morning."

"Good morning, Watcher Cameron! What may I do for you?"

"I need to do some research, and I need a timeline event pulled for me if you can, please."

"Of course. Which one?"

Grace handed her a piece of paper. "I need what happened just before this and what happened in the two days after."

The woman raised an eyebrow and looked up from her terminal at Grace. "Did you not work this one? Are you sure you want to see it?"

"I did, and yes, I am. I was pulled before I could see what happened."

The woman nodded, entering the information to locate what Grace needed. "It will be waiting for you at research station one, Watcher Cameron."

"Thanks," Grace said, heading past the desk to where the research stations were located. Each one was a soundproof room with no windows to facilitate any watching of footage or anything else the archives might have. Grace knew there would be no footage for this file, it would be impossible to have unless they pulled it from Observation, and that seemed unlikely. What they *would* have was a detailed report of the attempted change, what was done to stop it, and what happened afterward, and it was this report Grace was after. Sitting down in the chair, she pulled the report up on the terminal and scrolled through the brief discussing what the mission was about. She knew that part; she'd been the one to work it.

When Grace reached the section about what had been done to stop the mission, she read it over even though she knew what she'd done.

"Watcher Evans prevented the successful attack at Nairn by ensuring that the forces of the Jacobite army did not meet each other as planned due to O'Sullivan missing his contact target in the darkness when she caused his horse to startle. Watcher Evans also ensured that the Hanoverian forces became aware of the pending attack, leading them to skirmish with some of the Jacobite army who had continued with their original plan unknowingly."

Grace sighed, and although she knew she shouldn't regret this, she did. She'd regretted it from the moment she'd realized the connection to Euan's fate. It was the letter she'd forged and left with Cumberland that had been part of the downfall of this planned attack, the one that made sure the Jacobites would still lose at Culloden the following day as they were supposed to. Once O'Sullivan missed his target, Grace was pulled out, but according to the report, some of the Jacobites continued onward, and the revelation made her uncomfortable.

"After Watcher Evans' departure, some men were captured in the skirmish between the forces, though the main body of the Jacobite army had already retreated to regroup for the battle later that day. The private men were of the Atholl and MacPherson regiments, but one was an officer in the Cameron regiment. The private men were held, but the officer was summarily executed the following morning after being marched from Nairn to Culloden. This resulted in a delay of the battle by two hours with no change in the result."

Grace gasped, covering her mouth and squeezing her eyes shut, feeling sick to her stomach and desperate to get away from the words on the screen. She'd not been wrong, no, it was the thing she'd most feared when she'd come here. It was so much worse than she'd known, much worse than they'd told her. She'd always felt horribly guilty over what she'd felt was her indirect responsibility for Euan's death at Culloden, no matter what he or any of them said, but this was far worse. Euan was involved in the planning and execution of what would've been a successful attack at Nairn if she hadn't stopped it. It was successful because of *him*. Knowing his skills, the chiefs must have asked him to plan it and run it; something they hadn't done before. *That* was the change she hadn't been able to figure out and why she'd resorted to the letter. She wasn't indirectly the cause of his death in that timeline, oh no, she was personally responsible for it. In this timeline he was dead even before the battle, and it was because of her.

Grace kept her hands clamped over her mouth to stifle the scream welling up inside of her chest, her body shaking with silent sobs. The only way this would be worse was if she'd marched him there herself or pulled the triggers of the muskets that they'd executed him with, and as far as she was concerned, she might as well have. It may be a different Euan in a different timeline, but fundamentally he was the same. He was the man she loved, the one who'd so captivated her that she'd broken the cardinal rule for him. The man who, even this morning, had brought her a cup of coffee in bed but let it go cold because he was too comfortable snuggled up under the blankets with her to let her sit up and actually drink it. The same one who'd saved her life by pretending to betray everything he'd once stood for.

Grace stood up, the speed with which she did so tipping the chair over, and then began pacing to try to calm herself down. Once she felt she had sufficient control over her emotions, she hurried out of the archives, requesting entry when she reached Council Chambers. She was inside as soon as the doors opened wide enough for her to squeeze through.

"Watcher Cameron? What are you doing here? Is everything all right?" Councilwoman Rochford asked as she stood up, looking concerned.

"I need to speak with you right now. *Alone.*"

Rochford's concern seemed to deepen, but she nodded, gesturing toward the door Grace now knew led to the private gardens. Without another word, Grace walked over to them and outside.

"What is this about, Grace?" Rochford asked as she came out behind her, letting go of the formality now that they were alone.

"Why didn't you tell me?" Grace asked, turning to look at her.

"Tell you what?"

"That day when I woke up and asked you about Nairn; why didn't you tell me I'd actually caused his death?"

Rochford sighed. "Why would I? You were upset enough, and it made no difference at that point. Why add to it?"

"It makes a difference to *me!*"

"It should not."

The sound of derision Grace made was cold and bitter. "Easy for you to say, hm? *You* didn't kill your Companion before you met him."

"Grace —"

"No! Don't you *dare* try to excuse this or excuse me. What I did caused him to be captured and shot! He wasn't supposed to be there, Alice! You didn't tell me he was there!"

"Because it no longer mattered! He would never experience any of it again in any timeline. Once he joined with you here, it became as though he and his mother never existed there or anywhere after the point where we changed things to be as though he left with you, and that was the night before they left again for Inverness. He would never go back to that field to die."

"But he did *then!* The time I ran that mission he did!"

"The *only* time, Grace. The potential success of that attack never happened again because he was no longer there, then or ever. It can never happen again."

"I want to see it."

"What?" Alice gasped, aghast as she looked at Grace.

"I want to see what I did. I need to see it."

"That seems very unwise."

"I need to see what I did to him, what I caused. Send me as an observer, so I can't do anything."

"Grace, why? I am not sure you understand what you are asking, and perhaps if you took some time to think about this, then you would see that this isn't what you really want."

"Because what I did had a price, Alice, and someone else paid it, someone I love more than myself or anyone else. I need to remind myself that there are costs to this, costs I never see. I need to brand that into my soul, so I'll never forget or take for granted that what I do affects real people."

Alice sighed. "You are not going to take no for an answer, are you?"

"No, I'm not."

"Very well. You know where to go."

Grace nodded and left her, heading to Observation where new Watchers and Companions trained. They'd be sent as observers first, to see what things looked like and to watch an experienced Watcher at work, though this time the only work Grace would be watching was her own. Rochford had already sent the instructions ahead, and the archivists were waiting for her. As she got into position on the table, they placed the device on her head that she'd use to access past timelines without being able to be seen or make changes. Because it was now part of that timeline's history, they could easily send Grace back to that point in time without disturbing anything or even causing a repeat. With the change prevented, history would go back to what it originally was when the cycle repeated.

Grace closed her eyes, and when she opened them again,

she found herself on a road in the dark. She could see the fires of the Hanoverian camp, hear them celebrating the Duke of Cumberland's birthday. It was odd to hear those same celebrations from outside the camp instead of from within it as she originally had on this mission. In the next moment, men crept past her out of the darkness, watching the camp intently. She didn't know the others, but she spotted Euan in an instant, tamping down her first urge to grab him and pull him away. Grace followed them across the moor, not needing to hide, and from the darkness of the woods came a shot that hit the ground near Grace's feet. It sent her scrambling backward, and the men froze as Hanoverian troops appeared from the trees. The Scots looked at each other, nodded, and charged the soldiers with a shout. Shots rang out, but in some sort of strange miracle, all missed their targets. The hand-to-hand combat didn't last long as reinforcements arrived within seconds and surrounded them.

Euan and the men stopped fighting, knowing full well there was nothing they could do now. They might take a few before they died, but if they cooperated, they'd have a chance of being freed later and rejoining their fellows in battle. Their weapons were confiscated, their hands tied, and they were marched at the points of bayonets into the camp to be held prisoner and interrogated. Grace followed Euan as he was separated from the others.

"What is your name?" one of the Hanoverian officers asked.

"Alexander Cameron," Euan replied, using one of his two middle names.

"A Cameron! No wonder you were leading your little group. Always up to no good, the Camerons are."

Euan said nothing, keeping his eyes straight ahead.

"What is your rank?"

"I have no rank."

"Come now, that is not true. There is no way they would put a nobody in charge of a small attack group."

"What makes ye think I was in charge?"

"They all looked to you for what to do next, that is why. What is your rank!" he shouted.

Euan sighed. "Captain."

A gleeful expression spread across the faces of the other men in the tent. An officer was always quite a prize in war and Grace could tell Euan knew it meant his death, but if it bothered him, it didn't show on his face.

"Excellent! You will be quite the bargaining chip."

"No, I will nae."

"What makes you say so?"

"Because ye are nae going to leave me alive, and we both know that perfectly well, dinnae we? I am nae stupid, *Lieutenant*," Euan said, the word dripping with disdain as he turned a cold gaze on the other man.

"No, that is true, but we may be able to get something for you before we kill you."

Euan returned to looking forward, falling silent once more. Grace was glad they didn't seem to recognize him, otherwise they would've all rushed to collect the bounty on him and only prolonged his suffering.

"Hold them all here until we strike camp, then we shall take them with us to the next engagement. I am sure their fellows will be happy to see them again even if it is in chains on the other side of the field," one of the other officers said.

Grace closed her eyes and shook her head. It was only an hour until dawn, so he wouldn't be here long. Euan was forced down onto the ground to sit and await his fate, and she sat beside him even though he couldn't and didn't know she was there. She didn't speak, her heart aching too much for words. She wished she could touch him, bring him some comfort as he faced what was coming. Grace knew he'd always been prepared for this, always aware it could happen, but there was no outward indication as to whether the reality of it upset him.

It wasn't long before they came for him again, hauling him

up and tying him behind a horse for the march to Drumossie. The other prisoners were placed in a wagon at the back with the supply train. Euan winced as they yanked the ropes to make them too tight around his wrists, but he quickly smothered his discomfort so as not to give them the satisfaction.

"I am here with you, love, even though you don't know it and you don't know me," Grace whispered as she stepped up beside him.

"How did ye know we were coming?" Euan asked, his tone flat.

"We were delivered a letter that had been dropped by one of the aides to your officers in a tavern."

Euan's jaw tightened. Grace saw it, and she knew what he was thinking. It was such a stupid mistake. Why would anyone commit anything to writing?

"They didn't do it; I did. No one was that undisciplined," she said as if he'd hear her confession, absolving others of blame.

As the officer moved his horse forward, the rope snapped taut and forced Euan to walk with it. Grace could skip the trip to Drumossie but didn't, choosing to walk beside him the entirety of the way. He remained silent and no one seemed to harass him, but all these men had battle on their minds and there was no room for taunting when they would face the enemy in just a few hours' time. Once they were within sight of the Jacobite army, Grace's panic rose. It was the combination of having been here before, having been in the midst of what was to come, but she knew from the report that the battle would be delayed now so she wouldn't have to go through it again. A white flag was raised, and the officer who had Euan rode out toward the middle of the field while keeping him in tow. Four other soldiers followed him, their muskets on their shoulders.

At the sight of the white flag, officers from the clan regiments came forward as well. A white flag meant a parley and no violence. When they reached the middle of the field, the men looked at each other for a long moment across the open space between them.

"We have something that belongs to you," the officer said to the Jacobite officers.

"Aye. Will ye be releasing him?"

The officer gave a derisive laugh. "No, of course not. He is a spy. We have the rest of your men as well, the ones who accompanied him. I am here to let you know he will receive his punishment now, and because we are feeling generous and he has been cooperative, you may collect his body and return with it so that you might bury him as you see fit."

Euan's face remained unreadable, and Grace wanted to scream, hating how helpless she felt. The Jacobite officers nodded, knowing there was nothing they could do for Euan now. If they tried to rescue him, it could lead to many more deaths, and one life wasn't worth that, no matter how much they might like him. But the English were at least giving them the opportunity to see to the honorable burial of one of their officers. They turned their horses, riding away to inform their command about what was happening. The men in the regiments, however, already seemed to know what was coming.

"Euan! Bha thu treun agus cuiridh Dia fàilte ort. An urrainn dha do shlighe a bheannachadh agus is dòcha gun cuidich an t-anam sinn ann am buaidh!" Grace heard one of them shout. *Euan! You were brave, and God will welcome you. May he bless your path, and may your soul help us in victory!*

Euan's smile was slight. "Aye, lads. May he indeed, and I will do my best," he whispered.

The Hanoverian officer nodded to the four soldiers with him, who marched around to stand in front of Euan and begin priming their weapons. Grace stepped in front of them, knowing that her presence there wouldn't hurt her or stop the trajectory of those lead balls from their intended target. She'd done that once and couldn't do it again. Grace focused on his eyes, his face, and she watched his expression grow curious as he seemed to look directly at her.

"I love you. I'm so sorry," Grace whispered, tears streaming down her cheeks. "You don't know that I love you, you don't know me, but I do. I never would've done this if I'd known. I'm so very, very sorry."

Euan cocked his head just the slightest bit, and Grace realized he could, in fact, see her. She didn't let the surprise register on her face as she walked toward him. That wasn't supposed to happen, but if he could see her, then there was only one thing she could do now: distract him. Make it so he wasn't thinking about what was about to happen, stand before him so he couldn't see the guns. Euan didn't speak as she stopped in front of him, looking down at her as she looked up into his eyes.

"Are ye an angel?" he whispered.

"Yes," she whispered in return. "I'm here with you."

"Then I thank God for sending ye to bring me peace and take me to Him. I dinnae want to die alone."

Grace placed a soft hand on his cheek, even as her heart broke at his words and the lack of recognition when he looked at her. "You aren't alone. You never have been and never will be. I'm always here to protect you."

"Thank ye," he said. "Stay with me, please."

Grace leaned up and pressed her lips to his, feeling him meet her in it, soaking up that last bit of contact available to him in this life. The loud crack of the muskets startled her, and Euan's lips left hers as he fell to the ground, unmoving. It was clear he was dead, and she was thankful he hadn't suffered. Dropping to her knees beside him, she reached out to touch his body, but this time her hand passed through as it was supposed to do. Grace covered her face and sobbed as the Hanoverian soldiers cut him loose and then left him there. When the Jacobite soldiers came for his body, they put him over Absalon and took him back to his own men.

Watching through tears, Grace saw Duncan, Malcolm, and the others wash his body, while others dug a grave for him a good distance from where they'd soon do battle. They'd set it in the woods, the same woods where in another timeline he'd be reunited with Grace just before the battle, just before she'd give her own life to prevent this moment. The care with which they tended to him only impressed upon her the meaning of what he'd done for her when she was recovering after this same ordeal. Duncan, Malcolm, and Iain cried as they cleaned the body of their friend, and Grace knew they'd all soon be joining Euan.

Once the grave was dug, they carried him to it in a procession. One of them began a song, the others joining him, a song in Gaelic about brave warriors and what awaited them in death. Grace knew it was a sign of great respect that they were burying him this way, that everything had come to a stop to see to it. From the outside one might think they were burying one of the chiefs. Grace saw that someone had also taken pity on the beautiful Absalon, knowing he'd never let anyone but his beloved master near him, and they'd ended the stallion's suffering before it could begin so that master and mount would now occupy the same grave. Still singing, they lowered Euan's body into the earth and began to fill it back in. By the time they finished the song, the task was done, and Euan was buried. Malcolm sang the last lines of the song by himself now as the rain began to fall. Grace watched him as all the men filed away to leave Malcolm alone. As he finished, he looked up and at Grace, his eyes going wide for a moment before he let out an anguished sob. She knew he could see her now, too; she didn't know how, but he could, and she knew what she must look like to him, dressed all in white as she was. His expression was brokenhearted as she stepped to the edge of the head of the new grave.

"I see the angels have already sent one of their own to collect ye, my beloved friend, my brother, and I shall leave her to it. Safe journey to ye," Malcolm managed to choke out through his tears before he turned and walked away.

Grace closed her eyes and sighed, kneeling and placing her

hand on the freshly dug earth, feeling it sink in. The only thing stopping Grace from full grief was knowing she'd wake up from this and he'd be very much alive, as well as knowing he'd only suffered this fate once and never would again.

"I'm sorry," she whispered one last time. "Take me out."

Everything faded and Grace sat up from the table, pulling the device from her head and tossing it away from her as she lost all composure. It was more than just seeing his death; it was the anxiety from once again standing before guns and hearing them go off. She'd been able to push it back then, for his sake, but not now. She took a moment to compose herself, to get herself to stop shaking, before sliding from the table to find another Guardian to take her home. She hadn't used Caia for this, not wanting to face Caia trying to talk her out of it or seeing her upset for Grace's sake. Reappearing in their bedroom, she hurried toward the door, pulling it open and running down the stairs, out into the garden behind the house to find Euan there, still practicing.

"Euan ..." Grace sighed in relief.

He stopped, lowering the weapon as he turned to look at her with a curious expression. She knew he could feel her anxiety, her upset, could hear it in her voice. "What has ye troubled, *mo ghràidh*?"

Grace said nothing, closing the distance between them as fast as she could and throwing her arms around his waist, pressing herself to him. She needed to feel him breathing, hear his heart beating, feel the warmth of his skin.

Euan set the blade aside and wrapped his arms around her. "Ye are shaking! *Mo chridhe*, what is it? What is wrong?"

Grace shook her head, squeezing him a bit tighter.

Euan brought one hand up to rest on the side of her head, keeping her cheek against his chest as he kissed the top of her head. "There now, ye are all right," he whispered, stroking her hair. "I am here."

His last words broke her, and Grace burst into tears of anger, pain, and relief. He *was* here and she was beyond thankful for that, but she couldn't help her anger at what she'd seen.

"Shh, Grace," he said, his voice calm and comforting. "Please tell me what is wrong so I can help ye. Did ye have a nightmare?"

"Yes," Grace choked out. It had been a nightmare, all right. A real one.

"Ah. Ye are awake now, love, and ye are safe. I have ye."

"Don't let go, please," Grace pleaded.

"I will nae, nae until ye wish me to," he replied before he began singing to her in a soft voice while continuing to stroke her hair.

Grace closed her eyes, though it didn't stop her from crying.

"Did ye want to tell me about it?" he asked when he stopped singing.

"No, I can't."

"Cannae because ye cannae remember, or because ye dinnae want to."

"Don't want to."

"That is fine, I understand. I have had more than a few of those myself. I am sorry that such a thing happened to ye; ye have been sleeping so well lately."

"I can't …" she began, then shook her head. "I'm so … you were gone … and …"

"Gone? Did ye dream I left ye or disappeared somehow?"

"You died! You died in front of me, and it was my fault!"

Euan frowned. "Ach, Christ, *leannan*, I know how upsetting such dreams can be, but I am here, I swear it to ye. I am safe and so are ye. I am going nowhere, and I am certainly nae dying in front of ye or anyone else. No wonder ye are acting this way; ye want to feel me here, so ye know I am fine."

"Yes," Grace sobbed out.

"I am. Shh, I am. Come now."

Grace looked up at him, moving her hands from his back to his face. Those same blue eyes looked back at her, now untroubled and unafraid.

I dinnae want to die alone.

His words echoed in her ears and sliced fresh cuts deep into her heart. Alone. No one wanted to die alone, and he'd been no different. No matter what front he put up for others, no matter how prepared for it he'd tried to be, he'd been terrified of what was to come and she'd seen it in all the little ways no one else could've. Grace leaned up on her toes and kissed him, feeling his arms tighten around her and press her close to him. That there was none of the desperation she'd felt previously only served to help remind her that this was the reality, and not what she'd just seen.

"*Mo ghaol milis,*" he whispered against her lips as he rested his forehead against hers. "Dinnae be afraid, for we will never be without one another and ye know that. We are together, always."

Grace nodded. "Sorry."

"Dinnae be sorry, never be sorry for something like this. The moment ye no longer feel upset at the thought of losing me is the moment ye no longer love me."

"That will *never* happen."

"I hope nae," he said, smiling.

"It couldn't. I love you too much for that."

"Such things terrify ye," he said, pushing some hair away from her face. "Intense emotions like this mean ye are vulnerable, mean ye can be hurt, and ye just want to run from them. Yet, I am the only one ye dinnae run from. The love ye feel for me and the strength of it no longer frightens ye, but now the thought of being without it does."

"I could say the same about you."

"I will readily admit to it. I love ye with every fiber of my being, and as terrifying as that once was, it no longer is. It brings me comfort and peace, while the thought of losing that love is one of the things I fear most. I cannae imagine life without ye in it, and I thank God every day that I dinnae have to."

Grace closed her eyes and sighed. Euan had a way with words, he always had, a way of saying something so beautifully that it disarmed you. More than that, he was unabashed in expressing his feelings for her, unrestrained by anything but the language he could command to put words to it. He knew what to say to bring her back to him, to calm her, to keep her from withdrawing from him and from the world.

"Shall we go inside, and I can make ye a cup of tea to help ye?"

Grace nodded against him; her eyes still closed as she reveled in his overall presence.

"*Thig, mo bhòidhchead,*" he said. *Come, my beauty.* "It is time for me to be done for today anyway, and I cannae think of a better way to end it than over tea and biscuits with ye."

CHAPTER 2

Euan stopped moving as the blade hovered near his neck and grinned. "Very good, love. Ye are learning quickly."

"I have an excellent teacher. I think he's going easy on me, though," Grace replied, smiling back at him as she disengaged and pulled the blade away.

"A bit, but he has no desire to hurt ye, and ye are nae ready yet for him to do otherwise."

"I won't learn if you do that."

"Ye will, just as I did, and ye will learn as yer progress dictates. I will nae go easy on ye forever and, honestly, I am nae going all that easy on ye now."

"So you say."

Euan offered her a half-smile as he turned away from her, but in the next moment, he moved to grab her with the intention to catch her unaware, only to not find her there. In his momentary confusion, he paused, and that was all she needed. Grace swept his legs out from underneath him, throwing him flat on his back, and before that could fully register, the tip of a blade was against his throat and a knee was on his chest.

"Now, now. That wasn't nice," she said, her tone teasing.

Euan looked up at her, wide-eyed. "Well. Are ye nae full of surprises."

Grace laughed, leaning down to kiss him but not moving the blade. "You like it."

"I did nae say I did nae, as ye well know, but I had no idea ye had that in ye."

"You never asked."

Euan raised an eyebrow. "Is that so? I do believe I asked ye where ye learned to fight when we were in Oxford."

"You did, but all I did was punch him; you didn't ask about anything else. A little bit of fight training never hurt anyone."

"I quite agree, but I am nae sure that is part of the Watcher training."

"It isn't."

Euan's hand shot out and grabbed the wrist of the hand holding the blade, while his other hand pressed her leg flat on his chest before he rolled them over and pinned her wrist to the ground. Grace made a sound of shock and then winced as he squeezed her wrist, causing her to drop the dirk she held. Euan straddled her, pinning her hips to the ground, then grabbed her other wrist now that his hand was free and pinned it to the ground along with the other.

"Careful. I will always fight back."

Grace stared up at him, her expression part frustration, part something else entirely.

"Dinnae look at me like that when ye started it." Euan smiled, a dark edge to it that was always there when he'd been at this sort of training.

"And you're finishing it?"

"No," he replied as he leaned down closer to her, his hands still holding her wrists. "I am only just beginning," he whispered.

For a moment, Grace almost forgot to breathe. She sometimes hated how well and how easily he could do this to her, but she would never tell him to stop. When she didn't respond, he gave her a light, teasing kiss before he pulled back and stood up, pulling her with him.

"Is yer wrist hurt? I did nae mean to do so."

"No," she replied. "It's fine. It was more shock than anything."

"Good," he said, taking her wrist in his hands and rubbing it anyway. "I did like that move, though. I was nae expecting it of ye."

Grace smiled and shook her head. "I'm not entirely helpless."

"I know, but it does nae mean I cannae be impressed."

Grace had been working with Euan on broadsword and various other blades in the times between their missions, and according to him she was coming along quite well. It was for her benefit, of course, but also for his own. It gave him a sparring partner to work with, and teaching her helped keep him sharp. He may not use the skill in war any longer, but he most certainly used it in their work from time to time.

They were now on a rather extended break, just in time for spring and summer. After France they'd more than earned it, and there was still concern about Grace's mental state. A break allowed The Council to monitor her while also permitting her time to heal both emotionally and mentally. What she'd gone through was something none of them could imagine or understand, not even Euan, and he'd seen it. To be attacked mentally in such a way was a different sort of injury and torture. Grace knew it was impossible for him to miss the slight panic that still showed in her face if she forgot something she'd been told, what day it was, a thought, or even a word. None of it was anything but the normal ways a mind worked, but it didn't stop that momentary worry that something might be wrong. She managed it well, did her best to hide it, but it was still difficult for her. Eventually she'd get past it, but it would take time, and time was what The Council had given them.

There was now a chance to have something resembling a normal life, as temporary as it was. Their lives would never be normal, given who they were and what they did, but they could get as close as they were able. They had some trips planned around Scotland, and there was talk of perhaps an actual holiday someplace warm and tropical. Euan had been more than happy to spend an entire day losing himself amongst the books in the library at the University of Edinburgh and another day doing the same at the University of Glasgow. Films were screened, television shows binge watched, and sleep caught up on. They were entirely at their ease, so much so that Aileen had remarked that they were as relaxed as she'd ever seen them.

"I will take that as a compliment since impressing you is tough. People have to work at it," Grace said.

"Aye, that is true. Then again, I have seen much, so I am nae as impressed by things others might be. However, I think we are done for the day."

"What should we do then?"

"What would ye like to do?"

"How about a walk?"

Euan smiled, held out his arm for her to take, and they walked out of the yard into the woods just behind the lodge. She loved that they had this, could do this. Some of these woods belonged to them as part of the property, but they had the freedom to walk anywhere they pleased.

"I wanted to talk to you about something," Grace said.

"Oh?"

Grace hesitated, unsure of how she wanted to begin this conversation even though she knew they had to have it. "I went to the archives at The Council."

"Did ye? When?"

"The other day while you were training."

"Ah. What were ye seeking there?"

"Confirmation."

"Of?"

Grace stopped, her arm falling away from his, and it made him turn to look at her. "You were there."

Euan's posture changed in an instant, becoming more guarded. "I know."

"I saw it, your execution after Nairn. The one I was responsible for. After France, I suspected that it was worse than I'd thought, and I was right. That attack would've been successful because *you* led it. It was *you* I stopped, not them."

Euan frowned. "Why? Why did ye do that to yerself?"

"I had to. I needed to confirm what I felt, and I want to remember that everything we do doesn't happen in a vacuum."

"Ye could have picked something else or somewhere else if that was what ye wanted."

Grace shook her head. "Someone I loved paid the price. That was what I had to see."

"Ye did nae know me, and I did nae know ye. It was nae the same."

"To me you're always the same."

He sighed as he reached out to touch her cheek. "Ye did what ye had to do, and I will nae fault ye for it. I died well."

"How do you know?"

"I read about it. I realized after I decided to stay that if ye had a mission at Nairn, it was because they'd chosen to make use of me that time. I knew how it had failed, I was there, so if it was suddenly going to succeed, I knew it was because I had something to do with it. I did nae realize I was captured there until I read about it, but it made sense."

"Why didn't you tell me? You knew before we came here; that's why you mentioned it that night after you had that nightmare. You knew!"

"What good would it have done ye for me to say it?"

"Why does no one feel like I need to know things! I'm not fragile, Euan!"

"I know ye are nae and would nae suggest ye are, but this is different, Grace," Euan said, keeping his voice gentle in the face of his wife's rising temper. "Ye feel too much with this, with me. Ye cannae distinguish between other timelines and the man who stands before ye now. Ye said it yerself, just a moment ago: to ye I am always the same."

Grace sighed, not bothering to contest his assertions because doing so was pointless. "You didn't suffer. They buried you and sang the most haunting song about brave warriors. Duncan, Malcolm, and Iain washed your body."

Euan's expression grew sad for a moment. "I am nae surprised."

"They had so much respect for you."

Euan shrugged. "I earned what I had. Are ye satisfied now that ye know?"

"Not really. Satisfied because I have the whole picture, but heartbroken by all of it. I went as an observer, and I told you I was sorry even though you couldn't hear me. I walked with you from Nairn to Culloden, and I was standing in front of you when they shot you."

Grace saw Euan blanch at the mention of her standing in front of him as he was shot. She knew that hit far closer to memory than he'd ever want.

"You saw me in those last moments. I stood close to you, and you spoke to me. You asked me if I was an angel and thanked God for sending me because you didn't want to die alone. I was able to touch you, and you stayed looking at me. I kissed you and distracted you, so you weren't afraid, and you didn't see the guns before they fired. Malcolm saw me too."

"Really? I thought that was nae possible? Even if I did nae know ye, that would have brought some strange comfort if ye appeared how I imagine ye did. What did Malcolm do?"

"He said that he could see the angels had sent one of their own to collect you. And it's *not* supposed to be possible, but I feel like, as with everything, you and I are different and always will be."

"Does it make it better or worse for ye to know that ye were far more involved in what happened to me there than ye believed?" Euan asked.

"Worse," Grace replied, her voice strained.

"Then why do it? I understand what ye are trying to say, but we both know damned well that is nae truly why ye went there, Grace."

Grace trembled with the effort to keep herself from crying. "I wanted to tell you I was sorry."

"Did I hear ye? Did I know ye were there with me the whole time? No. Ye are torturing yerself. Ye forced yerself to watch it because ye felt like ye should, because ye felt so responsible for it that ye needed to suffer as some sort of penance, but ye dinnae. War is ugly, and people die; that is a fact. When that same attack failed, without yer help, I still died. I died the next day alongside my men because that is what happens in war."

"But the other times I wasn't directly responsible!"

"Grace," Euan said as he cupped her cheeks in his hands and forced her to look at him. "Listen to me: ye did what was required of ye, as I did. Would ye be this upset about it if it had nae been me? If it had been some other man killed there because of what ye did?"

"Yes."

"Stop. Ye are lying, and ye know I know when ye are lying. Answer the question truthfully."

Grace sighed. "No."

"Exactly, and that is how ye must treat this. Treat that man as though it were someone that was nae me, because it was nae. I am here with ye, alive and well. I will nae suffer that again because ye prevented that. Ye killed me in one timeline, but think of how many others ye have saved me in now?"

Grace nodded. "You're right."

"I hope ye will forgive yerself now, for I have never been upset with ye for it. There is naught to forgive."

"I might, eventually."

"That is at least a start," he replied, pulling her face close to his and giving her a gentle kiss. "No more of this. Leave it be, all right?"

"All right."

"Love, ye have enough to haunt yer mind without this, and I wish ye would nae have put that image in yer head."

"In a way, though, it hurt worse to know the truth, but I felt relieved to apologize for it. That you saw me gave me the chance to do something small to at least give myself a little bit of redemption."

"If it brings ye peace, then ye did what ye needed to. Please, swear to me ye will leave that behind ye now," Euan said.

"I will. I promise."

Euan took her arm again and continued their walk. "Why did ye nae tell me?"

"You would have stopped me."

"Maybe. That means there was no nightmare, was there?"

"No," she replied, quiet.

"It was all because ye went there. Ye saw me die, and that is what had ye so torn apart."

"Yes. I'm sorry. I just needed to know, and I don't think you would've told me if I'd asked you about it, just as you haven't with so many things. There is so much I don't know, Euan."

He stopped and turned to her, his expression darkening. "No. Dinnae tell me ye did that."

"Did what?"

"Did ye go into the rest of my past, Grace?"

"No," she replied, confused.

"Good. Stay out of it," he said, his tone as cold as it was sharp.

Grace looked at him in surprise, hurt by the way he'd spoken to her. "If you're so worried about it, you could always tell me instead. What are you trying to hide?"

"Have ye told me all?"

"I have always answered your questions honestly. I have nothing to hide from you."

"There is plenty in mine that ye dinnae need to be privy to, no one does, and it is all better left forgotten."

"*You* won't ever forget."

"And that is enough!" Euan shouted at her. "It is enough that it haunts me; it does nae need to haunt ye, too! Ye dinnae need to know about it to understand me, Grace."

"What did you do that makes you act this way whenever anyone gets near it?"

"Too much."

"But whatever it is makes you the man I married."

"No, it does nae! The man ye married was the man before war changed everything in him! The man ye met that day near the loch? *That* was who the war made me! If ye saw me at war, ye would nae know me, and I dinnae want ye to see that!"

"Euan, please calm down. I didn't see it, and I wouldn't do that; I wouldn't violate your privacy that way. I just wish you would talk to me and —"

"Fine," he growled, grabbing her upper arm and yanking her forward, bringing a startled sound from her as she collided with him. "Is this what ye want to see, Grace? Hm?"

"Euan!"

"Ye want to see what I become? Very well, I will oblige ye," he said, turning and pulling her along back toward the house by the arm he held. Yanking the door open, he dragged Grace inside. "Mam!"

Aileen appeared from the kitchen to find Euan holding a confused and frightened Grace by the arm. "Euan, what are ye —"

"When I came back that day from Fort William, do ye remember?"

"Aye."

"Tell her. Tell her what I looked like. Tell her what I said to ye."

"Euan, stop. Please," Grace pleaded. "You're hurting me!"

"Son, what has come over ye!" Aileen said, shocked.

"TELL HER!"

Both women jumped, the command in his voice clear, the same one he'd once used to give orders to his men, and it brought Grace to tears.

"Ye were covered in blood, head to toe. I thought ye were hurt, but ye told me none of it was yers. I asked ye what had happened, and ye told me nae to ask ye in a tone so cold I could nae imagine it had come from ye. Then ye walked away from me without another word."

"There. Is that what ye wanted to know, Grace? Ye want

to hear about me coming home covered in the blood of all the men I slaughtered the night before? Ye want to hear about how I enjoyed some of it? How I was nae sorry?"

Grace shook her head, crying too hard to speak, and Euan released her arm while shoving her away from him, causing her to stumble backward a few steps.

"Aye, I thought nae. Ye stay out of it," he warned, pointing at her.

Euan's eyes were hard, and his voice promised an unkind consequence for disobedience, though Grace couldn't be sure whether he meant for it to. Turning on his heel, he stormed outside, slamming the back door behind him as Grace fell apart, sobbing in both fear and pain. That wasn't her husband. He'd been right: he wasn't the man she knew.

"Oh, love, shhh now. He did nae mean to hurt ye, and he will be horrified when he comes back to himself," Aileen said as she hurried over to Grace and embraced her.

Grace shook her head, pushing herself away from Aileen. "I can't, please," she said, struggling to breathe as anxiety overwhelmed her.

"Grace, love," Aileen said, concerned. "Grace, are ye all right?"

"No, I'm … no … I can't …" Grace stammered before she turned and hurried for the front door, throwing it open and running out, leaving a bewildered Aileen in her wake.

CHAPTER 3

When Euan left the house, he stalked back into the woods, walking until he reached a ravine and couldn't go on without a bit of climbing, the forced stop leaving him pacing with fury. Why did she have to push him? Why did she need to know? Why couldn't anyone just leave the past be, let it be the past as he wanted, and understand that he didn't want to remember or discuss any of it outside of George's office? The names, the faces, the situations, the battles. All of it stirred up things in him he didn't want, things he wished he could forget for good. He hadn't wanted to admit that all he'd done during the French mission had affected him so deeply, but it had. Seeing Lochiel again, seeing Murray, Pierre — all of it had thrust him back in front of the things he'd worked so hard to push away. Some part of him almost wished those beings that had attacked Grace had come for him instead. He would've willingly surrendered all these memories; they could have them.

He'd so far managed to keep all this separated: his time with Specialist George and his time at home. Home was where he could forget, but now that wall had been breached and it all swirled around him. Malcolm, Iain, Duncan, Lochiel, the prince, and all the rest. What the field looked like when a battle ended, and the smoke cleared. Bodies everywhere, some twitching and groaning as they lay dying, the last of their blood oozing into the earth. The way it looked when all those bodies had been stripped of clothing and valuables; in Falkirk it had looked like sheep on the moor from a distance. It was only when one got close that they realized they were the unfortunate men who'd gone to fight for their government and ended their lives being stripped by looters in a Scottish field.

Euan dug the heels of his hands into his eyes to try to push it back down, to block it out, but his inability to do so made him scream with rage and sadness even as he broke down in tears. "STOP!" he screamed.

The sound around him, the woods, the remembered screams, the voices of his past, all fell blessedly silent, shattered by the force of his voice. Euan's chest heaved for air as he sank to the ground to bury his face in his knees and block out the sight of anything that might be lingering to torment him. What did he owe her or anyone? Did he owe her an explanation, a window into the memories he hated so much? George had told him that to share them might relieve the burden he carried, but he was terrified to speak the words. If he started, could he stop? Would she hate him when he was done as he hated himself?

"Euan, stop. Please! You're hurting me!"

The memory of those words hit him now from wherever they'd been kept when he'd been pushed too far, and it was only then that he realized what he'd done. The recollection only made it worse, made him hate himself more, and his tears came harder, faster. He'd hurt Grace, physically hurt her, and she'd been afraid of him. He scrambled toward the ravine's edge, unable to keep himself from being sick as the stress made his stomach revolt.

Turning over, he rested on his back, staring up into the trees, the leaves blurred by the tears that wouldn't stop. He *should* tell her. Maybe not about the battles themselves, but about everything else. The battles were something he couldn't speak of any more than he had to the Specialist, and he wasn't sure Grace needed those details. Maybe someday he could tell her about those but not now. Grace had spoken about going to Nairn as an observer, and he wondered if he could get The Council to let him do that with her. To let him show her instead of telling her.

But there was more to this, and he knew it. Though he loved being here, every turn brought memories of the men who were gone. He'd made peace with his survival and their deaths when they'd first returned, but his memories of them remained. Sometimes he swore he could see them out of the corner of his eye or felt that they'd arrive any moment, but of course they never did. The only other person here who had known them as he did was Aileen. He needed a friend, someone who might understand the horrors of war and why he'd want to keep the women he loved as far from it as possible. Grace couldn't be his only friend and confidant; it was unfair of him to ask that of her, and he hadn't. It wasn't that he didn't love her or his mother, or that they didn't do their best, but he had no wish to burden them with being the only ones to know. He didn't want them to carry that with them the way he did.

He'd need to speak to The Council to ask about the plan that was now forming in his mind because they were the only ones who could give him the leave to go through with it. Euan sat up and wiped his eyes, trying to get control of himself again. He needed to go home and apologize to both Grace and Aileen for what he'd done. He had to hope Grace would forgive him for it, though he wasn't sure he would if he were her. Pushing himself up from the ground, he dusted himself off and took a deep breath, releasing it before he began to walk back to the house. He had a decided course of action and that was helping to steady and ground him once more.

When he entered the house, the only thing that met him was silence, and it was unnerving. There was no one in the living room, no one in the study when he checked it. Euan moved to the stairs and ran up them to their bedroom. "Grace?"

There was no answer in return, the room as they'd left it

this morning, and he hurried back downstairs. "Grace?" he called out as he got to the bottom.

"She is nae here," Aileen said as she emerged from the kitchen.

Euan frowned. "Nae here? Where did she go?"

"I dinnae know. As soon as ye left, she ran out of the front door, and I have nae seen her since."

Euan closed his eyes and buried his face in his hands. "I have to find her," he whispered.

"Euan, what happened? I have never seen ye that way."

He shook his head and looked over at her, his eyes tired and sad. "I dinnae know, Mam, and that is the honest answer. She was asking me about things I did nae want to talk about, and it just took over."

Aileen frowned. "Oh, lad, how tormented ye still are. It eats away at ye still."

Euan nodded but said nothing.

"Are the sessions nae helping?"

"Some," he said, quiet.

"But nae enough."

"It is nae that easy, Mam. It does nae go away overnight, and France was such a blow."

Aileen sighed. "Go find her."

"If she wanted to see me, she would still be here."

"She needed time, as ye did. Ye terrified her, Euan."

"I know," Euan replied, his voice breaking. "God help me, but I never intended to."

"Ye are telling the wrong person." She held out Grace's arasaid. "She left without a coat. Dinnae make the same mistake," Aileen said as she handed it to him and walked away.

Euan tucked the garment under his arm and made his way back outside. He had a feeling he knew where Grace had gone, and the only way to get there was on foot. It was a way he knew well, and he made the trek without much thought. As he crossed the bridge and followed the path along the loch where he'd once lived, he was relieved to see Grace exactly where he'd felt she'd be. Sitting upon the boulder they'd once sat on together some two centuries ago, she stared out across the loch, her back to him. He knew why she'd come here, an attempt to find that young man she knew again after he'd been replaced by the beast she'd seen not long ago.

"Grace," he said, keeping his voice soft as he drew near her.

She turned around and instinctively backed away from him as far as the rock would allow. "Stop. You stay right there," she said, brandishing the sgian dubh that had become hers ever since he'd given it to her in France.

Euan stopped as she commanded him, though seeing that fear in her shattered him. It was fear that shouldn't be there, fear of him. Even worse was that she felt the need to have a blade to protect herself. "Love, I will nae hurt ye. I —"

"You already did."

"I know and I apologize, but I dinnae know what happened. I never meant to hurt ye, and I never would; ye know that. I was nae …" He trailed off as he searched for the words. "I was nae in my right mind at that moment, and that is the truth. Please, just let me talk to ye."

"You can talk to me from right where you are."

Euan closed his eyes and lowered his head for a moment. He deserved that, no matter how much it might hurt. "As ye wish. Grace, I did nae mean for that to happen. I felt ye were pushing for what I did nae want to give ye, and I became the man I have so wanted to keep from ye. It is nae me."

"I told you I wouldn't ask, wouldn't look. That I hadn't."

"Aye, ye did, but ye still questioned why, and ye see why now. I need ye to understand I cannae speak of the things that even I have nae come to terms with. I want to forget them so desperately; ye have no idea. Ye cannae understand that part, I know, but all I ask is that ye respect that there are things I cannae tell ye now."

"You're supposed to be seeing the Specialist."

"And I am," Euan countered. "Ye can check if ye wish to

make sure I am nae lying to ye. It is one thing to tell *him*, and another to look *ye* in the face and tell ye what I have done, what I have been through. France made it all worse."

"Worse how?"

"I had to see them again and remember all I had worked so hard to shove down, shove away, forget. Suddenly there they all were, living, breathing reminders of who I had been. People who knew about it, who had seen me, who had wanted that from me. Ye dinnae know what they said to me, the things they said to hurt me deliberately, and the ways they reminded me of what I had done and who I had to become when I did them."

"Who you had to become?"

"Aye. I had to become someone else, Grace. I had to in order to force myself to do the things required, the things the Euan *ye* know could nae do because they required a cruelty I dinnae possess. I hate it, I hate him and everything he did. Aye, he is Euan, too, but he is everything cruel and dark and violent in me. He is the one who could look men he had always known in the eyes and take their lives without a thought or sorrow. I had fought before when we were raided, but I had a reason then; I was defending my own. This was different."

"You had no need of it those times?"

"No. As I said, I was defending my home, my family, and my clan. The war was … It was nae the same. I was being asked to fight and kill for a cause I did nae believe in and a man as young as I was who I often did nae care for."

"What do you mean?"

Euan sighed. "Please, let me come to ye. I will nae hurt ye, ye have my word, and if I break it, ye have a blade to remind me."

Grace nodded, and with relief, he joined her on the boulder, draping the arasaid around her shoulders but careful not to touch her. He had no permission or right to do so, no matter how much he wanted it.

"I knew the prince, and I was unsure of him from the start. I did nae like him at all when I first met him."

"You never told me that, that you knew him."

"I never told anyone."

"Not even your mother?"

"No. She knew about the first time I met him but naught else. He wanted people to love him, but he just expected it, expected us all to fall in line and prostrate ourselves before him because of his name, and struggled to connect with the common men he led. He had only a concept of how to lead an army and relied on others to guide him. Nae only that, but he seemed to have little respect for the lives of the men who fought for him, at least at first, though that changed as things went on."

"So, in return, you didn't respect him."

"No, nae at all at the start though, again, that changed as time passed. Yet we were asked to fight for him, to die for him, when all many of us wanted to do was tell him to shove his rebellion up his royal arse and take ourselves home. At the same time, this was the man my chief commanded me to go to war for, and I had a duty to do. I hardened my heart and pushed away everything in me that would prevent me from doing what I must. I let all the worst parts of me come through instead."

"Surely you weren't like that the entire time?"

"No, of course nae. When it came time to do battle, to kill, I could nae be this Euan before ye now, for he would have thrown his musket and pistol down and walked away rather than do what was asked for men he did nae respect. When it was over, I would find a place to be alone for a time and put myself back together."

Grace reached out and brushed away the tears that had escaped. "He never went away, did he?"

"No," Euan whispered. "And he never will. I can bury him, but those battles are where he lives, in those memories that hurt so much. When I had that nightmare when we first came back, *he* was the one I was forced to become partnered with once more. I cannae go there yet, and I beg ye nae to ask it of me. *Please.*"

There was so much pain in that last word, more than he'd intended for there to be, a plea for mercy from the one he loved the most.

"Can you tell me what happened in the incident you made your mother tell me about?"

Euan nodded. It was already out there; he owed her that much. "It was after the siege of Fort William and just days before I met ye. We knew we could nae win at Fort William, for the prince would nae send the guns or reinforcements we needed. Lochiel tasked me with taking a few of them down with us as we retreated, and I did. A party that left the fort to get water and every sentry on the road back to Achnacarry."

"Euan …" Grace whispered in clear shock.

"It was their blood I was covered in when I returned home. Blood I was nae sorry to have shed and, if I am honest, still am nae. Many of them were Campbells," he said before he looked up at her. "Please, dinnae hate me for this, for I already hate myself enough for us both."

"I don't," Grace said, her eyes welling with tears. "Why would you ever think I would?"

"Because ye should; by all rights ye should. Ye should run far from me and from this and from all I have done because I am nae worthy of ye and never have been. I want to be the man ye believe me to be, but I cannae be. Nae entirely."

"How are you not worthy? Because you killed people? You were at *war*, Euan; it isn't as though you killed unarmed people. Those men were trying to kill you, too. Who is it you think I believe you to be?"

"The man who loves ye beyond measure. The one who sat on this rock with ye and sang to ye when someone had hurt ye, who asked ye questions about a time he never thought he would see. The one who would never hurt anyone if he could help it."

"He is the same one as the rest. You are not different people, Euan, all of it is you. The man I love is all those things, as well as a man who went to war and did what war required him to do to survive, and I'm not so naive as to think you never did anything. I knew you had, and I knew it when you sat here with me. I already knew the battles you'd been in and that you'd survived them; I just didn't tell you that because all that would've done was make you more suspicious of me. You would have pulled further away from me, and I needed you not to. Do you honestly believe I thought you lived through them because you just sat on a horse or hid somewhere?"

Euan was in tears now; he couldn't help it, and when she wrapped her arms around him, he held Grace to him tightly, letting the realization wash over him that his wife *knew*. Not the gory details, of course, but she knew. She knew, she understood, and she still loved him despite it.

"I never wanted ye to see that side of me," he said, his breathing ragged as he sobbed.

"I know," she whispered, "but I would've eventually. I got a glimpse of him in France."

"I can still hear them, I can still see it, and I dinnae want it!"

"I know, love," Grace replied, her voice still soft. "I know exactly what you mean."

"I am so sorry, Grace. I never meant to hurt ye, and ye know I would rather harm myself than ever cause any to ye, and after yer stepfather —"

"No," Grace said, cutting him off with a firm tone. "You aren't him and don't you ever say that or even think it. I was more scared than hurt. I'm fine, I promise, and I'll be more careful in the future when it comes to everything surrounding this. You don't have to tell me anything."

Euan looked up at her, exhausted. "I cannae promise ye will nae see that man again, but I *can* promise ye it will only be when it is needed. Had any of them done ye harm in France, *that* is the Euan they would have met, and it would nae have ended well. I would give no quarter, their blood would be the only thing to satisfy me, and they knew it. Lochiel knew it because he had seen it many times."

"I have no doubt about any of that," Grace said before she kissed his forehead. "All is forgiven," she whispered.

"Thank Christ," he replied, his voice breaking again.

"If you thought I was going to leave you over this, you're daft."

Euan laughed, mostly out of relief. "I must be daft then."

"I know you're struggling; we both are. There has been no time for us to deal with this, not really, not until now. We'll get through this. We are stronger than this."

"Aye, we are."

"Come with me."

"Where?"

"Just come on," Grace said as she slid down from the boulder.

Euan followed her to the tree line, where she sat down and leaned back against the tree. She patted her lap and Euan understood her instantly. He lay down beside her and rested his head in her lap, closing his eyes as she ran her fingers through his hair in slow, gentle strokes. This was something that always calmed him when he'd had a nightmare or was angry about something; it was relaxing and comforting. In a move that nearly set him to tears again, she sang that familiar song, a song he'd not heard since he'd sung it to himself that night when he'd tried to forget that he'd die soon. It was a moment that had never come, and he let the familiar tune and words carry him into sleep.

Chapter 4

"Councilwoman," Euan said as he walked into Council Chambers the following day, stopping before the assembled women to bow.

"Hello, Euan. Are you here to see the Specialist?" Rochford asked, though it was clear she was surprised to see him there.

"No," he replied. "I have something I need to speak to ye and The Council about. It is nae something I am sure ye will allow, but I wish to ask all the same."

"Go on," she said, giving him a nod.

"I would like yer permission to tell someone the truth about myself."

Councilwoman Rochford arched an eyebrow at his request. "Why? It is, of course, your choice to do so or not, and we know you'd not make such a choice lightly. Are you wanting to enlist this individual to help you in some way?"

"In a way, aye. He is kin to me ... well, sort of. He keeps the records at Achnacarry and is the descendent of one of my former friends."

"Oh! You speak of Malcolm?"

Euan's eyes widened. "How did ye know that?"

Rochford pointed at the tapestry, a small smile on her lips. "Ah, right."

"It actually begins a beneficial relationship between the Cameron Watchers and those who come after him."

"Is there a limit to what I may tell him?"

"No," she replied. "You may give as much or as little as you desire. I understand now why you feel the need to do this."

"Thank ye and thank ye for nae questioning too much."

She looked at him, her expression sad for a moment. "It does get better. It will."

"I know."

"Was that all?"

"No. After I tell him, I would like to ask if I might make use of the Observation training."

Rochford looked at him, her expression becoming very curious. "For?"

"There are many things I could tell Grace, but I dinnae wish to just *tell* her. To see them would truly give her the understanding she needs."

"But —"

"I have no desire to show her battle, Councilwoman, because I dinnae want to relive it myself. I cannae. I want to show her the things in between, the moments large and small that made up the whole experience. She is a Watcher. Where words would be enough for normal people, she needs to feel it, see it, touch it. She needs to be there. Ye of all people understand that."

"I do," she said. "It will be strange for you to see yourself."

"Aye, maybe, but I cannae let that stop me."

"I know what you mean. She needs to see you there; you need to be able to explain what you felt in those moments."

"Aye, ye are right. If things go well with Malcolm, I would like to take him, too."

"Oh, Euan, that is —"

"Nae normal, I know, but for a man of history as he is, think of what that will give him, the true understanding. I dinnae have to explain anything else or show him anything else here. That would nae be necessary."

Rochford looked over at the other members before looking over at him. "Give us some time to deliberate. In the meantime, go to Observation and they will help you line up what you wish for Grace to see."

Euan nodded and bowed before departing for Observation. He'd done this with Grace when they'd taught him about what missions would be like, and he'd been thankful for it. Now, he'd use it for an entirely different purpose. Sitting down with the archivist and beginning to go over dates, he found it odd to see the entirety of this part of the timeline stretched in front of him as a bunch of small points. There was nine months' worth of days to choose from. As he went over it with the archival staff, Euan asked for some parts of the conversations they'd see be edited out, removing mentions of his time in France, making the case that it was confidential information the two men with them wouldn't need, though he kept to himself that it was also something he wasn't yet ready to tell Grace about. He selected their attire, preferring that they not be there in modern clothing or even the standard Watcher uniform. Planning everything out now meant the archivist wouldn't need to remain in the room with them once they started.

It wasn't long before Rochford joined him there, looking at the points he'd picked with a nod. "A good selection. Are you sure you want to do this? To see them all again?"

"Aye. I see them so often in my mind anyway that this will be no different," Euan said, releasing a heavy sigh. "I wish there was a way I could bring them here."

"I know, but let me tell you something," she said lowering her voice as she sat down and looked around her to make sure the archivist had gone. "They are not gone, Euan," she whispered.

"What? Who is nae?"

"Your friends."

Euan's eyes widened, and he grabbed her hand from across the table. "How."

"Not in the way you think, not in the way you are. How much do you know about Malcolm?" she asked.

"Nae much, really, other than that he works for the current Lochiel."

"Did you know he was married before?"

"Was he? He has nae mentioned it."

Rochford nodded. "He was, though she died from
cancer when she was quite young. They had a son, and
his name is also Malcolm. He will take over for his father
eventually."

Euan looked at her sadly. "That is a horrible thing."

"Yes, but it was long ago. You will meet the son soon, and
he is who you are looking for."

When Euan looked at her in confusion, she went on.

"He is the same age you are. While you will be good friends
with his father, so, too, will you be good friends with him. He
is the Malcolm you seek, the one you knew."

"How is that possible? Are ye saying everyone comes
back eventually?"

"Something like that. Think of it more as the energies and
the traits of the ancestors flowing on to their descendants. It
is more complicated than that, but I will not bore you with the
explanation. It is irrelevant in this case."

"He will nae know me, surely."

"No, no, of course not. What he *will* feel is an instant bond
with you, as though you are a friend he has not seen in quite
some time. That is the energy of his past and being near you
will bring it out. He won't understand, but you will."

"How do ye know this lad is the Malcolm I knew?"

"As I said, they have a long history with the Cameron
Watchers from here on out. It was easy to piece it together
from his own statements. He said it himself, that he felt as
though he knew you the moment he met you. If you look at
his ancestry, it was exceedingly easy to figure out why."

"Do ye nae have the same for Grace and me?"

"No, sadly. We know, of course, what your ancestry is, but
I have not seen any point where your histories lined up, no

point when one of your ancestors knew the other. It is a rather fascinating mystery."

Euan smiled, shaking his head. "Rather like anything else having to do with us."

"So true," she said, chuckling. "The two of you are an enigma in so many ways."

Euan thought back to what Elizabeth had told him. There were things they would know later, long after they were gone, that not even this Council knew. "Thank ye for telling me this."

"Of course. I really should not have done so, but what will they do? Take away my birthday? You would have figured it out eventually."

Euan started laughing at her sarcasm. "Christ, ye really are from us."

Rochford laughed along with him. "Yes, and damned proud of it. I am sorry to say that I cannot tell you about the others … Duncan and Iain? Or any of the rest. But I am sure they are out there somewhere, somehow. At least the ones who had children before they left."

"Malcolm did," Euan said. "Duncan and Iain did nae. The three of them were my closest friends."

She nodded. "It will help you when he comes, I think. It is what you need. Friends, true friends."

"Aye," he replied, his voice soft and quiet.

"This will be ready when you are. The Council has decided you may take Malcolm with you. Both of them."

"I will meet him that soon?"

She nodded with a sly smile and rose to leave.

"Thank ye," he said. "Ye are an angel, Alice."

When he used her real name, she stopped and looked back at him. "You and Grace are the only ones who can get away with that. You know that, right?"

"Are we? Well, ye are kin after all. Hard to be so formal all the time."

"At least you leave it for when we are not in Chambers," she said with a wry smile as she left.

Soon afterward, when Euan arrived back home, he found a note stuck to his phone on his nightstand, telling him that Grace and Aileen had gone into Inverness to have a "ladies' day." He smiled, pulling it off the screen before picking up his phone to send Grace a text to let her know he was home and had gotten her message. He got one back almost immediately letting him know they arrived safely, were having a grand time, and would be back later that night.

Tucking his phone into his pocket, Euan looked around him, trying to decide where to start because if he was ever going to do this, now was the time. He made quick work of gathering the things he needed, pulling on a coat before heading out to the car. It was a short drive but a long walk, and Euan wanted as much time as he could get. As he pulled into the small drive at the caretaker's cottage, he noticed a car he hadn't seen before. Alice had been right when she'd said he'd meet the son soon, but soon was apparently right now.

Euan set the things he'd brought outside of the door to Malcolm's cottage before knocking. He knew he looked far calmer than he felt, nervous about what he was planning to do despite its importance. He needed to do it, even though he realized it was for far more selfish reasons than he'd let on. Euan knew Grace was likely aware of his true motivations when he'd told her he was going to The Council this morning but had been good enough not to say so. If anyone could understand what he felt deep down, it was his wife. They were so much alike, felt so many of the same things, and he knew she'd always understand him even when he didn't always understand himself. It was, after all, why they were here at Achnacarry. She'd grown to love it here as much as he'd always loved it, but she'd moved them here because she understood it was what his soul needed. Now he needed this, and once more she hadn't stood in his way.

The door opened and the older man looked surprised to see Euan on his doorstep. "Well, hello! I was nae expecting to see ye. Is anything wrong?"

"No," Euan replied, smiling. "Naught wrong, but I did have some things I wanted to discuss with ye about the history here, if ye did nae mind."

"Of course nae," Malcolm said, returning the smile. "Come inside."

Euan stepped inside the warm cottage, and it reminded him of his old home in small ways, though this one was far larger and more modern than his had been. He heard footsteps on the stairs and turned around as young Malcolm came bounding down them.

"Dad, who does that beauty of a car belong to?" he got out before he saw Euan. "Oh."

"Me," Euan replied, forcing a small smile. It was remarkable to him how much this Malcolm looked like the one he'd always known.

"Mal, this is Euan Cameron, the lad I told ye about who bought the lodge," Malcolm replied. "Euan, this is my son, Malcolm, though we call him Mal for short. He's just come back from university. Lochiel was gracious enough to send him after all my work over the years."

Euan's stomach knotted at the thought of another Cameron lad educated by a Lochiel, and he wondered what was expected in return before remembering that things weren't the same now. "A pleasure to meet ye," Euan said, extending his hand.

Mal took it, shaking it with a firm, confident grip. "And ye," he replied, smiling. "Ye look familiar … Do I know ye from somewhere?"

"I dinnae think so," Euan replied, though he very much wanted to say otherwise.

"Tea, Euan?" Malcolm asked.

"Stronger if ye have it and are up for sharing a bit," Euan replied.

Malcolm grinned. "A lad after my own heart, ye are. Take a seat. Would ye mind if Mal joined us, or is this of a more personal nature?"

Euan laughed as he sat down at the table. "He can join us."

Malcolm brought a bottle of whisky and three glasses to the table as Mal sat down across from his father. "Now, what can I do for ye, Euan?"

As Euan slipped off his coat and draped it over the back of the chair, he pulled something from an inside pocket. "Do ye remember when I first met ye, and ye told me that my ancestor had a bounty on his head?"

"Aye, I remember."

Euan nodded and slid the paper across the table. "Ye will want to see this, then."

Malcolm took it, looking at Euan in curiosity before unfolding it and then staring at it open-mouthed. "Where did ye get this?" he asked in something bordering on a whisper.

"It was given to me, pulled from the body of one of Hawley's men at Falkirk."

Mal turned to look at Euan, brow furrowed, seeming to get the underlying point his father hadn't.

"Who gave this to ye? How do ye know the provenance?" Malcolm asked excitedly, still staring at the document he held in his hands, a document over 270 years old and in nearly perfect condition.

Euan fidgeted for a moment. "One of the Fraser men gave it to me on my birthday. He pulled it from the body himself."

Malcolm tore his eyes away from the paper to look up at Euan. "What? What are ye playing at, lad? Come on, where did ye really find this?"

Euan leaned forward and looked Malcolm directly in the eyes. "I play at naught. What ye hold in yer hands was mine, given to me by my cousin, Murdoch Fraser, on 20th January 1746. My 25th birthday."

The curious look on Mal's face hadn't left, and Malcolm

frowned. "Euan, are ye all right? Ye are talking nonsense now."

"I am nae. I swear it," Euan replied as he pointed to the document in Malcolm's hands. "That is me. *I* am Euan Cameron, the officer who left with Lochiel and the Cameron regiment and never came home again. I earned that bounty for almost killing Cumberland at Clifton Moor by shooting him in the head. My pistol misfired, otherwise things would have been a lot different."

Malcolm's features held a sort of anger that Euan hadn't expected. "Ye should leave. I dinnae know what ye are playing at with this disrespectful stunt, but ye should leave," he said as he started to stand up.

"Dad, wait —" Mal began before Euan cut him off.

"Have ye heard tales of the Watchers, Malcolm?"

Malcolm froze in his movements and looked back at Euan, even as his son's eyes went wide.

"Aye, ye have. I had a feeling ye would have. Tell me, in yer accounts from the Cameron Culloden survivors, how many of them mention seeing a young woman with golden hair dressed in white?"

"I knew it," Mal whispered.

"How did ye —"

"Because I was *there*," Euan said, cutting him off. "Because that young woman is my wife, Grace. A Watcher."

Malcolm stared at Euan in shock before he spoke. "Those are just old fairy stories."

"I thought that once, too, and then she came to try to stop me from going to Culloden. It *is* real. Those stories are true," Euan said as he pulled up his sleeve to show Malcolm the mark on his left wrist.

The older man's eyes went wide, his face going pale, but a slow smile spread across his son's lips. "No ... that cannae —"

"Cannae be? I assure ye it can. She saved me from the battlefield that day. *She* died there instead of me, and her death brought me here."

"But ye did die! We have a record of it!"

"No, ye dinnae. Ye have a record of me leaving with the rest, that is true, but ye have no record of me dying. Ye cannae because I did nae die and was nae there for anyone to find and make record of."

Malcolm sat back down, picking up his glass to down the contents, and Euan couldn't say he blamed him. "This is impossible."

Euan offered him a small smile. "Nae impossible. Hard to believe, perhaps, but nae impossible. Ask me anything ye wish, something only I would know. Go on."

"Name one of yer friends. That is something nae in any records aside from the ones we keep under lock and key, records I know ye never could've accessed. Those relationships are well-documented from survivor testimony."

"Which one? Duncan? Iain? Malcolm? Findlay? There were some other men, too, from the other clans. Donald Macdonald, Big Duncan Mackenzie …"

Malcolm covered his mouth in shock. "Sweet Christ …"

"Or perhaps this," Euan said as he stood up and lifted his shirt to show his torso, pointing to the long scar. "I got this from a Campbell after I killed Alexander Munro at Falkirk. These smaller ones came from when Cope shot at us in Tranent churchyard with cannons and exploded a wall." Euan then dropped his shirt and pulled his hair back, pointing to a small scar near his temple. "This one came from the explosion of powder at St. Ninian's that nearly killed all of us, Lochiel included."

Malcolm reached out with trembling hands and lifted Euan's shirt again, touching the long scar to make sure it wasn't makeup, then gasping and pulling his hand back when he found it was real. "Merciful Christ … Ye are telling me the truth."

"Aye, and I have more ways to prove it," Euan said, leaving the table to go to the door. Opening it, he grabbed the things he'd set aside and brought them in, placing his broadsword on the table in front of Malcolm.

Malcolm stared at it before looking up at Euan. "The only ones who had these were —"

"Officers and higher, aye. That one is mine and well-used if ye look at it."

Malcolm pulled it from its scabbard and ran his finger across the flat of the blade. It was, as Euan said, well-used. There were burrs and marks where it had clearly collided with other steel, and it would be exactly like the ones they'd seen described in written accounts. He ran his hand over the basket, the Cameron arms engraved upon it, and even here the scars of battle were evident. This was no reproduction weapon banged about to look real. It was authentic. Mal looked at it in awe as he reached out his hand to touch it.

From the bag, Euan pulled other items, laying them out on the table. "If that is nae enough, perhaps my uniform is."

What Euan set before them was the coat, plaid, kilt, brooch, bonnet, and baldric of an 18th century Cameron officer. On the brooch was the crest and motto of the Camerons, the badge on the bonnet that held the feathers that marked him as an officer having the same. The baldric buckles were solid silver and engraved with a design seen only from that period. The tartan was the ancient sett and clearly not machine woven, while the coat was made of a sage green wool that matched the bonnet and the green in the tartan.

Malcolm picked up the coat, looking at it and noting the hand stitching and the antique construction, then began laughing with tears in his eyes. "Ye really are him."

"Aye," Euan said, allowing himself a relieved smile. "I am."

Malcolm stood up and extended his hand to Euan, who took it. "Then I truly do owe ye a welcome home to yer own land, lad, and it is an absolute honor to be able to do so."

"Thank ye. It was good to come home."

Malcolm surprised Euan by pulling the younger man into an embrace, one that Euan happily returned, before releasing him and sitting down again. "This is all incredible. We dinnae even have anything like this. None of those uniforms survived."

Euan sat down again and took a drink. "That one did because I was wearing it at Culloden."

Malcolm shook his head. "Culloden. I have only ever read about it, of course."

"Naught ye read could tell ye what it was truly like," Euan said, his voice soft and distant. "I will never forget it, and neither will Grace."

"Yer wife is a Watcher," Malcolm said in disbelief. "Then the woman with ye …"

"My mam? Aye, same one, Aileen Cameron. I was allowed to bring her with me. If I had nae, they would have sent her to England, and she would have died. That is why ye have no record of what happened to *her* either."

"Why have ye told me this?"

Euan gave a gentle shrug. "Ye keep the history and I can tell ye much," he replied, "but it is more selfish than that. Ye remind me of my friend. Malcolm was a good man, one of my closest friends. Ye are how I imagine he would have been if he had been able to …" but Euan stopped, unable to say more before looking over at Mal. "Ye look like he did when I knew him."

Mal offered him a warm smile but said nothing.

"I understand ye plainly enough," Malcolm replied. "There is the longing for the connection to yer kin."

"Aye," Euan said in a near whisper. "I want a friend here, someone who really knows *me* and nae the person I have to say I am to everyone else. Dinnae get me wrong, my wife is everything to me and I love her with all that I am, but she cannae be the only one. To do that is unfair to her."

Malcolm nodded. "I am happy to be that to ye if that is what ye wish."

"Thank ye. I know the Malcolm I knew is an ancestor of yers, and that is why I wanted it to be ye," Euan said.

"This is strange," Malcolm replied.

"Probably nae as strange as ye think."

Malcolm laughed. "I'm nae sure anything is stranger than this, though so many things make more sense now, such as why ye did nae know there was still a Lochiel."

Euan joined him in laughing. "That is very likely true, and aye, that would be why."

"What is it that ye do now? I mean, ye have no Lochiel to serve and no war to fight."

"I help my wife. I go with her to do as she must, and there are plenty of battles to fight there. I still use that," Euan said, nodding to the blade, "though only in practice now and I prefer it that way. Dinnae wish to lose the skill but happy nae to have to use it. At least nae here."

"And ye said she was there, yer wife? She was the woman in white so many Camerons saw?" Malcolm asked.

"Aye. Grace was sent to stop me from dying there, and she did. She was here for some days before we left, trying to convince me to stay behind, and she was at the party at Achnacarry the night before we left." Euan swirled the whisky in his glass, his gaze distant. "She tried to warn us, but we did nae heed her, and in the end, it all happened as she had said it would."

"Aye, there was mention of that in the accounts as well, that they had seen her with ye the night before ye left for the North."

Euan nodded. "She ran out after me into the battle that day. She took the balls meant for me, the bayonet meant for me. It killed her, and the energy of her death brought us both forward to the future, farther than here. They were able to heal her, and I was given the choice to remain or go back. Clearly, I chose to remain."

"A bayonet?" Malcolm asked, looking horrified. "That poor lass."

"Aye. Her body covered in blood on a table is a sight I will never be rid of. Ye would nae know now, though. She has no marks to show for it, thank God. At least nae physical."

"It will be fascinating to hear about life here from yer own words. What the people behind those names were truly like and the stories ye could tell of battle."

"Battle," Euan repeated with a hint of bitterness. "Aye, there are plenty of those stories, but I will ask ye the same as I asked my wife: Please understand if I cannae speak of them now. Someday I will, but right now …" He shook his head. "I have been here less than a year, and it is still far too close. I have already told ye more than even she knows. I also ask that ye please nae tell me how any of them met their ends. I dinnae wish to know."

"I understand. I would nae want to either if they'd been my friends," Malcolm conceded.

"I will see about it, but I may be able to get ye one of those papers for yer collection," Euan said, a wry smile creeping onto his face. "Ye should have one, I think."

Malcolm chuckled. "Ye relish that, don't ye?"

"Oh, aye. I am sad I missed."

Malcolm laughed harder. "I am sure *he* was nae."

"Probably nae," Euan replied, grinning now. "I got permission to tell ye all of this, so I will see if they will allow me to gather some things for ye."

"Who are 'they?'" Mal asked.

"The Council," Euan replied. "They are the ones in control of the Watchers and the ones who send them on their tasks."

"Fascinating," Mal said. "I would nae have thought it would be that way. Actually, I dinnae know what I would think it would be like, honestly."

Euan chuckled. "I can see if my mam would make a set of those clothes for yer collection. Ye could have the badges recreated easily enough."

"That would be incredible. Thank ye," Malcolm said.

"Other than that, I am more than happy to answer any questions ye would ever want to ask."

"I would nae even know where to begin."

"I know *exactly* how that feels, but we have all the time in the world," Euan said, smiling.

CHAPTER 5

After a few hours of conversation, Euan stepped outside, needing to take a break. It had gone far better than he'd hoped, and he'd made fast friends with both the older man and his son. Euan put his hands on his car, leaning forward and down, stretching his shoulders before standing upright again. Eyes closed and head down, he took deep breaths in to still his mind, as George had taught him to do whenever he began to feel anxious. There had been so many questions asked about life here, about things both big and small, moments that make up an everyday existence. To remember them was both amusing and painful all at once, because although the memories were good ones, he missed those involved in them.

"I know ye."

Euan jumped and turned around to find that Mal had joined him there. He'd been so focused within himself that he hadn't heard anyone else come out. "What?"

Mal smiled. "Didn't mean to startle ye. What I said was, I know ye. I knew ye the second I saw ye. I dreamt of ye when I was younger, and then just recently I did so again."

Euan looked at him, curious. "What was the dream about?"

The young man shook his head. "I dinnae remember, honestly. I just remember ye. Yer face. Ye were wearing that uniform, but yer face was the same."

"Ah, well, I think sometimes it happens that way when ye are meant to meet someone," Euan replied, though he took it as a sign that Alice had been telling him the truth about Mal.

"Aye, sometimes. That is why I did nae react the same way my father did. I already knew, and for some reason, it seemed the most natural thing in the world that ye should be here even when it is nae."

"It is most definitely nae."

"But that does nae mean it did nae feel that way all the same," Mal replied, chuckling. "I mean, this is yer home. Ye lived here, so of course ye should be here now. This may sound strange, so bear with me, because I feel I need to say this: It is good to see ye again, old friend. Welcome home."

Euan stood in silence, the two of them looking at each other for a long few moments, before they embraced as if they'd known each other all their lives. "Thank ye. I cannae tell ye how much it means to hear that."

Mal patted him on the back and then stepped back. "And here I wondered what I would do around here all summer."

Euan laughed and shook his head. "Still nae much to do?"

"Nae exactly, no. Would nae be anywhere else, though. There is nothing like an Achnacarry summer."

"Aye, that was true even back when I was first here."

"When ye were first here. Is that as weird to say as it is to hear?"

"Ye would be surprised how quickly ye get used to it. What did ye study?"

"Archeology," Mal replied, starting to laugh.

"How appropriate," Euan replied, joining him in that laughter. "To take up the records after yer father?"

"Eventually, aye. I very much look forward to meeting the infamous Cameron lady in white, though."

"She will nae be what ye expect," Euan said, a small sly smile appearing on his lips.

"What do ye mean?"

"Grace is American. Same age as we are and born the same year as ye."

"Really? I would've thought she would be from some past time."

"No. The only ones who are, in that sense, are the Companions like me, and nae even all of us are from the past. She speaks fluent Gaelic, though," Euan said as he gave a small shrug.

"Does she? An American speaking fluent Gaelic: That is nae something ye hear every day."

"I taught her, but I have a feeling my version might be different from yers if ye know it."

"I do know it, but enough will be the same. Aside from modern words for modern things, it has nae changed any."

"Probably," Euan said, walking back inside with Mal. "Ye cannae imagine the stories *she* will be able to tell ye."

"From her duties?"

"Oh, aye, but I have a few of those myself now. She has a degree in history from Oxford, so ye ought to have plenty to discuss."

Mal stopped walking and looked at Euan in surprise. "She has what! Do ye have any idea how difficult it is for a non-British student to get into Oxford?"

"No. It is different based on where ye are from?"

"Aye! On purpose! They only want the best. The qualifications they require from American students are absolutely insane, and ye are telling me that she nae only got in but also graduated?"

"Aye."

"Christ, I will be outmatched, I'm sure."

"She is nae like that; ye will see," Euan said as he sat back down at the table and studied his uniform. "It has been so long since I truly wore that."

"Did ye all wear the same?"

"No, well, we all wore the same tartan but otherwise no. We are all a bit different except for the badges."

Malcolm returned, joining them at the table. "I dinnae think we should ask more of ye today, Euan. Ye have given us so much already and ye look exhausted."

"Nae as exhausted as I seem. Relieved, perhaps, but I am used to nae —" he began before a ding from his phone caused him to stop and fish the device out of his coat pocket.

"It is really odd to see ye answering a mobile phone when we know who ye are," Mal said.

Euan smiled and shrugged, checking the message before he looked up at them. "The ladies are home. Would ye like to come up and meet them?"

"They would nae mind it being sprung on them?" Malcolm asked.

"I can let them know," Euan said, holding up the phone and waving it just a bit, his expression at once sarcastic and amused.

"Right, of course," Malcolm said as Mal laughed. "I would nae mind meeting them for who they are."

"Neither of them differ from when ye met them. It is only that ye now know the truth about what my wife does for a living, why she told ye she worked so much she never spent her money, and that my mam is nae named Margaret."

"I'd be happy to go," Mal said. "I have nae seen the lodge in ages."

Euan sent a message to Grace and then stood up, carefully folding his uniform and putting it away in the bag before he grabbed his broadsword. "Shall I see ye there then?"

"Take Mal with ye. I know he is dying to ride in that car of yers."

"That is absolutely true," Mal said.

Euan laughed and motioned for Mal to join him, which he eagerly did.

"I have always wanted one of these," Mal said, drawing a hand along the hood as Euan put his things behind his seat.

"It is a fine car, I will tell ye that," Euan said before he smiled and tossed Mal the key. "Go on, then."

"No, ye cannae be serious!"

"I would nae offer if I was nae."

Mal grinned like a child and ran around to the driver's side to get in. "Ach, God, look at ye, ye absolute beauty," he said in an almost reverent whisper as Euan got in.

"The clutch is a bit different, so just be wary."

"Got it," Mal said as he put his foot on the brake and pressed the ignition switch. As the car roared to life, he laughed with glee and looked at Euan. "Cannae ever get too used to that, can ye?"

"No, I love it," he said as he turned the music on and cranked it up, gesturing for Mal to go. Mal needed no prompting, though he eased it out of the cottage drive and Euan looked at him in amusement. "If ye are going to drive it like that, ye can just get out now. Ye should be ashamed of yerself."

Mal looked over at him, a sly grin crossing his face. "Right then, let's go," he said as he punched it and took off.

When they reached the road to the lodge, Euan had Mal wait at the bottom of the drive for Malcolm so that they wouldn't arrive before he did. Both of them were laughing, Mal with the exhilaration of driving a car he'd always wanted, and Euan with the pleasure of once again being in the company of another young man from home. When Malcolm caught up to them, the two cars went up the drive together, and Euan guided the two men inside through the front door after parking.

"Grace? Mam?" Euan called out.

"Kitchen!" he heard called back to him in unison.

"Wow, the old place looks fantastic," Mal said.

"Aye," Malcolm said, looking around. He hadn't seen it since they'd bought it. "Ye did a fine job with it."

"We tried to keep as much of it the same as we could," Euan said as he beckoned them to follow him. When they entered the kitchen, he found Aileen at the stove working on supper, but no Grace, though he could've sworn he'd just heard her. "Hi, Mam," he said as he kissed her cheek.

"Ye are lucky I was making something that would be enough for guests!"

"Ach, no, we could have just kicked them out."

"Euan Cameron! Where are yer manners!" she said, indignant, until she saw his smile. "Ugh, ye."

Euan laughed. "Mam, ye know Malcolm, but ye have nae met his son, Mal."

Aileen, laughing along with her son, turned to look at the two men, but her laughter ceased in a gasp as she set eyes on Mal. "My God … it is like looking at a ghost."

"I suppose the same could be said about ye, Mrs. Cameron," Mal said, smiling.

"Ach, and like talking to one, too," she groused with a half-smile. "Welcome to ye both. Malcolm, it is good to see ye again."

"And ye, Aileen," Malcolm said, his purposeful use of her true name bringing a curious look from her.

"They know, Mam. The Council gave me permission to tell them."

"Of course they did," Grace said.

Euan turned around as he heard Grace speak behind him, and the eyes of all three men fell on her at the same time. For Malcolm, it was as if he were truly seeing her, but Mal stared at her as though she were a painting come to life.

"It's good to see ye again, Grace," Malcolm said.

"And you," she replied, smiling, before she looked at Mal. "And you are?"

"Oh, sorry, love," Euan said. "This is Mal, Malcolm's son."

"Oh! I didn't know you had a son! A pleasure to meet you, Mal. I suppose you are both part of the super-secret club now."

"Aye, Euan told us. I am astonished, I will admit, as I did nae think those stories were true," Malcolm said. "Yer secret is safe with us, and we will assist ye in whatever ways we can."

"I appreciate that. It can get to be a bit of a lonely existence, and I'm sure that's why Euan got permission."

"I can imagine it would be, aye, especially for someone who has made such a shift as he has."

"I'm glad he has found a friend in you. The both of you."

Euan pulled her close and kissed her cheek, nuzzling it

to take in the soft scent of her skin and happy to reconnect with her physically after being apart from her all day. "Did ye have fun?"

"You know we did," she replied with a smile before she noticed Mal was still staring at her. "Is something wrong?"

"No, sorry, I just … I cannae believe it is actually ye."

"Me?"

"The woman in white from all of the records."

"What?"

"They saw ye, love. There was no way they could nae. The survivor accounts mention having seen a young woman in white. Ye," Euan explained.

"Oh. I suppose they would have, wouldn't they? I hadn't thought of that."

"It has never mattered," Euan reminded her.

"I grew up with those stories, wondering who ye were and what had happened to ye. Ye have long been a mystery we tried to solve, and now I know why we could nae," Mal said.

"I hope I don't disappoint."

"No, far from," Mal replied, his voice quiet. "Ye are better because ye are real, but ye are also more than ye were described."

Euan could tell Mal found Grace as captivating to look at as he had the first time he'd seen her, the way he often still felt when he looked at her. "I am glad we are all here. There is something I would like to discuss with all of ye."

Grace looked at him with curiosity, as did the others. "What would that be?"

"Naught bad," Euan said, feeling her relax against him with his reassurance. "The Council has given me permission to do something else. They are allowing me to make use of the Observation training to show ye things."

"What things?" Grace asked.

"My life," he said. "Nae all of it, I will nae show ye the battles, but I want ye to see the rest. I know ye, Grace. Ye have to experience it; I cannae just tell ye about it," he explained before he looked over at the two men. "They have given me permission to allow ye to join us."

"What!" Mal exclaimed. "What does that mean?"

"It means ye will come with us as if ye are going on a mission as we do. Instead of a mission, I will be taking ye through my time in the rising, and ye will be there as if ye are truly there. No one will see or hear us, but ye will see and hear everything."

"Ye are giving us a chance to actually walk through history, Euan?" Malcolm asked.

"Aye. In yer history and mine."

"How long will we be gone?"

"Nae long. A day, perhaps. Though ye will nae really be gone. Yer bodies will still be here while the rest of ye is elsewhere."

"When do we go?" Mal asked, excited.

"Whenever ye are ready. Nae now, but as soon as tomorrow if ye wish it."

Father and son looked at each other, and it was obvious that both recognized this was a once in a lifetime chance they'd be mad to pass up.

"Tell us what ye need us to do," Malcolm said.

"It is time for supper, so why dinnae ye all sit down and discuss it over the meal," Aileen said.

"Dinnae have to ask me twice," Mal said. "I'm starving."

"Now that ye mention it, so am I. What did ye make, Mam?" Euan asked.

"One of yer new favorites, Euan: mince and tatties."

"I have nae had that in ages," Mal said, grinning. "No wonder it smells so good in here."

"Thank ye, Mam," Euan said, smiling. "An excellent choice for a cold day."

"Ye were gone so early I figured ye would be hungry when ye returned. Come on, let us eat," Aileen said, giving Euan's cheek a gentle pat.

Over supper, Euan let Grace explain what Observation was and how it worked before they spent the rest of the evening talking together about all sorts of things. There'd been a lot of laughter, and Euan was happy to find that Grace got along with the two men as well as he did. Mal was quick to get over his initial shock once he realized she was just as normal as he was, and the two of them spent some time talking about Grace's schooling and some of the things she'd done with it, including missions.

The next morning, Malcolm and Mal arrived early, and Caia was there with another Guardian, who would see to Mal and Malcolm. She could get all of them there herself, but it would be easier on her to have the extra help.

"Gentlemen, this is Caia, my Guardian. Her job is to protect me when I'm out on missions and to take me back and forth to The Council when needed. She'll be transporting Euan and me, while Michelle will be taking the two of you," Grace explained.

"A pleasure to meet ye both," Malcolm said.

"The pleasure is mine," Caia replied with her customary smile.

"My name is Mal," Mal said, holding out a hand to Caia.

"I know who you are," she said, chuckling and shaking his hand.

"Do ye?"

"It is my job to know. Now, do not worry," Caia said. "Everything will be fine. Once you take Michelle's hands and close your eyes, you will feel a slight shift, and then you will be there. Are you ready?"

"Aye," both men replied, though their voices betrayed their nerves. The other Guardian held out her hands, and each of them took one. As soon as they closed their eyes, they were gone.

"I dinnae think I have ever watched that happen before with someone new to this," Euan mused as he took Caia's hand, hearing both Caia and Grace laugh before they, too, left.

When they opened their eyes, they were in the Observation room. They'd come straight here due to Euan's promise that he wouldn't need to show them anything else. Aileen had remained behind, not needing or wanting to see a replay of her own life.

"Jesus, that is the strangest feeling," Mal said as he opened his eyes, his jaw dropping as he looked around him.

"Welcome to Observation," Grace said as the two Guardians departed. "This is where new Watchers train, and where Companions train for their role with their Watcher. At first, we go out with an experienced Watcher to see what they do and how they work, to learn what's expected and what we might encounter. Often, these are missions already completed, so we know what the outcome is and what we should learn from it."

"This is incredible," Malcolm said before his eyes finally fell on Grace. "Sweet, merciful Christ," he whispered.

Grace stood there in the same white dress all Watchers wore at the end of their missions, and the very same white dress all the men whose stories they'd read had seen her in. The same one Euan had seen in those final moments. He'd known she'd appear in uniform because she always did, they all did, even him, just as he was now. He had no idea how it worked, but one appeared in uniform the moment they arrived, no matter what they'd previously been wearing, and when they left they were back in their regular clothing.

It was easy to see what the two men were thinking, the realization sinking in that they were sharing a vision that so many of their ancestors had seen before them. Mal shook his head and forced his eyes away from her, even though Euan could tell that all he wanted to do was look at her. She was even more beautiful this way, she was meant to be, and there should be no doubt now as to why Euan had struggled with his decision in the way he'd told them he had.

"What happens now?" Malcolm asked, recovering himself.

"We will all get on a table, they'll hook us in, and we'll go where Euan has chosen for us to start," Grace explained as she looked over at Euan. "Are you sure about this?"

"Aye," he whispered before he kissed her cheek. "I need to do this. I need ye to see at least some of it. I owe ye that much."

The archivist came in and helped to hook up the two men as Grace and Euan set themselves up.

"Now, all you need to do is close your eyes and wait for Euan to tell you to open them," Grace said.

Both men closed their eyes and waited. There wouldn't be the shift they'd normally feel if they were sent on a mission because this was different. Instead, there was a change in the feeling of the world outside. There was, quite suddenly, the warmth of a summer breeze and the familiar scent of the fields, along with the sounds of people moving and talking.

"We are here," Euan said.

CHAPTER 6

The two men opened their eyes to find familiar yet unfamiliar ground. Instead of the castle they both knew, there was the previous one, tall and proud in the late afternoon sunlight. They stood inside the castle yard, with people passing all around them, but none of them seemed to notice the four people now standing there. Both stood stock-still for a long moment, taking all of it in. They were really here, here in a history they'd only ever been able to read about. Their ancestors were here somewhere amongst these people.

Mal looked down at his clothing to find himself in the attire of a Cameron soldier. It was similar to what Euan had shown them but lacked the feathers in the bonnet and the badge that held them there. He carried no sword, but he did have a baldric with a dirk. He touched it incredulously and then started laughing with a giddy sort of joy. Malcolm was dressed the same and simply shook his head in near disbelief. Both of them looked at Euan and Grace, who stood there beside them.

Euan was in his uniform, as he would've been, his bearing changed entirely. He seemed somehow larger, his shoulders were back, and he stood straight. The buckles and badges caught the sun, and he looked nothing if not extremely intimidating. Grace stood beside him in the same blue dress he'd known her in, wearing the Cameron tartan arasaid in the traditional way: draped over her shoulders and belted around her waist. The bottom acted almost as a second skirt; the top was pinned at her collarbone to act as a cape with a hood if needed.

"When is this?" Malcolm asked.

"The day before we rode for Borrodale to meet the prince. I brought ye here first because I wanted ye to see what a supper was like here before everything changed. Come on," Euan said, taking Grace's hand and starting forward toward the castle.

As they walked inside, the laughter and noise from the hall was already at full volume, and the two men looked around them in awe. "This is amazing," Mal whispered to his father.

"Aye. Make note of everything, Son, for ye will never get this chance again."

"I promise I will let ye explore in just a moment," Euan said. "Ye should see it as it was."

Just as he said that, the younger Euan stepped out of the hallway from his meeting with Brenda. Grace gasped beside the current Euan, her eyes widening. To see him as he was, as he'd been before his entire life changed, was a surprise for her. He was different, his expression more open even though it was still guarded, his eyes not yet shadowed with the darkness of war. He wasn't easily missed even in this crowd of people, and she watched as he went to a table with a group of other men and sat down, passed a cup of wine as he laughed.

At the same time, Mal and Malcolm noticed their forebear. Malcolm Cameron, the officer, sat beside Euan, the two of them laughing and talking. He looked almost identical to the young Mal, who stood staring at him in utter surprise.

"It's like looking in a mirror, Dad. That has to be him."

"Aye," Malcolm said.

"It is," Euan replied.

"How old was he here?" Mal asked.

"About 30, I think. Married with 3 bairns at home. By this time, he has known me almost 20 years. He was 10 when we first met, and I was four when I came into Lochiel's service."

At that moment, the man himself emerged, and the entire hall rose to attention, bows and curtsies flowing before him, and Grace felt Euan's hand tighten on hers. She knew how hard it was for him to see this man now, after those visits with the Specialist had shown him just how deeply he'd been manipulated. She looked up at him and placed a hand on his chest to bring him back to her, and he smiled with gratitude.

"Christ, would ye look at that. It is The Gentle Lochiel himself," Malcolm whispered.

"Gentle," Euan muttered. "To anyone but us."

The two men shot him curious glances but said nothing, seeming to instinctively understand that if Euan wanted it revealed, it would be.

"Please, explore the castle as ye will. Grace and I will wait outside for ye."

The two men nodded and headed off as Euan pulled Grace outside and into his arms, just holding her.

"You don't have to do this," she whispered. "You don't owe me anything, and especially not this."

"Aye, I do. It is as much for ye as it is for me. This cannae harm me, and ye are here with me when ye were nae before. It will make all the difference in the world to me," he explained before letting go of a gentle sigh. "I told ye I was different."

"That young man is still there, and I see him more often than you realize."

"Do ye?"

"Of course. When you're truly happy, that's what you're like."

Euan smiled, but then it turned devilish. "Come with me."

"Where?"

"Ye will see," he said as he pulled her after him. When they reached the barracks, he ducked inside and brought her with him.

"Where is this?"

"The barracks where we slept," he said in a quiet voice before he silenced any other conversation with a kiss. Pulling her toward the cot he'd once occupied, he tossed the bags that rested there aside and dropped onto it with her.

Grace pulled back from him with a small laugh. "What are you doing?"

"Something I always wanted to but never dared."

"Which was?"

"Having a woman in here with me," he whispered as he kissed her neck.

"Euan!"

"Shhh … ye will get us caught," he said, grinning as he placed a finger against her lips.

Grace buried her face in his shoulder and laughed, but she wouldn't stop him. If they were back here, why not have a little fun with it and create other memories in places where they shouldn't exist?

"I have better ways to silence ye," he murmured, bringing her lips back to his.

Grace abandoned any desire to think about anything else, letting him and his desire for this carry her along, returning his kiss and wrapping her arms tightly around him. In return, she felt him melt into her, his hand cupping her cheek. When he pulled back to nip her ear, she let go of a tiny gasp, pressing her hips into his and hearing his soft groan in response.

"God help me, but if ye had been here when this actually happened, I would never have gotten anything done, and I would have been in some sort of trouble daily for it. Would nae have cared though; ye are worth every blow I might earn," he whispered against her ear.

"Maybe, but now it doesn't matter. Think about it, think about how the young man in there right now has no idea what his future self is up to in his bed. While he's there in service, you're here bedding me, and oh, wouldn't he be jealous?"

"Oh, aye, he would," Euan agreed. "He would nae be able to comprehend how smooth ye were beneath his hands," he continued, sliding a hand over her thigh under the skirts. "That lad never shall, for he is gone, and ye are mine alone."

Grace's back lifted slightly from the bed as he squeezed her thigh tightly, his fingertips digging in just enough to make her squirm. He brought his lips to her neck, placing a gentle bite on the tender skin and bringing an involuntary moan from her. There were times when he could be a bit rough, though he always seemed to know when that was what precisely what she wanted from him. This was one of those times, and he was delivering in all the right ways. Now that they were here, now that he'd started this, she had no other thought than finishing it.

In a swift movement, he grabbed one of her wrists in each hand and pinned them to the bed above her head, then clutched both in one of his own. He squeezed, and she winced just the tiniest bit, something that brought a dark smile to his lips. "Look at ye," he whispered. "Helpless here, and that is just the way ye like it, is it nae, my lovely? Nae only unable to resist me but also quite unwilling, the little bits of pain ye can feel only making it better for ye. What would anyone think if they knew, hm?" he asked before he kissed her, holding her bottom lip in his teeth for a long moment once he'd pulled away.

His words and his actions made it hard to think, but he wasn't wrong about any of it and he knew it. It was why he'd said it. While he loved to surrender control to her at times, there was no question as to who was in charge more often. He urged her to surrender, to let go, to enjoy some time where she didn't have to be in control of anything and could just feel, and she was always more than happy to do so.

Euan chuckled, his voice low and dangerous. "Naught to say, have ye? Well, as I can tell ye now want this as much as I do, there is only one thing ye need to do: Say yes, my angel."

Grace wanted to hesitate just so he could command her to say it — something she quite enjoyed him doing during this sort of game because he knew she ultimately *wanted* to say yes — but she wouldn't do so this time. "Yes," she whispered.

Euan didn't hesitate, and it brought a pleasured sound from them both. Grace knew how worked up he was, being able to act out a fantasy he'd always had of having a woman here in the barracks and thus breaking a huge rule, and it was clear in the tension of his body and every move he made. His hand tightened on her wrists even further, and it brought a small sound of pain from her for the brief moment she was able to feel it. His other hand now held one of her hips and pressed her against him, a loud gasp escaping her as it changed the feeling of what he was doing.

Before she could make another sound to follow that gasp, he smothered it with a passionate kiss, and Grace felt as though she were twisting inside out. Her hands tightened into fists, and the tension broke all at once, the near scream it brought from her stifled against his lips even as his was against hers. When his lips parted from hers, they were both breathing heavily, and he rested his forehead against her own.

"Are ye well?" he whispered.

"More than, I'd say," she said in return.

His laugh was soft, and he kissed the tip of her nose. "Good. Thank ye for helping me get to finally do this."

"You are very, *very* welcome."

"Ye wee vixen," he said with a slight grin before he let go of her and stood, pulling her up with him and helping her to smooth out her clothing.

"Is that a complaint?"

"Never."

"I didn't think so."

"Come, we dinnae want to be too long, lest they suspect something," he said, winking and taking her hand to lead her back outside.

By the time Mal and Malcolm came back out into the yard, Grace and Euan were standing there waiting for them as if they'd been waiting there the entire time.

"Did ye see it all?" Euan asked, nonchalant.

"Aye," Malcolm said. "It is an amazing thing to see what no longer exists, the things that did nae make it out of the fires and those that did. Ye can see them in their proper places."

"I will admit that I wish I had a camera or a sketchbook," Mal said. "I would love to have evidence of all of this."

"How would ye explain that?" Euan asked, his lips spreading into a half-smile.

"I know, I know. It's my job, though."

Euan laughed. "Come, it is time to go."

"You will just close your eyes again," Grace explained.

All of them did, and the familiar scent of the Highland breeze changed and carried a slight hint of salt air.

"Welcome to the prince's camp at Borrodale House," Euan said, his voice becoming quieter.

Before anyone could reply, Lochiel and Euan walked by them, Grace laughing at the reaction of the French soldiers upon seeing Euan, and Mal laughing at Euan being confused for Lochiel before they followed the two men into the house.

"Oh my God," Mal said as he entered and saw Prince Charles Edward Stuart himself.

Grace looked upon the young man with immediate suspicion. She knew, of course, what Euan had told her and what she knew from her own studies. But there was something about him that set her on edge, something she couldn't explain yet. The group watched as Lochiel tried to convince the prince to turn back, watched as the prince used emotional blackmail to force Lochiel into action. Grace scoffed and rolled her eyes at such a ploy, which brought a swift smile from her husband. While the eyes of the other two were on the prince and Lochiel, she was watching Euan, studying his expression, his reactions to the things being said around him. She knew him so well now that even his smallest reactions would tell her precisely what he was thinking and feeling, things no one here ever would've noticed. As the prince and Lochiel agreed on initial terms, she noted Euan's changed posture. He'd known then; she knew he had. When the prince suddenly addressed the past Euan, Grace's head turned to look at the young royal.

"How old are you?" the prince asked Euan.

"Twenty-four, Yer Highness."

"And what is your position with Lochiel that you are here at his side for such an important moment?"

"I am one of his officers," Euan replied.

"Euan is one of my best, Yer Highness, a captain, and he will fight for ye until he can no longer do so. He has trained for this since he was just a wee boy, and he is well-schooled in strategy, tactics, and combat. He accompanies me everywhere I go."

The prince nodded. *"Have you a wife and a family, Euan?"*

"Non, Votre Altesse. Juste ma mère. Je n'ai pas eu envie de prendre une femme," No, Yer Highness. Just my mother. I have nae had the inclination to take a wife.

The prince raised an eyebrow. *"Perfect French. As for not having a wife or family: good. That means you will fight harder when you have nothing to leave behind."*

"You son of a bitch," Grace muttered under her breath, making an involuntary move toward the young man, though Euan grabbed her by the arm to hold her back. "How dare he say something so callous," she whispered as she looked up at Euan, who said nothing in response.

"I will do as required of me, Yer Highness."

Grace noted the expression on Lochiel's face in that moment: a deep frown at the nonchalant dismissal of someone's life, and not just any life, but Euan's. It was a look Mal and Malcolm shared.

"We will move on now," Euan said, prompting them all to close their eyes.

The change in atmosphere and the sound of horses brought their eyes open again. They were at Achnacarry once more, this time in the darkness before dawn. All around them, men and horses gathered, women and children crying as they embraced their brothers, sons, and fathers, and to the side stood the surprising sight of the English prisoners from High Bridge. The four of them, however, were on horseback, with Mal and Malcolm on their own, and Grace sitting sideways in front of Euan. They were lined up right beside the younger Euan, and Grace noticed they even sat on the same horse, while beside him his company stood in formation.

"Are ye ready, lad?" Lochiel asked as he rode up alongside Euan. Beside them, the past Euan nodded. *"Aye, Lochiel."*

"Then let us away. Camerons! March!"

The order was called back, the pipes and drums struck up, and the entire mass moved forward as one. She watched as Mal and Malcolm looked around at the 800 men surrounding them, the sound of the music seeming to touch them deeply. They knew these songs, of course, and to hear them played as their own ancestors marched out to war had to be moving in a way she couldn't begin to understand.

"Get comfortable, ye are in for a day's ride," Euan said.

"Are we going where I think we are, lad?" Malcolm asked.

"To Glenfinnan."

"Christ, we are."

Euan laughed. "I wanted ye to have the experience of a ride with us when our spirits were high. Enjoy it, enjoy riding beside the men who sired those ye came from," Euan said as they rode through the gates.

Grace leaned back against him and nuzzled his chest, watching the younger version of Euan ride beside them, looking so serious about his duty. He was still that way, that same expression quite familiar to her from many a mission. He had a job to do, and that was his sole focus. Meanwhile, there was something there, something no one else would no-tice because they didn't know him the way she did. It was in his posture, the set of his jaw, the totality of his expression. It was obvious to her that he was troubled, that what loomed before him sat heavy on his heart and mind, and it made her want to reach out and touch him, to let him know she was there, and no matter what happened, a new life awaited him when all of this was over.

"Ah, and that is why I wanted ye here with me instead of on

yer own horse. I wanted the comfort of ye near me," he whispered, breaking her out of her thoughts and reminding her that the man this young man became was there with her now.

Grace smiled at the reminder that he could read her and feel her emotions just as well as she could do with him, saying nothing and turning her eyes forward to watch the scenery as they traveled. That the journey would take them on routes that could no longer be traveled would be a treat in and of itself, with some parts of it no longer open land, closing these ancient paths off to the modern world unless one walked them.

The former Malcolm moved to ride at the head of his company instead of at the side so that he could converse with Euan on the way. *"For Christ's own sake, Euan,"* Malcolm said. *"Ye look as though ye are about a funeral."*

"Maybe I am."

"Ours or theirs?"

"Theirs, I would hope."

"Aye, true enough, but then …" he said, pausing and looking around him before speaking again. *"Ye have to admit there are a fair few amongst us ye would nae mind being rid of."*

"I would nae admit that," Euan said, though he smiled.

"Would nae admit it, or dinnae think it?"

"If I said the last half, I would be lying, but I also am nae in the habit of making incriminating statements in front of 800 other men."

"Ye see!"

Euan laughed at him. *"Ye can be such a bastard."*

"I may be, but I am also yer brother, so dinnae forget it, ye arse."

"Ye would nae let me."

"No, I would nae," Malcolm replied, his grin mischievous. *"But at least now ye are smiling."*

Euan scoffed and gave a playful roll of his eyes. *"Ye always did relish taking me out of my focus."*

"Nae relish as much as specialize."

Beside the two men, their observers laughed along with them at such irreverent conversation, even the present Euan, and for the first time, Mal and Malcolm seemed to relax into it and forget they weren't really there.

"It was so beautiful, this ride," Grace said to Euan once conversation had lulled, her voice quiet.

"Aye, it was. Still would be if ye could do it, I imagine."

"It wasn't always like this, was it?"

Euan laughed, then shook his head. "No. It got worse as the weather did."

Grace wrinkled her nose. "Ugh, that had to be awful."

"Oh, aye, it was. Happy nae to have to do that again, believe me."

"Now you can do it in a car with a heater."

"I will never nae be thankful for that."

Grace chuckled and shook her head, reaching up to stroke his cheek before she pulled her hand back and looked at the young man still riding beside them. He was enjoying this ride, too, and it was written all over his face now that a friend had gotten him to relax a bit. They listened to some of the other conversations, laughing and letting Euan explain to them who the people they were talking about were. Somewhere along the way, Iain and Findlay took turns starting drinking songs, which got the men in the companies laughing and singing along.

"Right, lads! We are nearly there! Pipers!" Lochiel called.

The drums kicked in first, a song she didn't recognize even though the other two men did. From beside them, young Euan's voice rang out clear and strong to begin the song, and Grace looked over at him in surprise. She knew he could sing well, but not like this! He'd never sung this loudly around her, but she now wished he would, and the fact that she could understand the words he was singing made it all the more incredible. The current Euan now joined the former version of himself, singing the song now in the same way he had then, the two voices melding together in harmony. Grace closed her eyes to listen, and at the next verse, the rest of the Cameron regiment, along with Mal and Malcolm, joined in as they marched forward and began their descent into Glenfinnan, the beauty of the sound bringing tears to her eyes. Below them, in the glen, waited the prince and Clan MacDonald, who cheered when they saw their allies.

"I am nae a Jacobite, but God am I nae a proud Cameron at this moment," Malcolm said.

"I am, but even if I was nae, it would be hard nae to be proud," Mal said. "Look at us."

"Ye should be proud," Euan replied, "because we will strike fear into the hearts of the English and with damned good reason."

The small group remained on horseback to watch the men fall out and make camp, see the MacDonalds of Keppoch arrive, and observe Lochiel's conversation with Euan from a distance. When the Stuart standard was raised, Grace felt Euan's heavy sigh against her back. The countdown to the death of the Highlanders and their way of life had now begun.

CHAPTER 7

Euan asked them to close their eyes again, and when they opened them, they found themselves still on horseback, an icy wind whipping across the open space. It was bitterly cold, and even though the observers couldn't feel it, it was clear in the huddled postures and reddened skin of the men standing there. Sitting amongst the Cameron regiment, they were looking across a river at the men gathering on the other side. Beside them, a now healed Euan dismounted to join his men on the ground.

"The crossing into England," Mal said, almost to himself.

"Aye," Euan replied.

As they watched, he closed his eyes and sang as he walked forward into the river, bringing a small, sharp noise from Grace.

"That song … Euan, they sang that song when —"

"A good choice for such a thing," Euan said before she could finish so that she didn't have to say the words, following it with a gentle kiss on her temple.

As the rest of the Cameron men joined in, Grace looked over at Mal and Malcolm as they sang along with tears in their eyes. They knew what was happening here; but more than that, these were their ancestors. They felt this moment deep in their bones in a way no one else possibly could except for Euan himself. Without thinking, Grace joined them in the song. Though she'd only heard it once, the circumstances had burned it into her soul. Grace felt something wet hit her cheek and looked up to find Euan shedding silent tears as he watched himself and the others cross, not going with them this time, but remaining in Scotland. She couldn't imagine how hard reliving this must be for him, and it was the first time she'd seen him truly react to what he was watching. Taking his hand, she lifted it to her lips and kissed it, the gesture bringing his gaze to her instead of the men leaving their homeland.

"Thank ye," he mouthed, and she smiled in return.

The salute to Scotland as each man reached the English side also brought forth tears from the other two men watching, though they continued singing all the same. As the men now in England returned to formation, Euan looked away from them.

"I will nae take ye to England because there is nae any point. For us, it is time to go home."

In that instant, all of it faded, and they found themselves on the Observation tables. Disoriented, the two men sat up and looked around them. Back in their regular clothing, they looked almost disappointed, and an archivist entered to help them out of the equipment.

"Euan, I cannae thank ye enough for this," Malcolm said. "It was more than I'd imagined it would be, and there is such a swirl of things around me now. Pride, sadness, anger, awe. I cannae make sense of it."

"There is naught like being there," Euan said. "Ye saw what it was, what it was like, at least for us, and that is what I wanted for ye. I know it does nae help with yer records, but ye did get to see what ye wanted: what the people behind those names were really like. Though I did nae show it to ye, the prince himself changed along the way. He was nae at all like what the written history ye have tells ye he was, nae stupid or foolish or foppish or drunk. After I got to know him a bit, I did have respect for him and actually liked him for the most part. He had his moments, as we all do."

"Got to know him?" Malcolm asked.

"Aye. After Clifton Moor, he had a private meeting with

me where he asked to speak as equals, and we did. I left that meeting with a far better understanding of him, and as I told the Specialist, any time he saw me afterward he would greet me by name. I was asked to translate for him when he spoke to the men who spoke only Gaelic because I could translate it into French for him as well as English. He had a sense of fun and mischief, a strong sense of honor, but he had a presence about him, too. He could be studious and serious, could be princely in an instant. On the other hand, he was prone to melancholy and would, at times, call for me to talk to him when he was so. In the end, he was a young man with the weight of a dynasty on his shoulders, trying to do the best he could to fulfill the dream he'd been force-fed since birth."

"I had no idea ye knew him that well."

"Until now it was nae something I felt comfortable speaking about to anyone. Nae even Lochiel knew the full truth of it. My relationship with him and my feelings on all of it are mixed, at best."

"I am still amazed I got to see my ancestor," Mal said. "I could never accurately describe what that was like."

"Ye dinnae have to," Euan said, smiling. "I am glad ye could. I will have the Guardians take ye back now, and we can talk tomorrow."

The two men nodded as Caia came in to take them back. Grace sat in silence, and when they'd gone, Euan turned to look at her. "Now that the other two are gone, there is more I want ye to see. Just ye."

"Just me? Why?"

"Because so much of it is personal to me, things I dinnae want to share or discuss with others and cannae. It will be hard enough to do it with ye."

"Euan, please, don't. I don't want to do this to you, and my deeper understanding isn't worth what this will cost you."

He gave his head a gentle shake. "I want to. More than that, I need to. Are ye ready?"

Grace nodded, though she wasn't sure she was truly ready for it, and closed her eyes. The shift was quick, the sounds of Observation fading, and when she opened them again, it was to the darkness of a city street. There was a strange stillness for such a place, and what sounds there were seemed amplified off the stone walls in the placidity that belied the underlying tension. To Grace, it felt as though there were something seething around them, a turmoil about to erupt and shatter the hush that had settled like a thick blanket. Grace took a few steps forward, eyes narrowed as she searched for any sort of movement.

"Where is this?" Grace whispered even though she didn't need to.

"Edinburgh," Euan replied. "17th September 1745."

From the shadows, two young soldiers appeared, the sound of their boots on the cobblestones almost deafening in the dead air of the autumn night. They appeared unremarkable at first, just two regulars walking toward the guard post at the center of town. Grace noticed in almost an instant, gasping and pointing as she turned to look at Euan standing behind her.

Euan grinned. "Aye, lass, that is me. Excellent eye, as always."

"You look far better in that uniform than you have any right to," Grace murmured.

The statement brought a gentle laugh from Euan. "Hated every moment I was in it."

"Still."

"I will keep that in mind," he replied with a wink.

At that moment, a coach sped by them, and Grace quickly stepped out of its way to avoid being trampled, more out of instinct than actual danger. In what seemed like no time at all, 800 Cameron men swept past them, unopposed, fanning out in various directions, the bloodless capture of Edinburgh complete. Without a moment's hesitation, Grace followed them, staring in wonder at her husband wearing the uniform of his enemies. She understood what he'd done here and why because it was exactly what she would've done in his position.

"There was always a theory that you had help from the inside, but I never would've thought it was actually one of you. Cleverly done."

"It was exhausting," Euan admitted as he watched his past play out before him. "Especially coordinating two units after stealing the gate keys."

"You did what?" Grace asked even as she started laughing.

"I stole a set of gate keys and had some friends unlock it for me. That way, if one plan failed, the other would still let us in."

"Extra layers. I can appreciate that."

"Of course ye can," Euan said. "Why? Because ye would do it just the same."

"Oh, I absolutely would."

"It kills me to see ye in those colors, lad, even if the uniform looks well on ye. Take it off," Lochiel said.

Thank Christ," the former Euan said in relief, more than happy to obey the order, stripping off the coat and throwing it to the ground before spitting on it.

Grace glanced back at Euan with a raised eyebrow, as if to ask him if such a thing was truly necessary. When he responded with a smile and a shrug, she rolled her eyes playfully, shaking her head as someone tossed the other Euan a Cameron plaid to drape over his shoulder and ensure his clan knew him for their own. There was laughter from the Camerons when Euan revealed himself to Jacobs, and they cheered as Jacobs was hauled off, but none from Grace, who was troubled by what she was seeing. She felt a bit of sympathy for Jacobs; she never liked taunting people this way on a mission, though there were exceptions to that. Jacobs, however, wouldn't have been one of them.

"Aye, I know what ye are thinking, and ye are right, but I had my reasons for this."

"Which were?"

"If I acted too sympathetic and kind toward him, it would have made them suspicious of me, and that was the last thing

I needed. It might have given them cause to harm him to get information he did nae have if they thought he and I had been up to something. The other side of it was that I was exhausted and relieved, nae thinking entirely clearly, and it was hard nae to get caught up in it."

"I can see your points, and it makes sense. Sometimes you can be caught up in the cruelty of others."

"But I was nae cruel to him, nae in any way. I may have taunted him a bit to keep that distance, but none of it was cruel."

"No, it wasn't; you're right."

"Come, we are moving on from here."

The next jump took them to an almost silent military camp at night. The watch fires blazed, but there was no one stirring, the crackling of the flames on the wood mixing with the sound of canvas rippling in the gentle wind. Past Euan emerged from a tent, holding his side. His clothing was still bloody from the morning's battle, and she watched as he closed his eyes and exhaled as best he could. There was no need to ask where this was; she knew.

"Ye see? I am trying to bring myself back," Euan whispered.

She nodded as they watched Lochiel emerge to speak to the young man standing there in the darkness about the coming plan to invade England. Euan, of course, protested it, and she understood why he would. Though there were schools of thought that now believed they could've pulled it off, Grace still wasn't so sure about it, and there was no way the Euan standing here would've had the benefit of any of the information they did now. From where he stood, it was a disaster waiting to happen, and he wasn't wrong.

"How would 4,000 men stand a chance against 30,000 on their home ground?"

Lochiel said nothing.

"His advisors are foolishly urging it in spite of the numbers," Euan said, his tone flat.

Lochiel nodded. *"Men with no real military sense."*

"I could try to speak with him," Euan offered.

"No, ye will nae. Nae unless ye are asked. Remember yer place, Euan."

There was a sharp intake of breath from Grace at the verbal slap delivered to the young man who only wanted to help, the same young man who'd helped get this army here in the first place. Even now, the exchange angered Euan, and Grace could feel within herself the tension it was creating in him. Reaching back, she took his hand in her own and gave it a gentle, reassuring squeeze.

"Aye, Lochiel."

"As ye are awake, take the watch."

As Lochiel left him there, past Euan returned to the tent he'd come out of and emerged with his weapon on, his face white with pain. There was a quick jump without them closing their eyes, and it was now morning, camp had been struck, and the army was massing to go back to Edinburgh. Past Euan walked by them, and Grace watched him close his eyes as he willed himself to mount his horse.

"No, Euan, don't. Please," she said to the young man even though he couldn't hear her, following him and reaching out for his arm to stop him without a thought.

She knew enough to understand what he'd be doing to his body, and everything in her wanted to stop this. Her hand passed through him, confusing her for a moment, before she remembered where she was. She couldn't stop herself from trying to help him, protect him; it was second nature. When he mounted Absalon and screamed from the pain, Grace's hands covered her mouth, her eyes welling with tears. She'd never seen him in that kind of pain, and the distress was instantaneous. She felt the current Euan wrap an arm around her waist before he gently pulled her back away from the former version of himself.

"Dinnae fret, *leannan*," he whispered in her ear.

Lochiel rode to the front of the formation without acknowledging Euan or even asking after him, and Grace glared at the man's back. "How could he just —"

"He wanted to remind me of my place," Euan replied, the anger and hurt he still felt clear in his voice.

Another quick shift took them to the grounds of Holyrood to see the riders arrive back, victorious in battle against Cope and hearing the people cheer them. The Euan of the past watched in surprise as the men all saluted him, that moment of respect given in the absence of what should've been. Grace's eyes drifted to Lochiel's face, and she watched his expression grow dark as he realized what was happening. It was the moment his suspicions of Euan's true power against him were confirmed and part of the power struggle she'd witnessed between the two men in France once Euan himself had realized what he was capable of.

"Go mbeannaí Dia duit, gaisgeil Euan! Chlanna nan con thigibh a so's gheibh sibh feoil! Fàilte!" May God bless you, brave Euan! Sons of the hounds, come hither and get flesh! Salute!

The sound of the call brought Grace's eyes back to Euan and the men before him, and she watched as the young man he'd been tried to work up the nerve to dismount, an action he knew would be excruciating.

"No! Don't!" Grace shouted at him just as he forced himself to dismount.

The cry of pain as he hit the ground and his legs gave out, followed by the anguished scream as his hands hit the ground and jarred his broken ribs, made everyone wince. Grace burst into angry, pained tears as she made a move to help him, the sight of him in such agony too much for her to bear idle witness to. Euan caught her hand, the movement pulling her around and back to him, where she buried her face in his chest and sobbed.

"I know, *leannan*. Ye hate to see me in pain, ye want so badly to help me, and it hurts ye that ye cannae. Just remember that I made it through this. I am here now, safe with ye."

"I've never seen you in that kind of pain and I just ... Euan, I can't ... please ..."

Euan's fight against Malcolm and Iain's help played out beside them, and she watched in shock, silent tears still running down her cheeks. Grace had never seen Euan this way, and she didn't know what to make of it. This man was so under the thumb of Lochiel that he doubted himself and everything else, forced himself beyond anything he should've ever had to in order to prove he was worthy of the man's respect. She understood now why he'd told her he wasn't worthy of her and never had been. It was what Lochiel had always made him believe. He was worthy of nothing Lochiel hadn't given him and was barely worthy of even that. Grace's fury was tenuously contained, and she wanted to kill the man where he stood, just as angered by the fact that she couldn't do it as she was by his actions.

"Euan, ye are to let these men help ye to yer tent, and Archibald will see ye. I dinnae want to hear nor see ye fighting them. That is an order, are we clear?" Lochiel said as he strode up to the group of men.

Euan stopped fighting and was dragged inside a tent, and she heard a sharp inhale from the present Euan behind her. "No, archivist, stop it now!"

It was too late, however, and Euan's blood-curdling scream rang out in the next moment. Grace's eyes went wide, and she looked like she might be sick, before she covered her ears and turned away, squeezing her eyes shut and taking a few shaky steps away from him. Her chest was tight, and it hurt to breathe, the sound of his final scream too much for her. Euan hurried to her side, wrapping an arm around her to support her, in just enough time to catch her as her knees gave out.

"No, no, stay with me, *leannan*. Everything is all right. I am so sorry. I never intended for ye to see that part."

Grace's breathing was ragged, and in the next moment, she snatched the dirk from Euan's baldric. Without thinking, she moved to plunge it into the back of the source of all this pain, but Euan's strong hand grabbed her wrist and stopped the movement, his other arm hooking her around the waist.

"Grace, no. Ye cannae do him any harm here."

"Let me go! I just want to —"

"Beloved, stop. While I appreciate ye wanting to avenge me, there is naught ye can do for it now. Give me the blade."

Grace huffed in indignation but did as he asked, letting him take it back from her. After he replaced it on his baldric, he turned her face to look at him.

"I know what this must seem like, but he was nae always this way, as ye have already seen today. That is what kept me so off-balance. I never knew where I really stood with him."

"I *hate* him," Grace hissed.

"That is yer right, and ye have yer own reasons for it that have naught to do with me after France."

"You don't?"

"Aye and no. It is complicated."

"You are more than any of that, and you've proven it so many times. I wish he could see it; I wish they all could."

"Let us leave this moment."

The scene morphed again, and they were standing on the night watch with Euan, who was now healed from his injuries. Something stirred in the darkness and Euan drew his blade. *"Identify yerself."*

"I think you know me quite well."

As the figure of Colonel Francis Strickland came into the light of the torches, Grace surveyed him with absolute and immediate distrust, only to be proven right as she watched the man tell Euan to commit mutiny against his chief and his clan, as well as convince other regiments to follow him, disregarding the lives of others and thinking Euan could be bought with promises of money and titles.

"I knew it," she murmured. "I know a snake when I see one by now."

"Aye, and ye would be entirely correct. He was."

"You treasonous, self-serving, conniving bastard," Grace seethed. "After all the Camerons did for you …"

"I felt the same," Euan said, smiling at the curse. "But there is more to see. Let us go."

A new switch put them now amongst another military camp, the loud boom of a cannon heard. Past Euan emerged from a tent, Lochiel and Lord Elcho behind him.

"Falkirk," current Euan said before she asked.

"Euan," Lochiel called out.

"Aye, Lochiel," Euan replied as he turned to face his chief.

"I want ye to lead the men."

"Why? Are ye ill?" Euan asked, and his incredulity brought a small, bitter laugh from Grace. That he should be so in doubt of his skills as to assume that the only way he'd get to lead the regiment was because of Lochiel's illness was, to her, preposterous.

Lochiel chuckled. *"No. I will be there, but I think ye have more than earned yer chance to lead the Cameron regiment into battle. I want ye to call the commands for us."*

"Thank ye for yer confidence. It would be my honor to lead our men."

"Good. I have faith in ye, lad," Lochiel said as he departed.

The scene morphed, and Grace found herself standing amidst the Cameron regiment's front lines. She frowned in confusion, and while she saw the former Euan, she didn't see the current one anywhere. A loud crack and the rolling boom of thunder sounded before the skies opened up in a torrential downpour, soaking them all in an instant.

It didn't affect Grace, but looking at the former Euan, she saw water dripping from his bonnet and running down his face. His focus was singular; it was time for battle, and nothing else existed.

"Men at the ready!" he shouted.

Grace looked around her, desperate to get away from this before it started, the thought of being in the middle of another battle inducing intense panic and anxiety, but it was too late. The guns went off, and she jumped with a small scream. She turned to push her way through the lines of men, away from the front, but the scene suddenly shifted. Within seconds she was swept forward by a wave of charging Highlanders, and she shrieked in terror. It was too similar! She caught sight of

Euan and shoved her way forward to him, chasing after him. If she could get to him, she could tell him she was afraid and to take them out of this.

As he and the others collided with the Hanoverian soldiers, she realized that this was not her Euan. As he fought his way through their lines, he looked ferocious, detached, intent on dealing as much damage as he possibly could … until he stopped moving, eyes wide. Grace turned toward whatever he was seeing; what would make Euan stop this way?

"Euan?" a young man asked, his confusion plain even amidst the battle raging around the pair.

"Alex. No. No, ye have to get out of here or stand down!"

"I cannae! Ye are a traitor, Euan Cameron!" he shouted as he lowered his bayonet and pointed it at Euan.

"Alex, please, dinnae do this! Dinnae make me kill ye!"

Without another word, the young man he'd called Alex charged him.

"NO DON'T!" she screamed at Alex, but it was too late.

Euan took a slight step to the side, grabbing the musket and yanking the young man forward onto his blade, and Grace broke into heaving sobs.

"Why! Why did ye have to do it! Damn ye, Alex!"

Even as Euan stopped to respectfully close the young man's eyes in death, a flash of movement in her periphery caused Grace to turn around at the same time Euan stood. Almost on top of her, a man took a swing at Euan's midsection, the blade passing through her with no damage even as Euan screamed from the cut it delivered. Before she could process it, Euan's pained scream turned to one of rage as he came back with a savage swing that decapitated the other man. Grace stumbled backward, staring in horrified disbelief as Euan proceeded to destroy several more men wearing similar tartan.

Shaking her head, Grace backed away and ran from the grisly scene. Even as she ran, the scenery around her changed into the darkness of a nighttime moor. Activity was all around her, but her attention was quickly drawn to the sound of someone crying. Grace put her hand on her chest as she saw it was Euan, once again covered in blood, though some of it was now his own. On his torso, fresh and red, was the long cut that would become the scar he still bore, and Lochiel sat beside him, trying to comfort him in his distress about all that had just happened. Grace sank to her knees, feeling sick, and knowing that if she were in her real body, the stress of this situation would have her emptying the contents of her stomach.

The feel of a hand on her back made her jump, and she looked up to see the Euan she knew, his expression anxious. She threw herself into his arms, breaking down when he embraced her.

"I am so sorry," he whispered. "I could nae be here, could nae see this again. I am nae ready, but I should have realized ye would nae be either. This is too close. I should have faced it and gone after ye."

"Euan, who —" Grace began.

"Dinnae ask me, please," he replied in a soft voice. "Nae yet."

Glancing back at the broken young man sitting on the ground in front of her, staring into the distance with a haunted expression, his eyes glazed over, it was hard to believe that this was the same person who was now with her.

"Let me get ye out of this place."

Grace closed her eyes, and the feel of wind brought them back open. The former Euan stood on a terrace in the darkness between pools of light cast by the torches and fire pits there. There was silence aside from the crackle of the flames as they consumed the wood and the sound of the wind around the structure, and he was entirely alone. Grace approached him and saw him sway a bit on his feet. He was pale, dark circles under his glassy, exhausted eyes. He looked the worst she'd ever seen him; he hadn't even looked this bad at Culloden. A glint as the firelight met something reflective caught her eye, and she looked down to find a dirk clutched tightly in his hand as he stared into the blackness of the night beyond.

"Ye can do this," he whispered to himself as he looked down at the blade in his hand. *"It would be easy. Ye know where to put it to make it quick. If ye do it, then all of this will be gone. The nightmares will be gone, and ye dinnae have to do any of this anymore."*

Grace looked over at the present Euan, eyes filled with tears. "You wanted to … you tried …"

"For a moment, aye, I tried to talk myself into it. A moment when I was at my lowest. I had nae slept for days, for every time I did, I had horrible night terrors. I just wanted it to be over; I wanted to be free of all of it."

"Do it. Come on, Euan, damn ye! Ye can do this! No one is here to stop ye, and ye will be gone before anyone comes out to take this watch."

The former Euan raised the dirk with a shaking hand, lining it up in such a way that it would send the blade up and under his ribs once he let his weight fall on it. Closing his eyes, he took a deep breath to steady himself.

"Euan, what are ye about?"

The young man gasped and pulled the knife away from his chest at the sound of a familiar voice calling his name. Whirling around to find Malcolm eyeing him with a wary expression, he shook his head. *"Naught."*

Malcolm surveyed Euan in the firelight, taking a few more steps toward the young man. *"I dinnae believe ye. Ye are up to something."*

"No, I——" he began, his words ceasing as he watched Malcolm take note of the blade in his hand.

"Euan, what are ye doing? Please tell me ye were nae about to do what it seems like ye were."

The former Euan looked down at the dirk in his hand and dropped it, shaking his head even as he squatted down and covered his face with his hands, the realization of what he'd almost done washing over him and causing him to break down.

"Jesus, lad," Malcolm breathed as he stepped forward and

kicked the blade away to a safe distance before taking a knee next to Euan. *"Why? What in the hell were ye thinking?"*

"I cannae do this, Malcolm! Ye dinnae understand, ye cannae!"

"Tell me and maybe I will."

"I just want this to all be over. I cannae take the night terrors anymore, cannae bear to hear the screams and see them coming for me to make me pay for taking their lives!"

Malcolm sighed and put an arm around his shoulders. *"I am sorry ye are so plagued by what happened at Falkirk, but ye are being too hard on yerself. Ye did what needed to be done, and taking yer own life will nae change it, will nae bring any of them back. If ye do this, it will be more than yer own life ye would end."*

"What do ye mean?"

"This would kill yer mam, ye know that, dinnae ye? She cannae lose ye, nae like this, and nae a one of us could lie to her about how it happened because she would know. It would kill the men in yer company because they did nae have ye to lead them, and it would kill so many others, too. It would destroy yer friends and brothers, a pain none of us could ever recover from. We all need ye here, Euan. Ye mean so much more to all of us than I think ye realize."

Euan broke down in tears, sobbing even as Malcolm drew his friend close to him in an embrace.

"I know," he whispered. *"There are so many demons whispering to ye every day, every moment, and somehow ye manage to keep them from ye. I cannae imagine what it must be like, but I know I could nae do it. Ye are exhausted, I know ye have nae slept in days, and yer mind just cannae hold against them tonight, but I am here for ye, Little Brother. I will sit with ye until ye sleep or watch with ye and keep them in the darkness where they belong. Stay with me on this side of the world, for I cannae bear to lose ye again or know I would nae see ye in the hereafter."*

The young man nodded, broken but now reinforced by the strength of a friend. *"Aye."*

"Good lad. Tell me a tale, Euan; ye are so good at those."

The present Euan took Grace's hand, and she looked over

at him, an expression on his face she couldn't read, a mix of relief, gratitude, and sadness.

"I'm glad you didn't do this," she whispered.

"So am I, but then, something obviously made sure of that by sending Malcolm just in time to stop me."

"What do you mean?"

"Naught, that is for another time," he said, stroking her cheek and giving her a gentle kiss. "Come, two more."

The next jump returned them to horseback amongst the Cameron regiment on the road to Achnacarry. Almost home after Falkirk, they were singing and happy. They once again rode beside the younger Euan, who now looked far more rested and like himself again, as they entered the castle yard and were met by excited people welcoming them home.

"This respite will nae last long," Euan said. "We will be on the march to Fort Augustus soon, and then Fort William. After that is —"

"Culloden," Grace said.

"Aye. But soon, very soon, I meet a Watcher who changes everything."

Grace smiled at his words even as she watched the younger man swing down from the saddle. There was no one there to greet him, but he didn't seem upset about it as he turned to lead his horse away to the stables. The sound of someone calling his name stopped him, and he turned in enough time to catch a young woman in an embrace as Grace sat up with a frown. The two talked for a few moments before she tried to kiss him. Young Euan stepped back away from the attempt, took her hands, kissed one, said something, and then walked away from her.

"Who is that?" Grace asked, her irritation appearing in her voice despite her effort to hide it.

"Brenda," Euan replied. "She was … well … she and I spent a lot of time in each other's company, let us just say that."

Grace turned to scowl at him, and he chuckled.

"Ye can be mad if ye wish, my lass, but as ye can see, I did nae feel the same for her. She knew it, but that did nae stop her. At first, it was fine, and we both wanted only the occasional encounter. It changed somewhere for her; I dinnae know when. I was never with her again after we left for Glenfinnan."

Grace said nothing, struggling with what she felt in seeing this scene, trying to remind herself that he wasn't hers then and that, in the end, she was the one here with him now.

"Love, dinnae be angry."

"I'm not," she replied, her voice soft. "You had a life before me, as I had one before you; it was just jarring to see it up close like that."

"I am nae sorry for my choice, and I mean it. Ye are everything to me that she was nae. I had always felt as though I were waiting for something, for *someone*. Then ye arrived, and that feeling that what I had waited for was here was so strong it terrified me. It overwhelmed me. Worse, I felt it for someone all logic said I could nae have. I never felt that with her or anyone else."

Grace sighed. "I know. I know what you felt because I felt that, too. I wanted something, but I didn't know what it was."

"We know now, and we are together as we should be." Euan reached out and stroked her hair. "But ye see now. Ye see what it was like for me, why I dinnae want to talk about some of it."

"Yes," she whispered. "Euan, I am so sorry, for all of it."

"Dinnae apologize for what ye did nae do."

"Someone should."

"Perhaps, but that someone should nae be the person who is saving me from all of it, bringing me back to myself."

"When you were hurt —"

"Aye, I know. I am sorry for how much it distressed ye. Ye are usually so detached in Observation that I expected ye to be the same here, able to remember that this was the past and I was fine."

"I should've been, I just … I've never seen you that way, never seen or heard you scream in agony like that. My first instinct will always be to help you."

"As mine is with ye. Protect ye, love ye, care for ye in the ways ye deserve. I hate to see ye in any sort of pain, and ye are the same with me."

"Falkirk was —"

"Awful, and I regret sending ye there alone."

"The man I saw fighting wasn't the man I know."

"It is part of him when it is life or death. I will fight my hardest to make sure I live, and that is what ye saw."

"You seemed happy to take off that person's head after they cut you."

"Aye, well, he had injured me. He was also a Campbell, as were several of the others I dispatched right afterward."

"That explains a bit of it."

Euan chuckled.

"It breaks my heart that you were so close to taking your own life afterward."

"There were a lot of factors that put me there. I was nae in my right mind after so long without proper rest, and I felt horribly guilty about the things I had done. At the same time, I was facing this life I no longer wanted but could nae be free from until I died."

"So, you wanted to make that true."

"For that briefest of moments. Thankfully my sense returned. Last jump. Ye ready?"

Grace nodded before everything around her changed, plunging her into the deep blackness of a rural road on a winter's night, this time in her white uniform. Snow covered the sides of the road itself, lightly dusting the traffic path and undisturbed in these hours. Grace could see her breath even though she couldn't feel the cold and looked around her.

"Euan?" she called out, but there was no response.

Taking a few tentative steps forward, Grace felt uneasy as

she tried to spot him in the little light given by the quarter moon peeking through the clouds.

"Euan, where are you? Where is this? Please answer me!" she said once more in a loud whisper. "This isn't funny! Euan!"

The sound of footsteps got her attention, and she turned around in relief, only to be confronted by a man in a Hanoverian uniform. Stumbling a few steps back, Grace looked at him in confusion, watching his face as he performed the same futile act of trying to see anything in the darkness that she'd just attempted. He shook his head and turned around, only to find four men blocking his path. They'd appeared in such silence that he almost ran into them, and the man at their head left the soldier no time to speak or think, cutting his throat and not flinching as a jet of the man's blood hit his clothing before the soldier dropped to the ground.

Grace made a sound of shock and stepped backward so he wouldn't fall on her, watching as his body fell to the ground in the space between her and the other four. She stared at the body, horrified, before she looked back up at the one who'd done this. To her utter dismay, Euan stood before her, drenched in so much blood there wasn't a bit of him that wasn't covered in it. The look on his face was one she'd never seen before, and it was so foreign she almost swore it wasn't him at all. There was no remorse, no care, no shock at what he'd done. Instead, a darkness was there, his expression resolute and even pleased, but his eyes were flat and almost lifeless. He wasn't there, not truly, at least not the Euan she knew. Behind him stood Duncan, Iain, and Malcolm. Euan nodded to them, and they started moving down the road, right toward Grace. Euan clutched a dirk in one hand, and Grace backed away from him so fast that she tripped over her own feet, falling onto the ice-hardened ground. The impact brought a small sound from her, but she wasted no time in sitting up, scrambling backward as he strode toward her. Grace squeezed her eyes shut and turned her head away, feeling them walk past her.

She looked up and after them as they walked away from her, breathing heavily and shaking, trying to reconcile what she'd just seen of her husband with what she knew. She understood what this moment was now, the killing of the sentries between Fort William and Achnacarry, but the sight of Euan that way frightened her no matter how much she reminded herself this was Observation.

"Mo ghràidh," she heard Euan whisper near her.

With a gasp followed by a small scream, she whipped her head around and moved away from him before she could check herself, staring up at him from the ground.

Euan closed his eyes and hung his head, and she could tell that her reaction hurt him a great deal. "I am sorry," he said, his voice so soft it was near a whisper. "But this is why I told ye I am nae worthy of ye. I am nae, Grace. Ye saw what I just did, saw how little thought or care I gave it, and ye are right to react the way ye just did. I dinnae deserve ye, I dinnae deserve the chance ye gave me, and ye should go. Ye should send me back and find someone better, someone more noble, more befitting ye and what ye do each day. Someone far less steeped in blood than I could ever be."

Grace stood up and threw her arms around him, pressing her cheek to his, as she felt him shaking with sobs, quiet but deep. "Don't you *ever* say that again," she whispered. "Do you hear me? None of it. You're worthy of it to *me*, and that's all that matters. I don't want someone else: I want *you*."

"But ye feared me just now."

"That version of you, yes, but who wouldn't? You told me you became what you had to in order to do what was asked of you, and you just showed me how true that was. That wasn't *my* Euan, the one I'm holding in my arms right now, the one who was locked away so that he could be the killer he was expected to be."

"I just wanted ye to truly understand," Euan said. "It is nae that I want to keep ye out; it is that I have no desire to go through any of this again. I would have to if I told ye, and I cannae. Maybe someday, but I cannae do it now."

"I know. I understand, I really do. I always did. I didn't push you as much as you believe I did. You hold it so closely and get so defensive that your immediate reaction is anger. In your anger you hear things in what I say that aren't really there."

"Ye are probably right." He sighed. "And I need to get better about that. Ye mean no harm."

"No, I don't. I would never come here and get what you won't tell me. This isn't my life; it's yours. Only you have the right to tell me these things. I would never dream of violating your privacy like that. *Never.*"

"I know, and somewhere deep down I know it even when the fear and the anger take over, but it is hard to stop it once it happens. I know it is nae rational, and we are still learning about each other, ye and I."

"Yes, we are, and we'll get through this. *You'll* get through this. Let's go home."

CHAPTER 8

Over the next two weeks, Mal and Malcolm were frequent visitors at the lodge, talking to Euan and going over varying things in the records that he might help them piece together. Aileen agreed to make a replica of Euan's uniform for the museum, and the tartan she'd woven and originally brought with her would be enough for the kilt and the plaid while giving her the excuse to make more. When she'd mentioned that spinning and weaving had always been a task she'd enjoyed, Malcolm promised her some wool from the estate's own flock, making Aileen very happy.

Often, after they'd finished meeting with Euan, the three younger Camerons sat and talked about whatever came to mind, telling stories and laughing, or introducing Euan to all sorts of pop culture while leaving Aileen and Malcolm to talk in the kitchen before reconvening for supper. For the first time that either Grace or Euan could remember, there was a true sense of what a proper family felt like.

When Mal discovered that his new friend had yet to experience *Star Wars*, he brought the DVDs so that they could watch them. Euan absolutely loved the series, and that led to watching the newer ones, too. Euan, in turn, introduced Mal to the joys of his favorite musician, and Mal lamented not having heard any of it sooner before buying every album he could.

Mal made good on his promise to introduce Euan to a good group of modern Frasers, and Euan had very much enjoyed getting together with them, coming home full of names and anecdotes to tell Grace. But, as the days slipped by into April, the only ones who seemed to realize what was coming were Euan and Grace. While Euan took solace in new friendships and distractions, Grace became steadily more withdrawn. It confused the two men, but they were kind enough not to ask about it even when Grace stopped joining them for supper and conversation, and Euan explained it to them as best he could. When they were gone for the evening, Euan went upstairs to spend time with her, never wanting to leave her alone for longer than necessary because he was the only one she wanted to be around. Like him, too much time alone could put her too far into her own mind and the dark places hiding there. Sometimes they would read or talk; other times they lay together in silence.

When the day itself dawned, Euan and Grace rose early, going outside to watch the sun come up while sitting on the ridge looking down at the glen. He remembered well where he'd been when the sun had come up that morning, the rain coming down in sheets and the sleet beating down painfully as he did his best not to think about his coming death and how desperately he wanted Grace with him. There was no rain this morning, however, and the rising sun spilled golden light over the mountains, bathing it all in a new day. Euan hugged Grace tightly to him, her back against his chest as he kissed the top of her head. He could feel the tension in her and wanted to ease it in whatever way he could, bringing his lips near her ear and singing to her. As he did so, he saw her eyes close as she listened to him and felt her relax.

"You should sing more often," she whispered, keeping her eyes closed.

"Aye?"

"You have such a beautiful voice, and I always love to hear it."

"What shall I sing for ye next?"

"Whatever you want. It will be beautiful no matter what," she replied.

Euan smiled, starting a song in Gaelic as she snuggled into him. He sang as many songs as he could think of, staying away from silly or bawdy songs because it wasn't the time for them. In the mental space in which Grace currently resided, such a thing would only set her on edge or irritate her, and that was the last thing he wanted to do.

When they returned inside, they went back to bed for a short time, but restful sleep eluded them both, and when Grace woke up screaming, it broke his heart. He understood why, he'd had those nightmares himself and still did, but he hated that she also had them now. There was a part of him that still felt so very guilty, still felt as if he could've saved her from this by just listening and standing up to his chief. Instead, he'd capitulated and remained silent, just as he'd always done, and it would forever leave him feeling as though *he'd* done this to her no matter what anyone said. He'd exposed this beautiful soul to a horrible death, to the deaths of those all around her, and she was suffering for it now. He wrapped her up in his arms, rocking her back and forth as she sobbed, doing his best to lend her whatever strength he could. Facing this first anniversary was difficult, neither of them knowing what to expect, and all they could do was seek to calm each other by finding the positive in it. It was the day both of their lives changed for the better instead of the day when everything they'd previously known and understood had shattered irreparably.

On the other hand, he seemed to feel less anxious about all of it than Grace did. Perhaps it was the chance he'd had to confront Lochiel and truly see everything for what it was, the chance to vent the anger and grief he'd felt over the uselessness of it all to one of the men who'd caused it. That, combined with the Observation sharing, seemed to help, and he knew Grace had gotten no such opportunities.

Eventually they got up again because they had someplace

to be, and though Euan hadn't particularly wanted to leave the house today, it couldn't be helped. They had an errand in the morning that necessitated a drive to London today, which was a 10-hour trip by car. Euan finished loading their overnight bags into the back of the Range Rover they used during the winter and early spring and shut the back hatch. It was far more practical for the territory and the weather than the Astons, and they only used those at this time of year if they needed to. Grace had remained exceedingly quiet, and he couldn't say he entirely blamed her. She was still recovering emotionally from the French mission, and this was now stacked on top of it. There was so much going on in his wife's mind at the moment, and he wasn't as privy to it as he wished he were. She was so used to hiding everything from everyone that it sometimes took coaxing to get her to confide in him, and though it had gotten better, much better, in the last several months, there were still moments like these where she withdrew into herself and kept him out.

He went back into the house to find Grace standing in the kitchen, staring out of the window into the woods. Her hands were around a cup of tea that he was sure was now merely warm.

"Love," he said, keeping his voice soft so as not to startle her. "Are ye ready to go?"

"Hm?" she said as the sound of his voice brought her back to the present. "Oh. Yes, I'm ready."

Before she could move, he made his way to her and wrapped his arms around her from behind. "Are ye going to be up for this?"

"Yeah. I think it will be a good thing, a nice distraction."

"I agree with ye," he said before he kissed her cheek and continued to hold on to her. "It is fine, ye know, to feel as ye do. I do, too."

"I wonder when it will get easier."

"With time, when it is no longer so close. Never entirely, but less."

"Maybe we should go to the remembrance one of these times."

Euan stepped around her, giving her a look that told her he was questioning her sanity. "Why in God's name would ye want to do that?"

"It might help."

"I dinnae see how."

"We could see the solemnity, the memorial, the respect given to —"

"No. Ye know full well there is naught there for us but pain and horror. It is also far too dangerous now. Ye know why."

Grace nodded in reluctant acceptance. "Do you ever wish you could go back to say goodbye? Not as an observer?"

The question surprised him, as did the sharp pain it brought. "Sometimes," he admitted. "But then, what would I say to them? 'Sorry, lads, have to leave now to go be alive in the future while ye die.' There would be no way for me to say goodbye without changing what was. I said my goodbyes on the day we first came back here, and that will have to suffice. I was with them for a while during the Observation, and Mal is here now."

"Time is such a crap thing, isn't it?"

Euan let go of a small laugh. "Aye, it is. Speaking of time, we had better get on the road, or we will nae make it before midnight."

Grace dumped her tea into the sink and put the mug into the dishwasher before she took his hand and walked with him to the car. It had been decided that he'd drive, so Grace climbed into the passenger seat as he got in on the other side. They were both quiet until they reached the main road, though her hand remained in his as he drove.

"I looked at the route, and it takes me past some very familiar places."

"Does it?" she asked, looking at him with curiosity.

"Aye. Follows our route back from England almost exactly, except we went to Stirling after Glasgow instead of Achnacarry."

"Stirling. That's where you tried to lay siege to the castle, right? Before Falkirk?"

"Aye," he replied. "For two ridiculous months."

Grace's laugh was soft. "Tell me how you really feel."

"Ach, dinnae get me started, lass."

His reaction only made Grace laugh more. "What if I want to?"

"Get me started complaining about stupid tactics?"

"No, about this part. About England."

Euan was quiet for a long moment. They hadn't gone there in Observation because he'd seen no use in it. It was the first time she'd even mentioned anything about the Observation since they'd returned from it.

"I will if ye truly want me to … at least most of it. There are some things I cannae say."

"It isn't like they're secret anymore, Euan."

"No, it is nae that."

"Oh. I understand," she said as she realized what he truly meant.

"There are nae many, and I will tell ye all I can as we go."

"First, I want to ask you something directly."

He raised an eyebrow in question, and she continued.

"When we first went to Achnacarry and saw Malcolm, he mentioned you had a bounty on your head."

A smile spread across his face before he laughed. "Aye, I did."

"You didn't seem too afraid of it when I was there."

"I was nae. My own clan would nae turn me in."

"How much were they asking?"

"£100, an absolute fortune."

"Wow. What did you do to earn it, though?"

"Almost succeeded in killing Cumberland."

"What! No way!"

Her reaction made him laugh again. "He engaged us at Clifton Moor. I did nae know it was him, but he was running toward me, so I pulled my pistol and it misfired. Only found out later from his footman, whom we took prisoner, that the man I had shot at was Cumberland himself."

"Christ, Euan! No wonder they had it set so high!"

"I almost shot the heir to the English throne in the head, love. They were nae particularly enamored of me, so, aye it would be high."

"Still! Wait a second," she said, looking at him with narrowed eyes. "How did they even know it was you?"

"I told them."

"Oh my *God*, you are insane!"

"Well, it was nae like that, exactly. When the footman mentioned the shot, they all knew it was me because I was the only one who fired after the charge. Murray made a joke about Cumberland needing to change his breeches, and his little man got upset about it. He said he would tell his master we laughed about it, and I told him to go ahead, gave him my name, and told him I would nae miss next time."

Grace gave a playful roll of her eyes and then shook her head. "Somehow I'm not surprised."

Euan smiled and shrugged. "Ye should nae be. Why would I nae want to take credit for that one?"

Grace chuckled. "You're ridiculous."

"Ach, ye are just jealous I almost got there before ye."

"Maybe a little," she said before they both started laughing.

As they passed through different towns, he told her what he remembered of them or what had happened there. Where they had crossed into England. Carlisle. Penrith. Clifton Moor. Lancaster. Preston. Manchester, where they took their first English recruits, though their present route didn't take them through Manchester. Derby, which was also not on their route but was as far as they'd gone. There were so many stories, many more than he'd realized, though many of them were stories of everyday life on campaign. He found he loved her reactions to them, how funny she found all of it, and how fascinating some of those moments were to someone so far outside of them as she was. When he told her the story about the woman who thought they would eat her children, Grace laughed so hard she could barely breathe and had tears streaming down her cheeks. It was wonderful to see and to hear, to amuse her and pull her away from the darkness that lurked around this day.

"It still amuses the hell out of me that you were a spy in Edinburgh. That's not mentioned in any history anywhere."

Euan laughed. "Well, no, I dinnae think those who hid in the castle would have included that in the report they gave to their commanders later. Rather embarrassing."

"Oh, it definitely would've been," Grace said, sharing his laughter. "So, I was thinking about something."

"That is dangerous."

"Shut up."

Euan's lips twisted in a wry smile as she shook her head.

"I was thinking maybe we should make the move to Achnacarry permanent."

The surprise that swept across his countenance at her declaration had no chance of being hidden. "Really? Why? Ye dinnae want to go back to California?"

"Maybe as a vacation, to see my mom, but no. I really like it here, and I want to stay. It isn't like we've really gone back since we moved here or even really thought about it. I haven't missed it at all."

"Would ye keep the apartment then?"

"I think so. Mom could keep living there, and I can keep supplementing the rent. Would you want to stay?"

"Why do ye even need to ask?"

"Figured as much."

"I cannae say I am nae surprised by yer decision, though."

"Why?"

"It is just different here."

"You say that as though that isn't exactly the reason. I feel at home here, at the lodge, with you. The first place I truly felt at home. Everything I need is here."

Euan lifted her hand and kissed it. "Then if that is what ye wish, we will do it. Nae sure Mam will be pleased."

"She can go spend the winters with my mom if she wants to."

Euan nodded. "She could, aye."

"Settled then?"

"Aye, settled," he replied with a grin.

It was 8 p.m. by the time they entered London and made it to the Savoy where they were staying. They put their bags in their room, took a moment to freshen up, and made use of the ample time left in the evening for a bit of fun, starting with dinner and drinks in a nearby pub. Afterward, they began wandering around Westminster and Southwark, trying to find various places they remembered from missions just for the fun of seeing if they were still there. Euan entertained Grace in Southwark by pointing out places that used to be brothels, which he knew about from his stint trying to bust up the Wyatt rebellion.

Grace stopped and leaned into one of the doorways in a rather sultry manner, smiling at him. "Hello there, Highlander. How about a little fun?"

Euan looked at her, amused. "Aye, lass? And what fun would ye be offering me?"

"How much do you have?"

"Naught, sadly. Rebellion does nae pay."

"Shame," Grace said, feigning disinterest.

"Even if I had money, I could nae afford ye."

"Is that so? Why do you think that?"

"A lass as comely as ye does nae come cheap. Look at ye, freshly bathed, healthy, all yer teeth."

Grace laughed and then smothered it with a hand.

"Rosy cheeks and beautiful hair. Ye must be new at this."

"Or perhaps I'm just picky. Maybe I'm not really at this at all, and I'm a society lady just looking to do a bit of slumming."

"If ye were ye would nae ask for coin."

"Are you sure? It could be part of the game I'm playing, and if you're good enough, I'll give it back to you."

Euan laughed. "All right, stop it ye. Get out of that doorway and stop messing about."

"Aww, you don't like me?" Grace said with a mock pout. "How much do you think I'm worth?"

He paused, his laughter fading. "Worth? There is nae enough coin in the world to pay that price. I could nae put a price on ye and never would, for to me ye have none," he said as he closed the short distance between them. "I will nae cheapen ye by even entertaining such a thought."

Grace smiled. "I was only kidding."

"Aye, I know ye were, and I was amused by it, clearly. Ye simply asked a question that was impossible to answer."

"Impossible to you, perhaps. Maybe someone else would have an answer."

"Nae if they want to live," Euan said with a dark grin.

"Oh, I see."

"Now, get yer arse out of that doorway, Watcher."

Grace laughed and joined him, sliding her arm around his waist. "Fine, you win."

"Damned right I do. Shall we go see if we can sneak into the Abbey and sit ye on the coronation chair?"

"No!"

The horror with which she said it made him almost double over with laughter. "Aye, too much attention for ye. Come on, then."

In the morning, they rose to make their way to London Heathrow, and the two of them stood at the arrivals gate just past the baggage claims. Soon enough, their reason for the drive appeared and waved frantically before running forward and flinging her arms around Grace with laughter and tears.

"Hey, Van!" Grace said as she held tight to her friend, having desperately needed this sort of reunion just now.

"Hey, Gracie! Man, it's so good to see you, and that's a long-ass flight."

Grace pulled back, and both women laughed and wiped their eyes. "Could be worse. Could be Australia."

"At least you upgraded me to first class, so I had a bed. Most comfortable flight *ever*. Sneaky of you to not tell me though."

"That was Euan's doing, not mine," Grace said, chuckling. "He only told me after he did it."

Vanessa looked over at Euan, who'd kept his distance from the reunion of the two friends. "And you, my dear, are still as hot as ever. Thanks for the upgrade."

"My pleasure," he said, smiling. "Only way we fly when we go back to the States."

Vanessa grinned and hugged Euan as tightly as she'd done Grace, kissing his cheek, and Euan was happy to return the affection. "You guys are a sight for sore eyes! I've missed you like crazy."

"Come on, let's get out of here," Grace said as Euan picked up Vanessa's bags. "We're going to spend a few days here in London before we take you home. I thought you'd like to do touristy stuff since you've never been here."

"Yassss!" Vanessa replied, bouncing with excitement. "This is going to be the best vacation I've ever gone on," she exclaimed as the three of them laughed and made their way to the car. "Ooo, a Range!"

"Best vehicle for the weather at home. It is early spring, so we still get rain and snow," Euan explained.

"Really? But it seems so nice here in London."

"We dinnae live in London, lass," Euan said, chuckling. "Ye are headed to the Highlands."

"You say that like it's a different world."

"It is," Grace said. "You'll see."

"Intriguing."

The next few days were spent in London seeing the sights and hitting tourist locations. Westminster Abbey, The London Eye, The Globe, standing outside of Buckingham Palace — which Euan tolerated even though he'd fought a war against the ancestors of the family within. When they went to the Tower, however, Euan balked.

"I dinnae know if I should go in," he whispered to Grace as Vanessa was getting her bag checked.

"Why?" Grace asked him, keeping her voice as low as his.

"It is a prison, Grace. Being sent here was a legitimate threat, and several men I knew were kept here before their executions. *I* was meant to come here and probably die here."

"It isn't a prison anymore. What, you think they're going to arrest you?"

"Bounty."

"Euan, it probably doesn't even exist anymore, and even if it did, it's unlikely anyone here knows about it. Besides, why would they even arrest you? They'd have to think you were immortal for that to make any sense."

"Good point," he replied.

As they went inside, it felt a lot like its own rebellion to just walk through the gate, coming into a place he should've been sent to many times but never was and being able to walk back out again with no Englishman the wiser. It seemed much less threatening now, but then again, all the threat had been removed from it. Gone were the guards, the scaffolding, the moans and cries of prisoners, replaced by crowds of tourists interested in learning about the history of this place. He knew perfectly well that they could never truly understand the horror, the fear that the very name of this place had instilled in him and people like him only a couple of centuries before.

Sitting on a bench near the green while waiting for Grace and Vanessa to return with snacks, he watched one of the infamous ravens hopping about in search of food it could steal from unsuspecting children. The antics of the bird amused him greatly, and he was impressed by how many times it managed to be successful in its thievery.

"Please dinnae touch the ravens; they bite," he heard a woman say as one of the children reached out to touch it.

Euan raised an eyebrow and looked in the direction of a familiar accent to find a woman in uniform standing nearby. She was dressed in the same fashion as the men on duty and she looked quite pleasant, if not a bit mischievous, in her own way. Euan stood from the bench and approached her.

"First Scottish accent I have heard all day."

"Is it? Come to think of it, it is for me, too. A lot of French today, some Spanish, more than a few Japanese."

Euan chuckled. "Aye, I suppose ye get all sorts here now."

"Oh, aye, but it comes with the territory, so to speak." She took a moment to look him over and then gave him a curious look. "Where are ye from? The Highlands, clearly, but where?"

"Achnacarry, near —"

"Fort William, aye. I know it well."

"Do ye?"

"I would wager any Cameron in Scotland does. Or at least should."

"Ye are a Cameron?"

"Aye," she said with a nod and a smile, extending her hand. "Moira."

"Euan," he replied, shaking her hand. "Also a Cameron."

"Small world!"

"I dinnae know about that; we are everywhere."

Moira laughed. "True."

"Did nae expect to find one of us here, though."

"At least nae on this side of things?"

Euan laughed loudly; he couldn't help it. "Something like that, aye."

"Well, someone has to make up for the former lot, dinnae we?"

"Or be prepared in case it suddenly becomes a prison again, so we have someone on the inside."

"Ach, no, I dinnae think it will ever be that again, and if it was I think ye would find it easy to escape now."

"Maybe. All the same though."

"I would let ye out, never fear," she said with a conspiratorial wink.

"Ye see? Ye can take a Cameron out of Scotland but ye cannae take rebellion out of a Cameron."

"Probably more right about that than I would like to admit."

"That ye would nae like to admit it seems highly unlikely," he said.

"Depends on who I am admitting it to."

"Ah, well, ye would nae hide it from yer kin is what I am saying."

"Absolutely true."

"How did ye come by this posting?"

"Served 22 years in the army with good conduct and applied."

"Ye were a soldier? Well, I should nae be surprised by that either."

"Why is that?"

"Most of the Camerons I know are or were soldiers."

"Yerself included?"

"Aye."

"What branch?"

"Army. I was a captain," he said. It wasn't entirely untrue.

"Very nice. What do ye do now, Euan?"

"Now that part I cannae tell ye."

Moira raised an eyebrow.

"Classified."

"Ye are nae out of the service then? I thought ye were when ye said ye *were* a captain. Past tense."

"I am out of the army, but still serving."

"Ah, I get yer meaning. How very interesting. What brings ye here?"

"My wife has a friend visiting from America, so we are taking her about London."

"Oh! Well, that sounds fun."

"It is, actually. I have nae seen many of these things, and I had nae been here before today."

"I hope it is living up to expectations."

"As long as I get to leave at the end of it, it will."

The laughter from Moira at the quip made him smile. "I'm sure ye will be fine."

"Dinnae know. I was thinking of stealing some of those diamonds from within the building over there."

"If ye did that, then ye would be leaving on yer way to police detention, and there would be nothing I could do to help ye there."

"Fair enough."

"Euan! We have snacks! Who knew there were all these flavors of chips?" Vanessa said, bounding up to him with Grace not far behind her. "Oh, hello! Sorry, didn't mean to interrupt," she said to Moira.

"I'm used to it by now. Hard to ever have a full conversation here."

"That sucks."

"Sometimes, and sometimes nae. Depends on if it gives me a convenient out when I dinnae want to talk to people."

"Ohh, clever."

"Moira, this is Vanessa, my wife's friend," Euan said as Grace reached his side.

"A pleasure to me — oh! I know who you are! You're the one that was the first woman in this position, right?"

"Aye, that would be me! A pleasure to meet ye, Vanessa."

"And this is my wife, Grace," Euan said.

"Good morning," Grace said with a smile.

"I'm sorry those other guys were jerks," Vanessa said to Moira with a slight scowl.

Euan's expression turned curious. "What?"

"When I first arrived, I was subject to some pretty nasty abuse due to my gender, but that is all done and dusted now."

"Is that so? By Cameron justice?"

"What does that mean?" Moira asked.

"Do I need to kill them for ye?"

"Oh. Well, no. Ye would again be facing that situation where I could be of no help to ye."

"Pity," Euan muttered, "though they would have to catch me first, and I would nae do it in broad daylight."

"What was the other one?" Grace asked.

"I was thinking of going in and stealing ye the wee diamond crown ye liked so much," Euan replied, his words followed by a sly smile.

"Queen Victoria's crown?"

"Aye."

"Yeah, please don't do that," Grace said even though she laughed. "I can always have a replica made."

"Ach, ye are no fun."

The three women laughed before an alarm beeped on Moira's watch. "Ah, sorry, that's my cue to take my break. It really was a pleasure to meet ye all."

"And you," Grace said.

As she walked away, Moira turned around, walking backwards. "Ye behave yerself," she called out to Euan, pointing at him before turning back around, which made him laugh.

At least he knew he had kin on the inside.

Chapter 9

They left at dawn and the drive back to Scotland was uneventful, with Vanessa catching them up on events in between taking in the scenery. Once they got into Scotland proper and then out of the Lowlands into the Highlands, she gasped several times, remarking on how beautiful something was. As they neared Achnacarry, the road became a single track and took them through Gairlochy and along the edge of Loch Lochy. As they passed the turn-off that would take them to the castle, Vanessa was practically glued to the window when she noticed a sign.

"Hey, Euan, the Clan Cameron Museum, is that your family?"

"Aye, it is."

"Wow! So, they lived around here and now so do you! How cool is that?"

She saw Euan glance over at Grace with a small smile. "Uncanny, is it nae?"

"Oh my God, look at this place!" Vanessa said from the back as the hills and the trees surrounded both sides of the road that took them around the estate instead of through it, a longer way to go through Bunarkaig and Clunes.

On Grace's side, a stone wall ran the entire length of the road, and the trees formed a sort of arched canopy over the roadway. This early in the spring, they were still a bit barren from the winter, and the gnarled branches looked sinister. There were woods on either side that stretched back as far as she could see, blanketed in leaves or bright green moss.

"This section of the road is called the Dark Mile," Grace said from the front seat.

"Best road name ever," Vanessa replied, "and very apt. This place has to be pretty scary-looking at night."

"It's so dark out here that you couldn't really see it anyway."

"Not helping it sound less creepy, Grace."

Grace laughed, and suddenly the road to the lodge appeared on the right, seemingly out of nowhere, and they turned onto it. It was dirt and gravel as they made their way up and through the trees before it became paved out of sight of the main road to leave the impression that there was nothing there. To the right, the late afternoon sun filtered through the trees, setting the green moss that grew over everything ablaze with vibrant, bright color. As the lodge appeared through the trees and over the rise, Vanessa was, at first, too in awe to make any sound and just stared at it.

After a long moment, she whispered, "This is your house?"

"Aye," Euan said as he put the car in park and turned it off.

"This is incredible!"

"We like it," Grace said, laughing.

"I might never leave."

"Now you can see why I haven't," Grace replied.

"Legit don't blame you."

Grace got out as Euan opened the door for her and then did the same for Vanessa. "Welcome to the lodge and the Highlands, Vanessa," Euan said, smiling.

Though the sun was out, there was no mistaking that it was still very possible for it to snow up here. There was a bite to the air Vanessa hadn't expected, and she shivered before she turned and looked around her. The air smelled crisp and clean, and the sound of rushing water told her there was a stream nearby, or even more than one. Aside from that, there was a silence that she found both unsettling and amazing. She wasn't sure she had ever been anywhere so quiet, where the only sound to be heard for miles was birdsong, water, and the breeze rustling the trees. It was magical.

"Wow. Just wow," she whispered to herself.

Euan pulled her bags from the back, and Grace took theirs with Vanessa following them inside. "Mam!" Euan called out. "We are back!"

"Vanessa, love! Good to see ye! Welcome to Scotland," Aileen said as she made her way into the living room from the kitchen.

Vanessa didn't answer immediately, staring open-mouthed at her surroundings. The living room had a fire going in the massive hearth, and the furniture was for comfort and not art, with overstuffed couches and chairs, plush rugs laid out over wood floors and still beautiful even with its emphasis on comfort. She was so entranced that it took her a moment to realize she'd even been spoken to.

"Oh! Aileen! Hi!" she finally answered before she gave the woman a hug.

"Did ye have a good trip?"

"Thanks to Euan, yeah I did."

"Let us get ye settled in, as I am sure ye are tired and hungry."

"Absolutely! Well, hungry maybe. I think I'm too excited to be tired," Vanessa quipped as she followed everyone upstairs to the guest room that would be hers for the duration of her stay. It was larger than it seemed, bright and airy, with a window that faced out onto the drive and a beautiful view of the woods beyond.

After being given the tour of the rest of the house, they left her to shower, while Aileen fixed a small lunch for everyone to enjoy. It felt nice to freshen up and stand under the hot water, knowing she'd get to relax now, and her travels were officially at an end for a while. Grace and Euan had done a beautiful job renovating, with all the modern conveniences somehow looking antique to fit with the style of the house. Once she was done, she put on some yoga pants and a sweatshirt before going down to rejoin them, all smiles.

"Okay, so, can I just move in with you guys?"

Euan shrugged with a small smile. "We have the room, but there is nae much around here for work. Ye would have to go 60 miles to Inverness unless ye could find something down the road in Fort William."

"Worth it."

"The harder part would be finding a job to sponsor a work visa," Grace said, though she'd seemed to have to concentrate a bit more than she normally might.

"Ah, yeah, that would be hard. Are they hiring where you work?"

"Um, no, I don't think so."

Vanessa looked at her with great curiosity. "Why do you look so shifty suddenly?"

"I don't know? Just tired, maybe."

"Right. Also, do you know you have an accent now? A little one, but it's there. I mean, you already sounded English, but now there is a bit of Scottish in there, too, with certain words."

"Do I?" Grace asked, looking puzzled. "Hm. Hadn't noticed."

"Aye, ye do love," Euan confirmed with a grin before looking to Vanessa to explain. "And it is because we always speak in Gaelic here at home, rarely English."

"What? No way!"

"Aye. Grace, mo ghràidh, a bheil e doirbh dhut Beurla a bhruidhinn aig an taigh a-nis?" *Grace, my love, do you actually find it hard to speak English at home now?*

"Feumaidh mi feuchainn orm fhìn agus tha mi a 'faighinn a-mach gu bheil mi a' toirt mo bheachdan eadar-theangachadh gu Beurla seach an dòigh eile," Grace replied without even a pause. *I actually have to force myself, and I find I am translating my thoughts into English instead of the other way around.*

Euan laughed at her response, and Vanessa stared at her in shock.

"That's so cool! What did you say?"

"I asked her if she found it hard to speak English at

home now, and she said she has to force herself and translates her thoughts into English from Gaelic instead of the other way around," Euan translated. "A feeling I know well from my own experiences."

"Dude, that's so awesome and weird!"

"I can teach ye some if ye wish," Euan offered. "I can start ye as I did Grace, with the swear words."

Grace started laughing, and Aileen gave Euan a look, but Vanessa nodded eagerly. "Hell yeah!"

Aileen set out the small lunch she'd made, and there was small talk and catch-up with Aileen as Vanessa filled her in on their time in London and what they'd gotten up to there. After they'd eaten, however, Grace pulled Vanessa into the study, along with Euan.

"I ... um, Vanessa, do you know how you always ask me what I do for work?"

"Yeah?"

Euan looked at Grace. "What are ye doing?" he asked in Gaelic.

"I want to tell her. I trust her. The Council approved it just like they did for you," Grace replied in the same.

Euan's face registered shock, but he said nothing else, even as Vanessa looked between them in confusion.

"Do you really want to know?" Grace continued, switching back to English.

"Yeah, I mean, unless you're going to tell me you're a hitman or something."

"No, I'm not," she replied even though Euan laughed.

"Are you really a spy?"

"She is nae. Me, on the other hand ..." Euan interjected, still laughing. "Though Grace as an assassin of any sort is infinitely amusing to me."

"What! I KNEW IT."

"No, it isn't like that either," Grace said as she shot Euan an irritated look. "This is really complicated. My job is something my family has been doing for generations. There's a thing in the future called The Council. They were able to get rid of war and suffering and create a better world. They discovered that time isn't singular, there are multiple timelines happening at once, and history constantly repeats. Changes made in those other timelines could affect their future in a negative way, and my job is to go back and make sure history remains as it's written to protect the future."

"Wait … are you saying you're a time traveler?"

"Something like, yes."

Vanessa laughed. "Okay, what do you really do?" Her laughter stopped, however, when she saw that neither Grace nor Euan had joined her in it. "You're serious?"

"Very."

"Grace, that's not even possible."

"Yes, it is. I'll show you."

Just at that moment, the door opened, and Caia popped her head in. "Hey, all! You ready?"

"Ye were in on this, too?" Euan asked Caia.

"Umm, yes?" Caia replied, offering a sheepish smile.

Euan rolled his eyes. "Last one to know, apparently."

"You have no room to talk," Grace said to him before turning back to Vanessa and ignoring the slightly irritated expression on his face at the barb. "Vanessa, this is my Guardian, Caia. She's the one who watches me when I'm sent on missions."

"Hi!" Caia said in her normally bright tone, waving. "It is so good to finally meet you, Vanessa! I have heard so very much about you these last few years, and I was always telling Grace how much I wanted to meet you."

Vanessa stood up in a swift movement. "No, you're messing with me … right?"

"No," Caia replied as she came in and shut the door. "She is telling you the truth. Come, we will show you," Caia said as she held out her hands.

Grace took one, Euan took Grace's, and Vanessa stared at them apprehensively but took Caia's other hand.

"Now, close your eyes."

The moment her eyes closed, Vanessa felt the quick shift that, to her, felt almost as though her legs were giving out before everything was solid again. "What the hell?!"

"Careful when ye open yer eyes, lass. Ye will be dizzy," Euan said, placing a gentle hand on Vanessa's back as a steadying force.

Vanessa was thankful for the warning because he was right. There was an incredibly odd sensation of her brain trying to catch up to her, but when she got her bearings, she opened her eyes and looked around to find herself in another place altogether. "Oh. My. God. You were telling the truth!"

"Welcome to the future, Van," Grace said, smiling.

Both Grace and Euan were dressed differently than they'd been just a moment ago, with Grace in a long white dress and Euan in a tailored white suit with a Nehru jacket. The outfits seemed to change them in some way that Vanessa couldn't begin to describe, with Grace looking especially regal and strong.

"I can't ... You guys look incredible, like different beings."

"Do we? These are our uniforms, and they appear on us whenever we arrive here," Grace explained.

"So cool, though ..."

"Grace, The Council has given you permission to show her the tapestry. They're not in session right now, and the Councilwoman has gone out," Caia explained.

"Thanks, Caia. Come on, Van."

Vanessa followed along as Grace and Euan made their way through gleaming white halls before arriving at a set of giant doors that opened for them as they approached. As they walked inside, Vanessa stared around her in awe, unsure of where to look first. This was, quite possibly, the most beautiful room she'd ever been inside. The mosaic floors of blues, purples, and pearlescent colors were dazzling all by themselves, and the soft lighting did nothing to dim their sparkle while making the room seem relaxing.

"Vanessa, look over here," Grace said, pointing at a giant tapestry hanging from the wall, where several lines of different colors seemed to shimmer with faint movement.

"What is this?" Vanessa asked as she approached it, keeping her voice low as though she were in a sacred space.

"This is the tapestry that shows us all the timelines. Every line here is a different timeline running alongside our own, right here," Grace explained, pointing to it.

"So many!"

"Yes, and each line contains the exact same people and events. All the people are the same as they are everywhere else, sometimes with minor differences, but they all live the same lives across the spectrum."

"Whoa."

"The different, brighter points of light are major historical events, and if there's a change, we'll see it because it changes color. If something happens at a smaller point in history, that will actually cause the point to show up here, which is how we know something is wrong. The Council makes sure that the future they've created where there's peace and equality stays that way, and any change in written history that harms that goal is stopped."

"How?"

"They send a Watcher to make sure history happens as written. There are six Watcher lines, generations of women from the same family. I'm from one of those families, and I took over when my grandmother died."

"Is it dangerous?"

"It would be if we didn't go in what's called a mission body. It's like a super-advanced hologram, so we can't be hurt or die or anything like that."

"So, you get sent to where these major changes happen, and you stop it? That's your job?"

"Yes."

"How often does this happen?"

"All the time. It's why I'm gone so much."

"Jesus, man," Vanessa said, shaking her head in disbelief. "Thanks, Grace."

"For what?"

"For making sure the time we live in actually happens instead of it being something else."

Grace stood still for a moment, looking shocked. "You're welcome," she answered, offering a shy smile.

"Has no one ever said that to you before?"

"Not once."

"Not cool. I'm saying it now: thanks, Gracie. Wait, if The Council and the Watchers are all women, then what does Euan do?"

"I help her," Euan replied. "My job is to make sure she completes her mission. Sometimes that means working together on one target or playing different angles toward the same end."

"Wow. So, how did you get roped into this?"

"I ... well ..." Euan began, seeming unsure how to answer her question.

"I saved him," Grace answered for him.

"Saved him?"

"He was my mission once, and I had to save his life."

Vanessa looked at Euan. "Hold up: You're from the past?"

"Aye."

Vanessa started laughing and clapped her hands. "That's so amazing! How cool is that! I mean, that you could even find each other is awesome."

"It was nae like that," Euan said, his voice becoming quiet. "They sent her to find me, but they did nae tell her the real reason."

Vanessa noted the change in his voice and his expression and became wary. "Okay ..."

"They told her she had to stop me from dying in a coming

battle. They did nae tell her she had to stop me so that our future together could happen. She had to make a choice."

"To save you? I mean, she had to, right? That isn't really a choice."

Euan shook his head and looked at Grace, who seemed suddenly conflicted and upset. "I went to the battle despite all of her hard work. She had the choice to accept that she had failed, but she did nae. Instead, she ran out into the middle of the battlefield to save me."

"Jesus Christ! Grace, are you crazy?"

"Now, as she told ye moments ago, she cannae die when she is on a mission, but her choice to save me —"

"Wait … no … no, no, no, no, no —"

"She had to die," Euan finished.

Horrified, Vanessa stared at Grace, who wiped tears away from her own cheeks and couldn't meet her friend's eyes.

"We came back here; the energy when she died brought us back here. I had to choose if I wanted to stay with her, and I chose to stay. I brought my mam, as ye can see."

"But … but you're alive, Grace!"

"Thanks to the technology here, yes," Grace replied, finally speaking. "Without it, I most definitely wouldn't be."

Vanessa burst into tears at the thought of Grace not being here, of her going through something painful and terrifying alone, without being able to tell anyone who knew her about what had happened. Stepping forward, she hugged Grace tightly. "There is so much I didn't know! I'm so sorry, Grace," she whispered.

"I know. I wanted to tell you, but I couldn't. I got permission to do so, and now you know the truth. I wanted someone to know."

"Are you guys actually married?" Vanessa asked as she released Grace.

"Yes," Grace said, laughing through her tears.

"The Council gave Mam and I modern documents, so

it looks like we were born in yer time. One of those was a marriage certificate, but we did actually get married," Euan explained, smiling.

"What time did you come from?"

"Grace came and saved me in April 1746."

Vanessa's eyes widened. "Whoa. In Scotland, right?" she asked before something dawned on her. "Holy hell … that rebellion!"

"Aye, that one."

"What battle was it?"

"The last one: Culloden."

"DUDE."

"Where we live now, I used to live near there all my life. I served the chief, Donald Cameron of Lochiel, as one of his officers."

"You said you were a spy."

"I did do that, aye. I pretended to be a British officer during the war once so we could capture Edinburgh."

Vanessa considered him for a moment. "I bet you looked super-hot in that uniform, didn't you?"

"He did. Trust me, I've seen it," Grace confirmed as Euan's smile turned a bit wicked.

"Wait! This is like *Outlander*, but in reverse!"

"What is that?" Euan asked, cocking his head.

"It's a series of books and a TV show. The woman goes back in time to the same time you're from and meets the guy, and she stays in the past with him and stuff. I mean, there's more but —"

"I would nae have wanted Grace to stay with me there. Nothing good happened to us after Culloden."

"The whole point of one season is that they try to stop the rebellion from happening at all."

"Wish they had," Euan murmured.

Vanessa's mind was racing, but a thought jumped out at her, and she gasped. "Oh my God, do you know Jamie Fraser?"

"Who? I know the Frasers, they are like kin, but James is a quite common name. Could ye be more specific?"

"Van —" Grace began.

"You know Frasers!" Vanessa said, deliberately not hearing Grace in her excitement over the very possibility.

"Aye? As I said, they are like kin to the Camerons. One of my cousins is a Fraser, and they were with us when we got to Glasgow after England. I know a fair few of the new batch now, too, if ye want an introduction."

"I have so many questions."

"I will answer them if I can."

"You said nothing good happened afterward. What *did* happen?"

"The government came and burned everything on Cameron land, then hunted us down and killed any of us they could find. As I said, I would nae have wanted Grace to stay with me there."

"Did you kill people?"

"Why do people always ask that?" he mused. "Aye, I did."

"How many?"

"Right," Euan said, blinking as he was taken aback by the question. "That is a new one. I dinnae have an exact count, but there were four large battles, the hits at Fort William, the others before the war when we were raided …" Euan listed off as he pondered it. "A lot."

"Like 100?"

"Probably more."

"Holy crap, that's terrifying. Okay, new topic. Did you wear a kilt?"

"We all did."

"Do you still have it?"

"Aye, and I will wear it if ye ask nicely," he said in a teasing tone as Grace smothered a laugh in her hand.

"Did you get wounded?"

"Where do ye think all the scars ye saw came from?"

"Yikes. Did you hate the British?"

"Most of us hated them."

"Do you still?"

"No reason to now, so, no. Still hate the Campbells though."

"Who?"

"Never mind."

"Was it weird to come live in the future?"

"At first, aye, but I am happy I did. It is a lot nicer here."

"So, when we had lunch that day, you really *were* trying the food for the first time?"

Euan laughed at the memory. "Aye."

"Did it hurt to die?"

"I did nae die. She did it for me," Euan corrected, the sadness on his face telling Vanessa how much the incident hurt him to think about.

"Yes," Grace replied, her voice small and soft, answering the question before Vanessa could ask it. "But please don't ask me about it."

"I'm so sorry, Grace."

Grace shook her head. "It happened, and I got something wonderful out of it."

"Can I go to the past? Just to see history? You know I'm a history nerd."

"I'd have to ask, but maybe," Grace said.

Vanessa turned back to Euan. "So, that museum, are you in it?"

"No, I dinnae think so. Maybe, if there is a list there of those in the Cameron regiment, but I dinnae think they have any sort of plaque about me. I was naught extraordinary."

"I bet you guys have so many cool stories from working."

"You have no idea," Grace said.

"You *have* to tell me."

"Well, you're here for three weeks. Lots of time."

"I. Can't. Wait."

Euan laughed and shook his head at her.

"And you," Vanessa said, pointing at him, which stopped his laughter as he looked at her with a raised eyebrow. "You need to dig that British uniform out because I totally want to see it."

"Dinnae have it," Euan said. "Last I saw it, it was on the ground on a street in Edinburgh where I threw it once it had served its purpose."

"Damn it."

"Sorry to disappoint," he replied, following it with that same teasing smile he'd given her earlier.

"No, he isn't," Grace said, giving him a gentle shove. "At all. We should go anyway. We can talk more about this at home."

Just as Grace spoke the words, one of the doors at the back of the room opened. Both Euan and Grace looked surprised as a woman in a white dress and long hair like Grace's walked inside, not seeming to notice them. She ran a hand through her hair with a tired sigh, but she stopped short when she saw them and looked at them in shock.

"Oh, hello. I did not know you would still be here," she said to them, looking uncomfortable.

"Vanessa, this is Councilwoman Rochford, the head of The Council. She's also a Watcher," Grace said, introducing the woman, who then smiled.

"Good to meet you. I'm Vanessa, Grace's friend."

"I know who you are," the Councilwoman replied. "Alice Cameron, good to meet you."

"Wait, what? I thought Grace just said your name was Rochford?"

"About that …" Grace said as the Councilwoman laughed.

"These two are my ancestors, technically," she explained. "Rochford is the name I go by as the Councilwoman, but when I'm out as a Watcher, I'm out as a Cameron, just as Grace is. I only get to be myself when I go home or when I work."

"Whoa. That's a trip."

"Tell me about it," Grace said.

"Where did ye go?" Euan asked Rochford.

"Cannot tell you that, you know better," she said before she chuckled. "I did make a secondary stop though," she continued as she pulled a piece of paper from her sleeve. "You can give that to Malcolm."

Euan took it from her and unfolded it before laughing. "Ye are brilliant. He will love this, but I am sorry ye had to go there."

Rochford shrugged. "Better me than you."

"What is it?" Vanessa asked.

Euan held it up to show both women the bounty flyer for him, though this one was stained in one corner by the blood of the man it had once belonged to. "I promised Malcolm a copy."

Grace rolled her eyes but smiled anyway, and Vanessa stepped closer to look at it. "Dude, you … you were an outlaw?"

"Aye, proud of it, too, when it happened."

"Does that say you tried to kill the Duke of Cumberland!"

"Indeed, it does."

"Hang on, is that blood?!"

Euan glanced at it, then shrugged. "Probably."

"You are so hardcore."

Rochford laughed. "You will find out soon enough just how right you are." When all three of them looked at her curiously, her eyes widened, clearly having said something she hadn't intended to. "Oh. Um …"

Euan folded his arms and raised an eyebrow. "What does that mean, exactly?"

Rochford seemed to take a moment to think of something to cover up her mistake but then decided not to bother. "Grace, although you have not asked yet, yes, she can stay, and yes, we will handle it."

"Handle what? I don't even know what I was supposed to ask?" Grace queried.

"You were eventually going to ask if there was some sort of way you can help Vanessa stay with you. The answer is yes. You would not be the first Watcher and Companion to have a trusted friend and ally at their service as a sort of assistant. A person who handles the things you cannot: groceries, bills, taking Aileen places. You are gone so often that it is easy for the small things to slip your mind. I have a friend doing that for me and my Companion."

"Would you want to do that, Van?" Grace asked as she and Euan both looked at Vanessa, who was staring at Rochford in surprise.

"Well, I mean, is that all I'd do? Just sort of be your manager?"

"You would be whatever they needed you to be, within reason," Rochford answered. "For instance, mine makes sure bills are paid on time, the house is kept up with any repairs, other service calls are handled, groceries are bought, and my children are tended to."

Grace looked back at Rochford. "You have children? I didn't know that."

"Yes, I do. Not something I ever thought of telling you because it does not really matter."

"Well, one of them will be a Watcher, right?"

"No, one of them will be the mother to the future Watcher, not be one herself."

"Would I need a work visa and stuff?" Vanessa asked, drawing the conversation back to the former topic.

"You would have one. There is no need to be concerned about that."

"Do we just pay her salary out of our wages?" Euan asked.

"No, we pay her because she is working for you to assist you in doing your jobs. That, of course, falls within our purview, just as security for the lodge does. Do not worry about the amount, it will be more than fair."

Vanessa was quiet, trying to process it all. "Do I have to decide right now?"

"No, you may decide whenever you wish, even after you return home. Take your time; it is a big choice," Rochford said, smiling. "It is a lot of responsibility, but those who do it always find it is worth it."

"We'll discuss it later. We should let you get back home," Grace said to Rochford.

Rochford nodded in gratitude. "Goodnight then. Good to meet you, Vanessa," she said as she walked toward the main doors before stopping and turning around. "Oh, and yes, you can go to Observation with her, but do be careful what you show her, Grace."

"Got it," Grace confirmed before Rochford left. "Right, let's go, shall we?"

"This has been the coolest and weirdest night in my whole life," Vanessa declared.

"I would say it would remain so, but due to what ye were just given leave to do, that would be a lie," Euan said as Grace laughed.

"Everyone ready?" Caia asked as she came back in. "Let's get you home."

CHAPTER 10

"I'm not sure I can look at anything the same way now," Vanessa said as she opened the door to the study and walked out. "I mean, everything I know about anything is —"

Her words were cut off when she collided with someone else in the hallway who had been coming into the study as she was coming out. She gave a small scream of shock as she fell and landed on top of her opposition.

"Oh my goodness, I am *so* sorry!" she said as she pulled back to find herself looking down at Mal.

"Uh, hi. Terribly sorry about that, should have looked where I was going. Nae usually the way I like to find myself in this position."

From the doorway, both Euan and Grace burst into laughter at Mal's comment. "Mal, this is Vanessa, Grace's friend from America. She is here to visit us for a few weeks," Euan explained through laughter.

The two of them remained unmoving before Vanessa shook her head and backed up to sit on the floor. Mal got up and held out his hand to her to help her stand, which she took with a smile. "Malcolm Cameron, but ye can call me Mal like everyone else does. My father and I share the same name."

"Vanessa Farron," she replied. "Nice to meet you. Are you related to Euan, too?"

"No. Well, nae like that anyway. We are from the same clan, but that is as far as it goes."

"Oh, I see." Vanessa rubbed her eyes. "Sorry, a bit off right now."

"Jet lag?"

"Time lag," Euan said, and Mal looked at him. "Aye, she knows."

"It can be a bit disconcerting. Trust me, I remember," Mal said.

"You know, too?"

"One of only three outside people who do," Grace said. "His father knows, and now you. My mom knows because her mom was the Watcher before me, and Aileen would obviously know."

"I'm glad you trust me enough to tell me," Vanessa said with a yawn, "but I think I want to take a nap. I'll come back, though. Hopefully you'll still be here," she said to Mal.

"I can be if ye wish," he offered with a smile.

Vanessa nodded and left the study to go upstairs.

"Poor lass looked exhausted."

"She has been on the move since she arrived and we were up at dawn to get home," Euan said.

"Ye and dawn. I swear it is ingrained in ye to leave at that time."

"Will nae deny that. It was always a good time to leave if ye faced a lot of travel."

"Fair enough. Anyway, I came here for a reason, and it was nae to be shinty tackled by yer friend."

Euan laughed. "Shinty. Now there is a game I have nae played in a *very* long time."

"We will have to remedy that. I was thinking that perhaps we should do a sort of gathering here at Achnacarry in the summer."

"What sort of gathering? Ye are nae trying to overthrow the queen, are ye?"

Mal chuckled. "No, I actually rather like her. I have a feeling she is a smart arse underneath all that propriety. This would be just a clan thing, a chance for some of us to have the experience of all being together like we were once."

"Ye mean like at Glenfinnan and Falkirk," Euan replied.

"Aye," Mal said with a nod. "Except without the killing."

"But that was the fun part!" Euan said, straight-faced for a moment before laughing at the looks on the faces of the other two. "I am kidding."

"Ye see, when ye say things like that, I cannae always tell."

"Ye would be right to assume I fell somewhere in the middle of that."

"Right. Anyway, what do ye think, Euan? The Frasers would come for certain; we could maybe get some MacDonalds and Murrays."

"It would be fine even if it was just the Frasers," Euan replied with a small shrug. "But, aye, I think that sounds grand. What would ye have there?"

"I think mainly just getting outside to enjoy the sun, but we could also have some sort of session for those of us interested in the history. Whisky and food, of course, and a night out under the stars around a fire."

"Aye, I am certainly up for it if ye are. It will be nice to do so and know there is nae a day's march or a battle ahead of us. Nice to look around and know that the faces ye see will all be there the next day."

"It would be, aye, and ye *will* see them," Mal said reassuringly as he put a hand on Euan's shoulder. "I promise."

"I could use a cup of tea," Grace said, breaking the tension that had started to settle.

"Ach, me too," Euan said as they all headed for the kitchen. "And some biscuits. Is yer father here, Mal?"

"Aye. He would nae miss a chance to come up now."

"Why do ye say th —" Euan's words stopped as he hit the entrance to the kitchen, his jaw dropping.

This reaction earned a curious look from Grace, who stepped up next to him and then stopped. "Oh."

Euan backed away from the kitchen, pulling Grace with him and away from the sight of Aileen and Malcolm talking quietly in the kitchen, with some flowers he'd brought for her lying on the kitchen island between them and one of her hands in his.

"I … I dinnae know what I think about that," Euan said in a whisper.

Mal's laugh was quiet. "I was surprised, too, but then at the same time, I wasn't."

"I think it's sweet," Grace said.

"It is nae yer mam!" Euan countered.

"Even if it was, they aren't doing anything. Not like we walked in on them making out or something."

Euan scowled at her.

"Well, we didn't," she muttered.

Mal smothered a laugh. "It is a *wee* bit awkward."

"It is not. You two are being ridiculous."

"Aye, a bit," Mal conceded. "My dad has nae even thought about such a thing since my mother died. It's kind of nice that he is now; it just happens to be yer mother, Euan."

Euan sighed. "It is just odd to think about. She always said she never wanted another after my father."

"She's only in her mid-40s, Euan. That's a long time, and it has already been over 20 years," Grace pointed out. "It may have been easier to keep to in a place where she knew everyone already, but now her whole world is different."

"Would ye marry another if I died?" Euan fired back.

Grace paled, her expression a mix of hurt and shock. "No, but we're not the same, Euan. You know I couldn't marry someone else even if it *was* something I'd consider," she replied, her voice full of the same hurt her face held.

Euan blinked, realizing what he'd said. It hit too close for her, this being a situation they'd almost faced and only just weeks ago. She couldn't marry another because they'd both be dead. "Love, I —"

"Don't," she said in a whisper, cutting him off before turning and walking away from him, heading upstairs.

Euan swore under his breath. "I should nae have said that."

Mal gave him a curious look. "What was that about? What happened?"

Euan sighed and shook his head. "There is a bond between the Watcher and the Companion, created when the Watcher saves them. If the Watcher dies, so does the Companion, or the other way round. If I died, so would she. She could nae marry another because she would nae be alive to do so."

"Jesus, that is intense."

"Aye. Worse is that it was something that almost happened on our last mission."

Mal sucked in a breath through his teeth. "Ye are in some shite, my friend."

"Very much so," Euan admitted.

"So, what should we do about …" Mal said, trailing off with a nod toward the kitchen.

"What *can* we do?"

"We can either act like petulant children who cry and scream about the memories of our loved ones while forbidding them from having any sort of relationship like that with anyone …"

"Or …"

"We act like grown men, realize that they deserve to be happy, and if they make each other happy, then so be it."

"The second option seems preferable."

"It does, aye."

Euan folded his arms and leaned against the wall, considering something. "As a bonus, if it does go well, ye and I would actually be kin."

"I'm fine with that."

"Me too."

"Still want that cuppa?"

"Aye. Chocolate biscuits are calling my name," Euan said as he pushed away from the wall. "May need a nip in mine though after this."

Mal laughed, which made Euan laugh, too. "I'm with ye."

"Wait, I know what to do," Euan said, winking at Mal. "So, I got something from The Council," Euan began, his voice louder than it needed to be.

Mal immediately understood it was a warning they were coming and played along. "Aye? What is it?" he replied just as loudly.

Euan turned and walked into the kitchen with Mal to find that Malcolm and Aileen were no longer talking, and Aileen was putting the flowers in a vase. "Hello, Mam, Malcolm."

"Lads," Malcolm replied with a nod.

Euan pulled the paper Rochford had given him from his pocket and handed it to Mal. "Got this," he replied, continuing the conversation as though the pair of them knew nothing at all.

Mal unfolded it as Euan grabbed the kettle and filled it with water. "Christ, ye got one! Dad!" he said as he placed it in front of Malcolm.

Malcolm grinned and picked it up. "Ye brilliant lad! This will go well with our records. Nae as pristine as the one ye first showed us though."

"Aye, but that makes it more authentic, right?"

Mal swallowed his laugh and turned it into a cough.

"What is it?" Aileen asked as she set the vase of flowers on the countertop.

Malcolm handed it to her before Euan could stop him, and he froze behind her with the kettle in his hands. Fortunately for Aileen, her son had seen fit to teach her to read when he'd learned, but that was about to be unfortunate for Euan and he knew it. She turned around and looked at her son, who looked for all the world like a child caught doing something he shouldn't.

"Mam ..."

"Euan Alexander Cameron, I cannae believe ye!"

"Ye knew I had a bounty on me! Ye heard Malcolm say it when we first met him!"

"I did nae know how ye earned it! Is it true? What this says?"

"Aye, it is," Euan replied as he set the kettle back on its stand and flipped the switch on.

"Ye tried to kill the bloody Hanover prince? Are ye mad?"

"It is nae like I meant to or sought him out. It just happened."

"Just …" Aileen trailed off before making a frustrated sound. "I am like to box yer ears now, ye *idiot* boy!"

Mal and Malcolm watched the exchange with extreme amusement, and Euan looked sheepish.

"Ye could try."

"Oh, I would do more than try. Ye are lucky ye were nae killed!"

"To be fair, I was that lucky a lot of times."

"EUAN."

"That was the wrong thing to say," Euan said as Mal fell apart with laughter.

Aileen slammed the paper down on the counter and glared at her son, which silenced Mal in an instant. "Ye can joke all ye want, but it was nae *ye* who had to sit praying yer child came home to ye! *Ye* were nae the one who scrubbed blood and bone from his clothing when he came home dripping with gore! It was nae *ye* who watched him become a cold shell of himself! *I* did that! And now ye want to joke about how ye almost died many times over and had a bounty on ye, which would have most certainly meant ye met a traitor's death?"

"Aileen," Malcolm said, "it is nae as though the lad sought it out. It was war."

Euan didn't know what to say for a moment and looked pained. "I know ye did, Mam, and I am sorry ye had to do any of it, truly I am. I hated it as much as ye did."

"But it is a joke to ye, is it?"

"No," Euan replied. "It is a defense. I need to laugh about it so that I dinnae cry and scream. I need to make it less than it was if I am to have any chance of getting past it. I have to."

His words took some of the anger out of Aileen, and she nodded. "Ye are right. I am sorry I yelled at ye."

"It is still hard on all of ye," Malcolm said, placing his hand over Aileen's on the counter. "To Mal and me, it has been 270-some years gone. To ye? Only a year. This will happen."

"I never knew what ye did, Euan," Aileen said.

"I know," he said, his voice soft. "I made sure ye did nae,

and I still dinnae want ye to. This is the past, Mam," he continued as he gestured to the flyer. "Over and done. It cannae hurt me now, and I am alive and well here, as ye are. That is all that matters."

"Is this what ye do when ye are gone now?"

"No. I use my mind and nae a weapon. I outsmart people; I dinnae kill them. It is nae allowed, except in certain circumstances."

"Which are?"

"If our target is in danger. In France, Grace was my target, and had anyone tried to harm her, I could have killed them and would have."

"I thought ye said ye cannae be hurt?" Mal said.

"Aye, that is normally true, but something happened there. It is complicated, but Grace was cut off and as normal there as ye are here now. She was nae safe, and The Council could nae get her back, so they sent me after her. She became the target for me, and that gave me leave to do whatever I needed to do to protect her."

"Ye did nae say something had gone wrong!" Aileen exclaimed.

"Hard to explain, Mam, but it did. It is fine now, but it was close."

"That is why ye said … oh hell …" Mal said, putting the two pieces together.

"Exactly."

"What?" Aileen asked. "Tell me."

Euan sighed as the kettle whistled and he turned to shut it off. "She almost died, Mam, and that means I almost did too."

Aileen gasped, turning away from him.

"We made it, and it is all right now, Grace just …" He paused as he tried to think of how to explain it. "Did ye notice how she seems to get anxious if she forgets something?"

"Aye," Aileen replied, her back still to him.

"It is because the beings that cut her off from us started stripping her memory while she slept. She would wake up sick and in pain with a fresh loss of memories. It got to the point where she forgot marrying me … and then she forgot *me.*" He couldn't keep the strain out of his voice at the last words, making obvious the hurt it still caused him.

"Oh my God," Mal whispered.

"The goal was to take everything from her until all that was left was her memory of dying. They did that, or at least they thought they did. They had her in a place we could nae reach, and they put her back on that battlefield. They made her suffer the pain of her injuries again, but this time she did nae know why she was being hurt or for what. All around her were the men who died that day, frozen in place like some macabre movie on pause. They used my image to lure her, to encourage her to touch them, because if she did it would kill her."

"Who would do something like that? Why?" Malcolm asked, astonished.

"Torture. They wanted her to suffer before they killed her." Euan paused, wondering whether he should say it, but decided he should. "They knew that if they killed her, I would follow. That would mean that the Watcher who trapped them where they were could nae do so because she would nae exist. If Grace died, the Cameron Watchers died with her."

"Christ, that's sadistic," Mal said.

"Aye, but that is what the plan was. They hate the Watchers, but they hate the Cameron Watchers especially. They want us dead. I heard them once. 'Death to the Camerons,' they said. Grace is the first Cameron Watcher; if they killed her, it was the end of everything. They would have destroyed The Council."

"Are ye still in danger from this?" Aileen asked as she turned back around.

"Always," Euan admitted, not about to lie to her now that he'd put this out there. "Every Watcher is. But we know what they are and how they operate now. That will keep us safer. They cannae get to us here, but that is why ye will never see us at Culloden again. They have an opening there and they have already tried to use it."

"The spectre ye saw," Aileen whispered.

"Aye."

"What can we do to protect ye, Euan?" Malcolm asked, his face serious.

"Our security here is excellent, but if ye see anything strange, tell us. If ye see people where they should nae be, tell us, even though they are nae supposed to have the ability to manifest outside of their space. Especially if they look like one of us. That is how they work. They look like someone ye know, but are nae them, and if ye are paying attention, ye can tell. Their eyes are entirely black, no white to be seen. Extra people looking for them will never hurt."

"I will keep a watch for it; ye have my word," Malcolm said.

"And mine," Mal added.

"Thank ye. When I asked The Council for permission to tell ye, they told me that ye were the start of a long and beneficial relationship between the Cameron Watchers and yer family. I have a feeling this is why."

"I will feel safer with ye watching, too," Aileen said.

Euan smiled before he turned and pulled tea bags from the canister, putting them in cups and pouring the hot water over them. "It is fine with me."

"What is?" Malcolm asked.

"Ye two," Euan said, watching the surprised looks hit the faces of the pair. "Aye, we know. All of us do. Go on with ye; ye have my blessing."

Mal laughed. "Aye."

"Ye too, lad?" Malcolm asked him before his son nodded his agreement.

"Euan, are ye sure?" Aileen queried.

"I am. Ye are young yet, Mam. Ye have mourned for 20 years, and it is time for ye to set it aside," Euan replied as he took her hand and kissed it. "Father would nae want ye to do such a thing; he would want ye to be happy. It is fine, I swear it to ye."

"Thank ye," she said, squeezing his hand before he released hers.

"I need to take this to my wife and apologize for being an arse," Euan said as he finished making the cup of tea and put it on a small tray. "If ye will excuse me?"

"If ye have been an arse, ye had better take one of these, lad," Malcolm said, pulling a flower from the vase.

Euan took it with a nod of thanks, placing it on the tray, walking out of the kitchen and up the stairs. "Grace?" he called out in a quiet voice as he entered the room. When his eyes adjusted to the dimness, he saw her curled up in one of the chairs by a window and walked over to her, holding out the tray with the flower and the cup of tea. "A peace offering."

Grace took the tray as she sat up but said nothing and set them on a table.

"I should nae have said what I did, and I am sorry for it. I was nae thinking."

After a long moment, she looked up at him. "No, you weren't."

"It is easy to forget we are nae normal."

"Is it?"

"When this is our reality, aye. To everyone else it might be hard to forget, but nae us because we live with it every day. Just like how we cannae die on a mission, we are so used to it that we no longer think of it."

"I wouldn't, you know," she said, her voice soft but the hurt in it clear.

"Would nae what?"

"If we were normal and you died, I wouldn't …" She stopped and shook her head, closing her eyes.

"No," he whispered, reaching out and stroking her cheek. "I know you would nae, just as ye know I would nae, but dinnae think about what will never happen. We know what happens to us."

"Do you ever wish we were normal?"

"No," he said, sitting down on the floor in front of the chair, leaning back against it, and tilting his head back to look up at her.

"Why?"

"Because if we were, I would nae be here and would nae be with ye. I would have died as I always did, with the knowledge something waited for me but never getting to find out what that was."

"That's true."

"Besides, I have never been what ye would consider normal. Normal is boring," he said, his words making Grace chuckle and bringing a soft smile to his lips. "There is my lass. I gave them my blessing."

"Did you really? That's very good of you even if you don't mean it."

"I do mean it. Ye were right. She deserves to be happy again, and I will nae stand in her way. Nae after all she has done for me."

Grace smiled at him and leaned down to kiss his forehead. "You never know. Maybe it won't work out."

"It will," he said, and Grace gave him a curious look. "I just feel it. Cannae explain how, but when those feelings do come, they have never been wrong."

"Well, then you get a brother instead of a friend."

"Fine by me."

Grace laughed a bit. "With the way you two already are, I don't think anyone would know the difference anyway."

"Aye, well," he said, shrugging. "Come down with me? I still really want my chocolate biscuits."

"Oh, I think we're out of HobNobs."

Euan's face fell, and he sat up, turning around to look at her. "What? I dinnae remember eating them all! Did ye?"

Grace laughed at him. "There are two sleeves in the cupboard."

Euan looked at her with annoyance. "Dinnae tease a man about his food, woman!" Grace only laughed harder, which made him laugh, too, before he turned back around. "Ye are a cruel wife."

"No, cruelty would have been to hide them and then tell you we were out."

"Ye would nae …"

"Is that a challenge?"

"No!"

Grace smiled. "Better mind yourself then."

"Mind myself … oh, sin e." *That's it.*

Grace had no time to respond as he reached up over his head to grab her around the shoulders and pull her forward, then down into his lap where he tickled her.

"Mind myself, is it?"

Grace started laughing and squirming as he tickled her. "Yes!"

"Wrong answer!"

She let out a small shriek as he upped the ferocity of his attack. "Okay, okay, I surrender!"

Euan let go of her, and she lay in a breathless heap on the floor, still laughing as she tried to catch her breath. "Come downstairs and be social, ye blasted Watcher," he said, laughing as he stood up and left the room.

CHAPTER 11

The next morning, Vanessa came down and grinned when she saw Grace reading at the kitchen table. "Morning, Grace! I thought maybe you and I could binge *Outlander*, and Euan can watch with us."

Grace looked up from her book and shook her head as Vanessa sat down. "No, we can't."

"Why?"

Grace released a soft sigh. "Because that was his life, Van. Those events, the atmosphere? He lived it. Not just the season with the war, but all of it. He won't want to relive that and, to be honest, neither do I."

"Oh, I hadn't thought of that. I mean, I knew he would understand it and all, but I didn't think about the fact that he was familiar with it on a next-level type thing so you're right. You know you thought Jamie was hot though."

"I did," Grace said, a sly smile spreading across her lips. "Then I got my own."

"Oh, okay, rub it in, why don't you," she said with mock bitterness as Grace laughed. "Where is he, anyway?"

"He took Aileen into town. They'll be back later."

"Cool! Just you and me, huh?"

"Yep. I was thinking maybe it would be a good time to take you to Observation for that history you wanted to see."

Vanessa gasped in excitement. "Really! I am so down. What would we see?"

"Anything you wanted, really. I mean, I can take you into some of my missions if you want. There are some people in there I know you'd be dying to see."

"Do I need to do anything?"

"Not really. You're already dressed, so we can go now if you want."

"Let's do this thing!"

Grace laughed. "Caia will be here in a second."

"How does she know when to come?"

"I told them earlier to expect us today and to have Caia come in the morning. She could always hang out if you weren't ready to go."

"She just hangs out?"

"Sure. She's human, you know. She just happens to be from the future."

"Cool. She seems super nice."

"She is," Grace said, smiling. "Aside from you she's one of my closest friends and has been since the day my grandparents died. She'll be with Euan and me our entire lives."

"Whoa, really?"

"Yep. We're her assignment."

"And I feel very lucky to have it," Caia said as she walked into the kitchen. "Good morning!"

"Hey, Caia! Tea?"

"Oh, I would love some, thank you!"

Grace got up to make her a cup, and Vanessa looked at Caia curiously. "So, how do you get this particular job?"

"You mean being a Guardian?"

"Yeah. Are you born to it, like Grace was?"

"Oh, no. There is a pretty rigorous program we go through before we even get to attempt training. If we pass training, then we wait for an assignment. The positions do not come open often, so you do a lot of other things while you wait. I worked in medical for a while and the archives. All of it helps you to better understand the entire process and be of the most help to your assigned Watcher. They won't have to explain it to you when they need something instantly, you will already understand where to find it and how to get it. They need us to be on top of things while they're in the field and rarely have time to hold your hand through a task."

"Wow. Pretty cool that you ended up getting to do it."

"I agree! I love my job, and I am lucky to have Grace and Euan as my assignment. I have had to fill in with a few people who were not so personable. When I got the permanent assignment to the newest Watcher, I was really excited. Someone my own age to work with!"

"Do you get to see their missions, too?"

"Goodness, no! I only know what they tell me when they come back."

"We always try to tell her as much as we can, though," Grace said, bringing the cup to Caia.

"Thank you, and yes, you do. I always appreciate that."

"Were you there when Euan came?" Vanessa asked.

Caia stopped with the cup halfway to her lips, looking sad for a moment before she nodded. "Yes, I was."

Grace gave Caia a questioning look. "You were?"

"I was in the room when he woke up; he just did not see me."

"What did he do?"

"Screamed. I have never heard anything like it. It was …" Caia paused as she tried to search for the words. "All of this pent-up pain and anger, and then he started crying, all because he was thinking of you."

"How do you know that?"

"People only cry like that when their heart is broken," Caia said. "I have seen it enough to know. It was the same way you cried when you woke up."

Grace looked down, clearly trying to keep a check on herself. "I remember it clearly, that moment and all of those things I felt, the sense of failure and the loss of someone I cared about more than I was ready to admit."

"I was there, too, when he would come and talk to you."

"What?" Grace said as she looked up. "You never told me that he'd come and talked to me."

"I am sorry. I thought I had. He came every day and would sit and talk to you about what he had learned that day and sing to you. It would break my heart for him when he would plead with you to wake up, to return to him, and he did it every time. He wanted you to know he was there, and it did not matter that we told him you could not hear him and would not know. He came anyway."

Grace closed her eyes, fighting with her own emotions. "He still does," she whispered. "Sing to me, that is. Whenever I am feeling anxious or sad."

Vanessa wiped tears from her cheeks. "And I thought he couldn't get any more perfect."

"He isn't perfect. None of us are."

"He's perfect for *you*," Vanessa countered.

"She is right," Caia said. "You did not see him when France went wrong. He was so afraid, and then he was angry with the Councilwoman when he found out where you had gone. He had not been right from the moment you left. He could not be still, could not be easy, and then he suddenly said he could not feel you with him. I should have known then that something was wrong, I should have believed him, because if I had he could have gotten there sooner, been with you from the start."

"No one knew what was going to happen, Caia. Please, don't blame yourself. There was nothing you could have done. I was in danger the moment I left, and the fact that they sent him against all protocol when they did is what saved my life in the end."

"Wait, what do you mean? I thought you said you can't die, Grace?" Vanessa questioned.

"Normally I can't. Something really bad happened on our last mission, and I was suddenly very much a regular human being who could die. It was a place where people certainly wanted me dead."

"Euan wasn't there?"

"Not at first. See, he's not supposed to go back into his former lifetime, and this mission was only two years after he was supposed to have died so he was required to stay behind no matter how much he hated it. When it went wrong, they broke protocol and sent him after me."

"Thank goodness we did," Caia said.

"Besides me, he was the only one who could've pulled that mission off," Grace explained. "It involved everyone he used to know, so he knew their game intimately and managed to stop them."

"Well, they are not sending you without him again," Caia replied.

"Really?" Grace asked.

Caia nodded. "They will not take the chance with you, and you know why now. That attack specifically targeted you, and there is no saying they would not try again. Euan will always be with you."

"I'm actually really glad to hear that," Grace said, her smile one of relief.

"You two work best together anyway," Caia said with a small shrug. "There is not a pair that comes close to touching you in terms of success or amount of work. The Council is not blind to that, certainly."

"This job sounds crazy dangerous, Grace," Vanessa said, wary.

"It isn't Van, not normally. Exhausting, strange, and lonely sometimes but usually not dangerous. If Euan is with me, I don't need to worry about anything."

"Certainly not," Caia agreed.

"Anyway, we should go," Grace said. "We're going to scare Vanessa away."

Caia chuckled. "Ready when you are."

Grace and Vanessa stood up and took Caia's hands for transport, though Vanessa was ready for the shift this time.

"That's still weird," she said, keeping her eyes closed.

"You get used to it after a while," Grace assured her.

When Vanessa opened her eyes, Grace was once again in uniform, and she shook her head. "You … wow."

"What?"

"You just look so different in that dress."

Grace looked at herself in the two-way mirror and then back at Vanessa. "What do you mean?"

"I don't know. There's just something about you when you're wearing it. You look unreal somehow."

"Hm, I don't suppose I really notice because I'm used to it. Anyway, come on, hop up," Grace said, pointing to the table.

The archivist came in to help Vanessa while Grace hooked herself in. "This feels like a weird version of *The Matrix*."

Grace laughed and then looked over at Vanessa with a grin. "You ready for this?"

"Hell. Yes."

"Eyes closed and here we go," Grace said. "Okay, open them."

Vanessa opened her eyes as instructed and looked around her. The sound of steel clashing caused her to turn around, and she looked at the two people for a long moment before she recognized the both of them. "Wait, is that —"

"It is."

"You had a mission with Queen Elizabeth!"

"We did, though she was Princess Elizabeth here," Grace explained as she nodded to Euan, who was teaching the future queen to use a sword.

"DUDE. I … OH MY GOD."

Grace laughed. "I brought you here first because I know how much of a fan of hers you've always been. I actually quite enjoyed this one."

"What was she like?"

"Smart, sarcastic, wary, and tempestuous. She could get angry very quickly."

Vanessa watched them go through the motions, watched

Elizabeth smile and laugh as Euan tried to correct her grip or her footwork. "She's totally flirting with him!"

"Oh, she absolutely is and did so every chance she got. I wasn't worried."

"Yeah, you shouldn't be, and I can't really blame her for trying. Why were you here?"

"To make sure she didn't join Wyatt's rebellion."

"Whaaat."

"Yep. She was going to this time, but we made sure she didn't, and Euan ensured the rebellion still failed."

Vanessa looked at Grace in shock. "Why?"

"Because it had to. That's history."

"How did he do it?"

"I don't know," Grace admitted. "I never ask because I don't want to know."

Vanessa nodded. "You know what? Knowing him, I get that. Can I get closer?"

"As close as you want. They can't see you. Think of it like being a ghost in a movie. This is the past, a past mission we worked, so it's not really happening."

"This is so cool," Vanessa said as she walked up to the two of them and looked into the true face of a woman she so admired. She then saw the mission version of Grace walk by them, stopping to reverence the princess, saw Euan watching her and Elizabeth seeing the way he watched her before Grace rose and continued on her way. "You looked really pretty in that outfit!"

"Thanks, Van," Grace said, smiling. "They don't give us horrible clothes. Remind me to show you what I brought back from France when we get home."

"Sweet!" Elizabeth suddenly stepped closer to Euan and Vanessa backed up with a disconcerted expression. "Hey ..."

"Cameron, why do you look at her that way?"

Grace looked at the scene unfolding in front of her curiously, not having seen it before.

"What way, Yer Highness?"

"In a way that says you wish it were night and you were alone with her."

Euan looked at her with a small questioning smile. *"What makes ye believe that is what I am thinking?"*

"You do not look at anyone else that way, not even me, and I have seen that look on the faces of plenty of men who were more than happy to tell me that is what they were thinking about me."

"Should I think that of ye?"

"If I wanted you to, then yes."

"Ye cannae command me in that way."

"I can command you in anything. You serve me, remember?"

"Nae that."

"Do you not think I am worthy of it? Everyone else seems to."

"I think ye are beautiful, as does everyone else."

"Oh, hell no," Vanessa said.

"Shhh," Grace replied, having drawn closer.

"But not beautiful enough."

Euan shook his head. *"That is nae my thought at all. What would ye want with me? I am naught to ye, and ye are meant for princes, nae stable hands."*

"So, you do think I am enough then," she said as she placed a hand on his chest, which made Vanessa gasp.

Euan didn't move. *"If my heart was nae elsewhere, then perhaps."*

Elizabeth frowned. *"I could dismiss her."*

"If ye did, I would leave too."

"You could not unless I gave you leave!"

"Ye would have to catch me first."

"I would have you brought back here! In chains if required!"

"And ye think that would get me to do as ye wished, do ye?"

Elizabeth looked momentarily taken aback.

"Ye cannae force someone to love ye, Yer Highness. That is nae how love works."

"What is love?" Elizabeth said disdainfully. *"Love brings pain and death. It is nothing."*

Euan looked at her sadly. *"Yer past makes ye say that, but it is nae so. Dinnae base yer thoughts of it on what ye see around ye in those in yer station. They play at love. Look to those beneath ye to see what love truly is."*

"To you?"

"No," Euan said gently. *"Nae to me. I cannae give ye what ye seek."*

"What if all I seek is what you wish to have with Mistress Evans each time she passes you? It is in your eyes. What if all I seek is to know the touch of someone who is not forced to wed me for alliance or duty before I am forever consigned to that fate?"

"What I wish to have and what I do have are two entirely different things, Yer Highness. I may look at Mistress Evans, but she is nae mine to have. If that is what ye seek …"

"No way," Vanessa whispered. "Grace, uh, we should go."

"Yes?" Elizabeth said, wanting him to continue.

"I am nae the one for ye," Euan said with a bow. *"I apologize, but I have no wish to show one without the other. It is nae the way I am. I am sorry that ye face such a situation, but I cannae be the one to educate ye in such ways."*

Grace smiled wryly. "Liar."

"Seriously?"

"You really think he wasn't using those looks to his advantage, Van? I also know perfectly well when he's lying."

"True."

Elizabeth stepped back away from him. *"I think I am done for the day,"* she said as she pulled the gloves from her hands angrily. *"Yer Highness —"*

Elizabeth shook her head and thrust the hilt of the sword toward him before she stormed off, and Euan sighed.

"See," Grace said, "easily angry."

"I thought for a second he was going to do it."

"I didn't. Come on."

Grace took them farther back next, and they found themselves in a long gallery, standing across from a set of doors. "This will be really brief."

The doors opened, and a man stepped out with a woman on his arm. "Holy crap!" Vanessa exclaimed.

"Yep," Grace replied.

In front of them stood Henry VIII himself, still a fairly youthful and trim man. On his arm was Catherine of Aragon, and as they walked out, a retinue of young women trailed behind them.

"Look, there's Anne," Grace said, pointing.

Vanessa squealed in excitement. "This is crazy! Look at their clothes!" But then she noticed someone at the end of the line: Grace. "No way …"

"Yes, I really wanted to stop that whole thing, but I couldn't. They weren't my mission anyway."

"That sucks."

"It does sometimes, yes."

Vanessa grabbed Grace's hand and pulled her down the hallway until the royal party stopped moving, running up close to look at their clothing. "So intricate."

"They were beautiful. And heavy. Where do you want to go next?"

"Did you ever go to ancient Rome or anything?"

"Yes. And Egypt."

"Dude, I totally want to see that."

"Sure," Grace said, smiling.

Grace took her to both of those missions, letting her see Cleopatra, Egypt, Rome, Caesar, and Antony. Those figures hadn't been her missions either, she'd explained, but she'd seen them, and that meant Vanessa could. Vanessa watched all of it with great interest, studying what they looked like, how they spoke, how they moved, and marveling at the similarities and differences.

"Right, so, next? Show me how you first saw Euan," Vanessa said.

Grace didn't bother to hide her look of surprise. "Why?"

"I want to see what you saw."

Grace nodded and when Vanessa opened her eyes next, she found herself standing at the edge of the loch with Grace, and the gunshot immediately followed, with Euan running out of the woods with the others.

"He shot you!" Vanessa exclaimed. "What the hell, dude!"

"No, he didn't. Duncan did."

"Right. Okay, let me rephrase. Show me when you first *really* saw him."

Grace smiled and hurried along the loch road, Vanessa behind her. Taking her hand, she pulled Vanessa close to a tree. Across from them was the mission Grace, looking at the same thing.

"There," Grace whispered.

Vanessa followed her gaze and saw Euan in the loch in the same way Grace had seen him that day. "Oh. Oh wowwww. Holy crap, dude."

"Mmmhmm," Grace replied, laughing softly.

"How did you not tackle him?"

"Not part of my job."

"Still."

Grace grinned and shook her head. "Don't think he would've taken kindly to that. Well, at least not at that point."

Just then, the mission Grace turned around while the current Grace laughed harder. "I get to watch this time."

"Watch wh —" Vanessa's eyes went wide as Euan turned and walked out of the loch. "Oh, my Lord."

"Yeah, definitely glad I didn't watch this then," she said as Vanessa stood there with her jaw on the ground.

"I'm not going to ever be able to look at him the same," she said.

Grace nudged her, and Vanessa laughed. "Where else can we go?"

Grace paused to think for a moment. "Oh! I know! Close your eyes!"

When Vanessa closed her eyes and then opened them, they were standing on a dark city street. "Where in the hell are we?"

"Edinburgh, September 1745."

The sound of two men talking got Vanessa's attention in enough time to see them walk past her and stand near a guard post. It took her a moment before she realized one of them was Euan.

"Ohhh, I knew it! I knew he'd look hot in that uniform!"

"He absolutely did."

"Did I now?"

Both women screamed and jumped, only to hear Euan laughing behind them.

"What are you doing here?" Grace asked, hand on her chest.

"Ye said ye were coming to Observation, and since we got back a bit early, I thought I'd join ye. Spying on me, are ye?"

"She was only verifying for me that you did, indeed, look hot in that uniform," Vanessa said, trying and failing to not remember having seen him nude just moments before.

Euan laughed again. "While I appreciate ye saying so, this was awful. I had to spend four days pretending to be English. If I slipped up, I was dead. Though, dinnae get me wrong, I am nae upset ye came here for this."

"Well, since you're here, maybe we can see something I wanted to see but couldn't," Grace said.

"Which is?" he queried as he took her hand and kissed it.

"I want to see the fight at Versailles."

Euan raised an eyebrow. "The broadsword fight?"

"Yes."

He considered it for a moment and then nodded. "If ye wish. I did rather wish ye had seen it then, so I suppose now ye can."

"Wait, there was a sword fight?" Vanessa asked.

"Oh, there was indeed," Euan said, flashing one of his wicked grins.

As soon as they closed their eyes, they were shifted, and when they opened them, they stood in the gardens at Versailles. "Oh! Versailles! Rad," Vanessa said.

Mission Euan stormed past them, pulling off his frock coat and tossing it to the ground as the other men followed him, and everyone else stopped to look.

"Is this location agreeable to ye?"

"*Aye.*"

"*Euan,*" Lochiel said. "*Are ye sure ye want to do this?*"

"*Oh, aye. He was nae the only one slighted.*"

Lochiel nodded and drew his own broadsword before he handed it to Euan. "*Ye will be in need of this then.*"

Euan nodded. "*Thank ye,*" he said as he took a few practice swings with it. "*Shall we?*"

At the first strike, Vanessa jumped, but Grace watched intently. When Euan grabbed the man's arm and yanked him forward to break his nose, Vanessa let out a little scream, and Grace grimaced.

"Oh, that had to hurt," Grace said.

"I would imagine so, aye."

In the next instant, the man had charged with the small knife, and Euan had flipped him over his shoulder and onto the ground. He now had the knife and moved the tip of his sword to the man's throat, looking every bit as though he intended to run him through.

"Oh my God!" Vanessa shouted.

"*Hold!*"

All attention went to the king, and Euan stepped away from the man as the current Euan spoke, "Put us just in the gardens alone, please."

Suddenly, the gardens were empty of people except for the three of them, and Grace looked at him curiously. "Why did you do that?"

"I had no wish to hear again the words that came next."

Grace nodded, but Vanessa shook her head. "Were you really going to kill that guy? Did you?"

"I really was, aye, and no, I did nae. Unfortunately."

"But …"

"It was a duel, Vanessa. Those dinnae tend to end well for at least one of the people involved."

"Why did you fight him?"

"Well, first, he tried to kill Grace. Second, he accused me of abandoning my men at Culloden."

"Oh, hell no, he didn't."

"Oh, aye, he did."

"Okay, yeah, he totally deserved killing."

Euan laughed. "Aye, it is a shame I could nae. Are ye planning to go elsewhere ladies, or may I take ye home for tea?"

***

When they got back, Vanessa noticed Mal was there, sitting in the back garden and sketching something. Excusing herself, she went out to join him. "I promise not to fall on you this time."

Mal blinked and looked up, then chuckled. "I did nae hold it against ye."

"That's good. It's a pretty bad first impression to make."

Mal shrugged. "I've seen worse."

"Have you?"

"I'm a scientist of sorts so, aye. Trust me."

Vanessa let out a small laugh. "What kind of science?"

"Archeology."

"Nice! I bet you're loving all of this stuff with Euan and Grace."

Mal nodded, turning his eyes back to the view in front of him and continuing to sketch it. "Aye, it's pretty amazing. Euan said ye went to Observation with Grace and he was off to fetch ye. Did ye have fun?"

"Loads! I got to see some of my heroes. Which was both weird and awesome."

"Where did ye go?"

"I saw Elizabeth I, Henry VIII with Catherine of Aragon and Anne Boleyn, Cleopatra, Antony, and Caesar. It was fantastic."

"Christ, ye went all over," Mal said, grinning. "Maybe I will have Grace take me to Rome sometime. I'd love to see that as it was."

"I bet you would," Vanessa said as she looked down at the sketch of the glen he was working on. "That's really good."

"Thank ye. It helps if ye can sketch when ye find things. We take photos, but it's good to have my own copy to look at as well when I'm writing up a report."

"Makes sense. Are you going back to school soon?"

"No, I'm done. Home for good."

"What school did you go to?"

"University College London. One of the best schools for archeology outside of Cambridge and Oxford."

"Nice!"

"What about ye?"

"English major at UCLA."

"Good one. How did ye meet Grace?"

"I think it was just before she became a Watcher or maybe right after because she wasn't gone much at all then. She'd just gotten back from Oxford."

"I still cannae believe she went there, but go on."

"Yeah, she's seriously ridiculous. Anyway, she stopped a guy creeping on me at a party by sitting with me. We started talking and haven't really stopped."

"Euan said ye are her closest friend."

"Only friend," Vanessa replied. "At least her only non-work-related friend."

Mal looked at her curiously. "How do ye mean?"

Vanessa looked at the house, then back at him, lowering her voice. "Gracie … She didn't have a very good childhood. Her stepfather hit her all the time, and she just sort of closed herself off to survive it. If people are close to your heart, they can hurt you, and she's had enough of that. I persisted because I liked her, and eventually I got in there, but most people don't have that kind of patience, you know?"

"Jesus. I suppose I cannae blame her in that case."

"It was why I was so surprised when she turned up with Euan and said they were married."

"From what I understand, it was just as much a surprise to them."

"Really?"

"Aye. They were tied together by all The Council stuff, but when they got home, they had a marriage certificate saying they had gotten married a year before."

"They weren't really married," Vanessa said, almost to herself. "Oh man, that makes so much sense."

"No, they were nae. It would be like ye and me knowing each other a few days and then someone saying, 'Right, ye are married now, and yer lives depend on each other.' They did nae really know one another."

"Awkward."

Mal chuckled. "Well, clearly there was something else going on if she chose to save his life."

"She really cared about him; she's told me that. I know they did really get married in Edinburgh, and they knew they loved each other when they did that; she told me that, too."

"Aye, that was a bit later. I have no doubt about how much he loves her, or how much she loves him. It's pretty plain, is it nae?"

"Yes, absolutely," Vanessa agreed. "He's the only one who could've gotten to her in that way, and I think he still is and likely always will be. I mean, she may open up a bit, but he's the only one who will ever really know everything."

"If I am honest, I think he is a bit the same way. He will tell ye things, but to get to what he's truly feeling? That's difficult. I think there are parts of him only she sees, and that's the way he prefers it."

"He's a good dude, though."

"Aye, he is. Strange to think how close we all came to nae knowing him, isn't it?"

Vanessa frowned. "Wow, that's true. Sometimes I forget he's over 200 years old."

Mal laughed. "I dinnae think he is. I mean, he is from that

far back, but he is nae that old. It does nae work that way."

Vanessa chuckled a bit. "So, I have a chance to stay here, but I don't know if I should take it."

Mal set the sketchbook aside at the sudden change of topic. "Aye? Doing what?"

"Working for Euan and Grace, being a sort of steward, I guess. Making sure their normal lives are organized, maybe helping take care of any kids they might have. Whatever they need."

"And ye would nae want to?"

"It's a lot to consider. I have a job, family, other friends. I'd have to leave that all behind."

Mal nodded. "Ye have two of those pieces covered here. Maybe nae family, that's a tough one, but ye would have a job and friends."

"Well, yeah, Euan and Grace are my friends, Aileen, too, but that's all."

"Ye can count me in that number."

Vanessa smiled. "That's sweet of you."

"I suppose the way I would think of it is this: what ye would get against what ye would leave." Mal picked up his sketchbook and turned the page. "Let's write it down," he said, drawing two columns and putting job, family, and friends in both. "What do ye keep if ye go home?"

Vanessa considered it. "Familiar things. The beach. Warm weather."

Mal wrote them down and then put a bracket around it with the note 'things you can reach by plane,' which made Vanessa laugh. "And if ye leave?"

"Friends. Scotland, because, oh my God, I love it here already. The chance to wear cold-weather clothes for once. A lower-stress job. Some serious adventure from hanging around these two. What seems to be a slower pace of life."

Mal nodded and looked up at her. "Does nae sound like ye lose much. Ye can get to warm weather places in only an hour or two flight from here, just so ye know."

"And the rest?"

"The rest I cannae disagree with ye. Adventure is certain. Slower pace of life is definite."

"They did say it was a different world here."

"It is, for sure. Depending on how much they pay ye, yer family could always come visit ye."

"They could. I guess lots of people move far away from home and survive it."

"Aye, they do, and so would ye. If it is what speaks to ye, if being here feels right to your soul, then ye should do it. I know that is why Grace stayed here with Euan. It felt like where she was supposed to be. They are nae going back."

Vanessa raised an eyebrow. "Really?"

"From what I understand, they made the decision to make the move here permanent nae too long ago."

"Can't say I blame them. There's nothing in California for him, and she doesn't have much either except for me and her mom."

"They have peace here," Mal said quietly. "Given the work they do, I think that is what they need. It was odd to come back here after my dad and I went through Observation, so I cannae imagine what it was like for her to come back to a major city filled with people every time she finished a mission."

"Me either. I don't think I could do it. Their job, I mean."

"Nor I, but we are nae asked to. Ye have to be a certain kind of strong for that work and nae many possess it."

Vanessa smiled at him. "You know, you probably weren't one of the awkward scientists, were you?"

Mal laughed. "No. I actually had a girlfriend until just before graduation."

"Oh no! What happened?"

"Ach, well, she did nae find it appealing to come live here, and I was nae going to live elsewhere. I had a job waiting for me here. Truthfully, we had been drifting apart for a while."

"Still hurts though."

"Aye, it does. I think I am out of that for a while," Mal said.

"I feel you. I can't promise not to fall on you, but I *can* promise not to hit on you."

Mal started laughing. "I appreciate that, thank ye. Though I dinnae know if I should be offended that ye would nae."

Vanessa laughed now. "I didn't mean it like that."

"I understand ye," he replied, winking. "I am always happy for more friends. Besides, if things work out with Aileen and my dad, it would be a bit awkward to be shagging my sister-in-law's best friend."

Vanessa blinked, then burst out laughing. "Oh my God, that is so wrong, dude."

Mal joined her in laughter. "I only say it as I see it, lass."

"It's cool. I'm on the lookout for Jamie anyway. I need to find a henge or something. Do you know where one is?"

Mal grinned and shook his head. "Ach, nae ye as well."

"No, not really," she said, chuckling. "I mean, I would freak out if I really saw him, but Euan said he knew a lot of actual Frasers."

"I dinnae recall seeing him in records, but James was a pretty common name. There may have been one, but nae the one ye are thinking of. The actor though, I think he lives in Scotland still, so ye may see him, especially if ye are about Edinburgh. And they film here in the Highlands, too, so there's that."

"Oh! Good points!"

"See? More reasons to stay."

"Thanks, Mal."

"For?"

"Talking me through it. It helped."

"Good. Always happy to do what I can."

"Maybe you should have been a psychologist instead of an archeologist."

Mal made a face. "Oh, hell no. Dead people are much easier to deal with."

Vanessa snorted with laughter and shook her head. "I love you so hard already, Mal."

Mal grinned and then laughed along with her.

CHAPTER 12

A couple of days later, Euan disappeared after breakfast but refused to tell Grace anything about it. When he returned, he came into the house with a mischievous smile. "Grace, love! I need ye to come with me!"

Grace stepped out of the study with a concerned look. "Why? What's wrong?"

"Naught wrong. Put yer boots and coat on and come out front."

Grace eyed him with suspicion but went upstairs to do as he'd asked, and Euan returned outside. Waiting for him was a horse that was almost mahogany in color, and he swung back up into the saddle, patting the horse's neck. In the next instant, Vanessa was outside with wide eyes.

"Oh my goodness! Is this yours?"

"No," Euan said, chuckling at her reaction. "Why do ye act as though ye have never seen a horse in yer life?"

"I haven't really. I mean, I've seen them on television or from a distance at work, but never this close," she explained, reaching out a tentative hand toward it and then yanking it back.

"Really? That is a shame. We will have to take ye on a ride before ye leave here." Euan watched the movement of her hand with a curious expression. "Ye may touch her if ye wish; she will nae bite ye."

"I can? Really? It's okay? I won't upset her?"

"Dinnae think so, no. If she were that skittish, she would

nae be a horse to be ridden yet and still being trained."

Vanessa edged closer and reached out her hand in a slow motion, touching the neck with her fingertips first, then placing her entire hand down with a smile when the horse stayed put. "Ohh, she's so pretty and soft! I didn't think they felt like this," Vanessa murmured as she stroked the mare's neck.

The mare tossed her head, and Vanessa squeaked, yanking her hand back, which made Euan laugh. "She was telling ye she liked it," he said through laughter.

"Oh," Vanessa said with a nervous laugh before she reached out to pet the mare again. "What's her name?"

"Oighrig."

"What does that mean?"

"I think it translates to something like Effie in English?"

"Cool! Aww, Effie, I like you. Do you know how pretty you are?" Vanessa asked in a sing-song voice. When Effie nickered, Vanessa grinned. "Yes, you do. You have such pretty long hair. I bet we could braid it and make you the coolest horse in the stables."

"I dinnae know about that," Euan said. "Nae that she would nae let ye, she probably would, but I dinnae think Lochiel would be keen."

"She's his?"

"One of his, aye."

Grace came outside, stopping short in surprise. "What's this?"

Euan smiled at her reaction. "A surprise for ye. I thought ye might like to go for a ride with me. I feel the need to be out in the open."

Grace's smiled widened, and she walked across the yard as he leaned down and extended a hand to her. Removing one of his feet from the stirrups, he let her place her foot there, pulling her up as she pushed up. Once she was seated in front of him, he resumed his proper footing.

"We shall see ye in a while, Vanessa. The house is open to ye to do as ye wish, but if ye desire a walk in the woods or the like, ye should call Mal to go with ye because he knows the land."

"Will do!" she said as she turned and went back inside.

Euan turned the horse and started them back down the drive, and there was a long moment of silence between them as they enjoyed the quiet of being together.

"What made you think of this?" Grace asked.

"I rather enjoyed having ye with me on that ride during Observation, and I thought it might be nice to get out and be alone together for a time since the day is sunny and fair."

"Where did the horse come from?"

"Malcolm gave me permission to exercise those in the castle stables. Now that he knows who I am, he does nae have much of a worry about whether I can handle them," Euan replied, chuckling. "It will be nice to do that every so often when I can. This one is Oighrig."

"That's really nice of him. I'm glad you told him."

"So am I."

"What made you decide you wanted to?"

"I wanted at least one other person to know the truth about me because I did nae want ye to be the only one I could ever speak to about anything. It is nae right to make ye solely responsible for my company, and I knew he would understand who I was and what it all meant."

"That's fair. I see the logic in it."

"I assume that is also why ye told Vanessa?"

"A little, but mainly it was that I was tired of lying to her. She's been there for me through so much, and it felt wrong to keep her in the dark."

"I can understand that," Euan said, nodding. "Lying is a very difficult and exhausting thing, especially to people ye care about."

"It is. I often feel like it's all I do."

"No, it is nae. When we work ye play yer part and do as ye must, but when we are here at home, ye are always yerself."

"But who is that? I wonder if I even know anymore."

Behind her, a wry smile appeared on Euan's lips. "I

wish I could say I did nae know precisely how that feels."

"I know you do," she said, her voice quieting. "But that was so much worse."

"Ye know who ye are, love. Ye dinnae change and have nae; ye are still the woman I met here. Kind, generous, funny, and full of empathy. When we work, yer name may change, but that is all and ye are yerself when we are alone. Outside of our time together on a mission, ye play a character ye create, but the real Grace, *my* Grace, is always there under the surface. Here at home, I have never seen ye be anything other than what I have always known ye to be."

"Sometimes I wish I had met you before everything."

"Before everything? What do ye mean?"

"Before the war, before my grandparents died, before Eric. All of it would give me more time with you."

"Ah, I see. Aye, so do I, but then I think ye would nae have liked what ye found."

"Why not?"

"Ye saw me at Edinburgh after Prestonpans, Grace. Ye saw how desperate I was to make him proud, for him to respect me and to prove myself worthy. I am nae sure ye would have had the patience for that man, the one who could nae see what everyone else could. Or did nae want to is maybe a better way to say it. Ye would have demanded I see it, and I would have denied ye at every turn. My desire to please *him* would have superseded my desire to please *ye*, as much as I hate to admit it."

"Would it have? You really don't think you would have had the capacity to both love me and serve him?"

"Ah, my darling one, I would have loved ye with every bit of me, just as I do now, but the strife his control over me would have caused would have been a wedge between us always. I know ye, ye would have begged me to stop chasing what I could nae have, and I would refuse ye because if I just tried harder, I *could* have it. We would argue about it, and it would drive us apart."

"I would hope I was more understanding, but maybe you're right that it would've been that way after a while. I want you to know that you *were* worthy of his pride, his respect, and always were."

"Aye, I know that now. Perhaps I would even venture to say he did nae deserve my service and my loyalty to him after all he did."

"You're not wrong to say so. You were still under his thumb when I met you, though."

"Oh no, nae as I had been, for I had already begun to see how things truly were. That started in Edinburgh after Malcolm spoke some hard truths to me. When I met ye, I was already so disillusioned with all of it but did nae know what else to do. It was my life; how could I change it? It was nae like it is here. I could nae just quit and find other employment."

"He never would have let you anyway."

"No, he would nae," Euan said, remembering his conversation with his mother. *He would have killed ye before he let ye go, and in the end that is exactly what he did.*

"It still angers me that anyone could do that to another person."

Euan offered a gentle shrug in response. "I am nae sure I can be angry about it anymore. All I can do is work on finding myself without his shadowing me. 'Ye are what I say ye are, Euan' was what he used to always tell me."

"But he would never really tell you what that was."

"He would tell me whatever suited him at that moment."

Grace's sigh was heavy. "I wish I could help you."

"Ye do. Every day ye help me because ye are here, because ye love me for myself and nae what I can do for ye. Ye trust me, let me know ye are proud of me, encourage me. Ye understand me, and ye dinnae ask anything of me other than to love ye in return. I have the freedom to just be, to think, and to figure things out. Ye cannae understand what that support does."

"What if —"

"I told ye once: Asking that question never helps."

"I know, but what if when you find out who you really are, you discover you don't really love me at all? That you aren't happy and I'm not what you want?"

Euan frowned, though she couldn't see him. "That is nae the kind of thinking I am doing. I love ye beyond measure, and that will nae change. Naught can take that from ye; no one could change it. I will always be with ye, love. I will nae leave ye, and I know that is what ye fear."

"Because that's what happens."

"What is?"

"The people I love always leave."

Euan sighed and kissed the top of her head. "That is nae true, *leannan*."

"It is for me."

"It is nae any longer. Look at what is around ye, Grace. Ye have me, my mam, Mal, Malcolm, Vanessa. Ye have a family now who loves ye, and none of us are going anywhere."

"Vanessa hasn't decided to stay."

"She will, and ye know that as well as I do."

"I don't know what I would do if you ..." Grace began before she stopped.

"Ye need nae fret about it because I will nae, so dinnae let such a thought trouble ye for even a moment. The things I did in France, I did them for ye as much as I did them for the mission. I wanted to save ye, and to do that I had to do something I had once sworn I never would: I had to betray Lochiel."

"It was for you, too," she whispered.

"Aye, it was. I needed to show him I was better than he thought me to be, smarter, stronger. I needed to take my life back, and I did, but if nae for ye, then it never would have happened. Without the strength yer love has given me, I never would have been able to do it. Please understand; I would give up everything, do anything, betray anyone I had to in order to save ye and keep ye with me. Never will I let anything happen to ye, let anyone come between us, or take ye from me. I would face the devil himself and his entire army, I would kill them all, and naught would stop me from getting to ye."

Grace was silent, but he saw her lift a hand and wipe tears from her cheek before she turned her head and kissed his shoulder. Euan passed the reins into one hand and wrapped his arm around her, pressing her close to him and kissing the top of her head again. He held the peace of it for a long moment before he spoke again.

"There is something I want to talk to ye about."

"Oh?"

"Ye asked me in Observation, when ye saw me after Falkirk, who it was I had killed. I want to tell ye."

"Euan, you don't have to, honestly. You have been so against it. Please don't dredge it up because you think you're obligated to tell me."

"No, I want to. More than that, I *need* to."

"All right, if you're sure. Go on."

"His name was Alexander Munro. The Munro and the Camerons were nae allies, but we knew each other well enough. Alex and I frequently crossed paths, and I liked him a great deal. He was kind, nae the sort ye thought would be a soldier, but he did what all in his family did and had done. That day, as I was fighting my way through Hawley's lines, he was suddenly there. I told him to go, to leave, begged him, but he called me a traitor. He lowered his bayonet, charged me, and I killed him; I had to, or he would surely have killed me. I cursed him for making me do it, for nae leaving when I told him to, but the battle was nae over and I took a cut from a Campbell, the long one on my torso. I killed him and any other Campbells in front of me. In a way, I suppose they paid for his death and my anger."

"That's awful, and I'm sorry that happened. I can't imagine being in that situation."

"It is more than awful, lass. His death haunted me and still does sometimes, and I can still hear the sound he made when I ran him through, this guttural and strangled groan. When ye hear something like that, ye cannae ever forget it. I was plagued by nightmares, and I spent two weeks nae sleeping more than an hour or two so that I could avoid such a thing. If I was exhausted, I could nae dream, and ye saw for yerself what that made of me. I went on that way until I collapsed where I stood."

"Oh, love," Grace said. "What an untenable situation."

"I know, but grief and fear are nae things ye can reason with. This was nae the first time I had killed men I recognized, but for some reason this was different. I was torn; proud of what I had accomplished in leading our men to victory and yet nae because I killed someone I knew. How could I be proud of that?"

"They are two different things. You can be proud that your skill led to a victory, but that victory didn't kill Alexander. It wasn't as though he was your only opponent. As you said, if you hadn't killed him, then he would have killed you, and clearly he was intent on doing so if he charged you with a bayonet."

Euan felt her involuntary shudder at the mention of a bayonet, and he didn't blame her. The things were utterly horrendous in what they did to a human body. "Ye are right. I had nae thought of it that way. To me they were the same thing, but I can see how ye are saying they were nae."

"It was as you always tell me: You did what was required of you to survive. I'm not sure Alexander would have had the same grief over killing you. He called you a traitor."

Euan blinked, his mouth opening slightly. Why had he not thought of that before? If Alex believed him to be a traitor, then killing him would have been a great victory for Alex instead of something to be mourned. To Alex, he was already worth nothing, so there would have been nothing to grieve.

"Christ," he whispered. "How did I nae see that?"

"You saw him as a friend; he saw you as an enemy. If someone is an enemy, you don't feel bad for doing them harm. How many Campbells are you upset about killing?"

"None, but they deserved it."

"Yes, to you they did. Again, because they were your enemies and you felt they deserved to die. Were you sad when they did?"

"No, I was glad, proud to have been the cause."

"Exactly. Just as he likely would have been proud to be the cause of yours. Another traitor killed for daring to revolt against the king Alexander served."

Euan shook his head. "I cannae believe I did nae even consider it in such a way."

"When you're so close to it, sometimes it's hard. You couldn't cut through the grief and the guilt to see it."

"But ye could because ye were so outside of it with no emotional stake. In a strange way, just that realization alone seems to have set me free from the burden I carried."

"A burden you never should've taken on."

"Aye, ye are right," Euan said as they reached the end of the drive, and he turned them to the left to continue down the road.

"I feel as though I should tell *you* something now," Grace said.

"Ye are nae required to do so."

"I should. If we are going to have these kinds of talks, I need to give as well as get."

"Before ye do, I want to say I hope these sorts of talks help both of us feel better and come to terms with our pasts. Specialist George has been urging me to share this all with ye for quite some time, and I want us both to let these things be and move forward free of them."

"Me too," she said, nodding.

Euan felt her tense in his arms, felt her anxiety within himself as she tried to work up the courage to speak the words she knew she wanted to. "Take yer time, beloved. There is no need to rush yerself."

After a long moment, she finally spoke, but her voice was strained. "I know that you're aware Richard was cruel to me, and my mom told you about the last time he hit me before I went to my grandparents."

"Aye."

"It was so much worse than she realized. It wasn't always physical abuse. He would mentally abuse me, too."

"One usually goes with the other, does it nae?"

"Sometimes. Sometimes it's just the rage and the need to be violent. For Richard, it was about control more than anything. If we were afraid of him, he always had the upper hand over us. He could do whatever he wanted."

"Please dinnae tell me it was more than hitting ye," Euan said, though he couldn't stomach even the thought that the man had gone beyond violence and into another kind of physical abuse.

"No, thank goodness. He never did that," she said in a rush.

Euan exhaled in relief. "Thank God for that. What would he say to ye?"

"That I was stupid, wouldn't amount to anything, that I deserved to be hit and put in my place. Then he started telling me that I must like it, so he would hit me more or harder. If I spoke up, I was disrespectful. If I didn't, I was proving how stupid I was because I had nothing to say. I was weak for not fighting back, but if I did then how dare I? If I did, it would be worse."

To hear this hurt him a great deal, but Euan knew she had to say it. She wanted someone else to know, just the way he did. What happened to her was much the same as what had happened to him, though Lochiel had never used violence against him in the same sort of way. At least not more than anyone else faced in his time.

"Ye got to a point where ye did nae know what to believe anymore. Ye could nae win."

"Exactly. I started to shut down, to try to make myself small so that he might not see me, but he always did. I was his favorite target for anything that upset him, from a bad day at work to something on television. Honestly, I almost think he hoped he'd kill me at some point."

Euan's hands tightened on the reins, and he wished he could get hold of Richard to show him what it felt like to be abused in such a way. He was fairly certain the man had never been beaten, and he should've been. "But he did nae. Ye survived him. He made ye stronger instead of weaker; he just did nae know it."

"It doesn't feel that way sometimes," Grace admitted. "I doubt myself so often. I hear his words in my head if I cry, telling me I am weak and pathetic. He made me close myself off to anyone because I didn't want them to hurt me the same way he did. If they weren't close to me, they wouldn't know what to say to hurt me."

"Dinnae let him haunt ye any further, my love. Ye are free of him, and there is naught he can do to ye here. I would kill him before I let him put another hand on ye, and I would be glad of it. To cry does nae make ye weak; it shows ye are strong enough to allow yerself to feel and show it to others. I dinnae know if ye have noticed it, but ye did nae keep Mal at arm's length when ye met him. Ye accepted him right away and offered him yer friendship. Ye never would have done that before."

"You're right. I hadn't realized it, but you're right, I did. Maybe it was because he was with you, and I knew I could trust him because you would never bring anyone around who would hurt me."

"No, I would nae, and whether it was because he was with me or nae is irrelevant. Ye could have chosen to stay distant, but ye did nae. Ye are making progress even if it does nae seem so to ye."

"I suppose."

"What happened to make ye feel that those ye love will always leave ye?"

"My dad did. My mom did. I mean, she gave me to my grandparents and stayed with Richard even after what he did to me. My grandparents did, too, eventually."

"Yer father and yer grandparents did nae do so willingly, Grace. Death came, and they had to go. I am sure they would have remained with ye if they could have."

"It doesn't make it hurt less."

"Of course nae, but there is a difference, and surely ye must see that. Besides, if yer grandmother had nae done so, I would nae be here."

Euan heard Grace gasp softly. "You're right."

"I will never leave ye. Nae even in death," he said, his voice soft. "Ye will always have me. Forever."

"Thank you. I think that was the most important thing you could've said to me."

Euan smiled and kissed her head again. "I will tell ye so as often as ye need me to. To know I will always have ye at my side brings me a sort of comfort I could nae begin to describe. I hope it is the same for ye."

"It is."

"I was thinking, when Vanessa returns home, we should go to Skye. I would like to spend a few days camping there with ye, and I can show ye how we did it."

Grace smiled. "That sounds wonderful, actually."

"I thought it might. However, I dinnae think this horse is getting much exercise just walking along. Let us give her some fun and let her run, shall we?"

CHAPTER 13

The rest of Vanessa's visit was spent seeing the sights during the day and relaxing at night. Euan and Grace were able to regale her and the others with stories from their work, though some of them were just Grace alone, as she had far more to tell than Euan did. They took Vanessa to Inverness, Glasgow, Edinburgh, and to some of the castles and other places that had been in various films. They'd gone hiking through Glen Coe and Rannoch Moor, walked a bit of the Ben Nevis path, with Grace and Euan deciding they would come and do the entire climb in the summer months. Along the way, Euan would often point out places he knew or had been and where things were different now. In Edinburgh, it greatly amused Vanessa to find the spot where she and Grace had seen Euan during Observation.

Aileen began making the replica uniform for Malcolm, but she also took the time to teach Grace and Vanessa about preparing and spinning the wool, dyeing it, and weaving it into cloth. It was something that, as Euan's wife, Grace would've done had she lived there with him. Once the cloth was made, Aileen moved on to teaching both young women how to construct the clothing, from how to measure a man for certain pieces, to cutting the fabric and sewing it all together. There were more than a few nights that the three women could be found sitting around the kitchen table, each with a piece of clothing in her hands, sewing and chatting with each other, or singing waulking songs Aileen taught them. It made Euan happy to see, and he knew it made his mother happy to pass these things on to his wife. It would've been Grace who would sew his clothing after weaving the cloth, piecing it all together with delicate stitches that showed her love and care for him. Had they been married before he'd gone off to war, those pieces of clothing would have been built with her prayers for his safety woven into them, christened with her tears at the thought of his never returning to her. He would've spent each day knowing that the very fabric touching his skin had been made by her, and it was this which kept her with him every moment he was away from her, as close to him as her own hands upon that same skin. To Euan, it was touching that the uniform going to Malcolm and the museum would have parts of it made by his wife. It gave more meaning to it, at least for him.

Vanessa enjoyed every minute of these days with Grace and the rest of the crew at the lodge. There was a beautiful simplicity in all of it, a sort of peace she didn't know she was missing until she had it. While the days out to the cities were fun, she loved the days where she stayed here. Days where she and Grace watched movies or silly television, laughing or crying at what played out before them. Long walks where the two of them talked about anything that came to mind, with Grace being far more open than Vanessa had ever known her to be. She spent time getting to know Euan better, happily talking about books or poetry when she discovered what an avid reader he was. He taught her how to play chess, or at least tried to, and showed her some moves to defend herself if the need ever arose. There had been time with Mal, too, their friendship becoming ever closer. She related to him in ways she hadn't expected, and they were a lot alike. He made her laugh so hard she would cry, though she could do the same for him. She played video games with him, the friendly competition amusing to the others in the house. Mal told her about some of the history of the land and the area, showed her some of his favorite places to walk, and shared some of the Celtic fairy tales he'd grown up with, including the tales of the mysterious Watchers.

A few days before she was due to return home, Vanessa came downstairs in search of Euan and Grace. They were often in the study at this time of night, after everyone went to bed, reading and simply being in each other's company. The door was open, and when she entered, she saw Euan seated at one end of the couch and Grace reclining with her feet in his lap. Both had a book in their hands.

Vanessa knocked gently on the door frame, and they both looked up. "Hey, guys. Can we talk?"

"Of course," Grace said as she sat up. "You can shut the door or leave it open."

Vanessa walked inside and shut the door, making her way over to a chair by the fire and sitting down as she smiled. "You two always look so comfortable."

"A lot of time spent in places with only books to entertain ye will do that, certainly." Euan chuckled. "I happen to like the quiet. It can get too loud for me at times."

"I can imagine," Vanessa said.

"Is everything okay, Van?"

"Yeah! Totally. I've really enjoyed my time here, and I think this is the most rested and relaxed I've ever felt, to be honest. You're right, it's another world up here entirely, and this place is magic."

"I am glad ye have enjoyed it," Euan said. "It was what we wanted when we bought this place, somewhere to retreat and relax, and we designed it for exactly that purpose."

"It's pretty hard to come back from wherever you've been and walk right into a modern city. It's jarring in a way you don't expect," Grace explained. "This place makes it much easier."

"This whole time I've been thinking about what the Councilwoman said, about working for you. It's always been in the back of my mind, you know?"

"You aren't required to do it, Van. It isn't a predestined thing."

"Oh, I know, and that's why I wanted to really take my time and think about it. To view my time here as a preview instead of a vacation, to let myself feel like I really lived here to see if it was the right thing for me."

"That was a good idea," Euan said.

"I think I want to take you up on the offer if you still want me to do it. I know Aileen does some of it, but I have a feeling she won't be living here much longer, and you'll need someone here when she's gone."

"Aye, I have a feeling ye are right," Euan said.

"Are you sure, Vanessa? I mean, *really* sure? It's a huge commitment you're making. You'll have to leave everything you know and lead a bit of a double life."

"I know," she said. "Mal really helped me think it through. It isn't like I can't go home on a vacation or even have people visit me. I've lived there my whole life, and it's time to do something different. The bonus part is I get to live with my best friend and her husband who has become just as much a friend to me as she has."

"Thank ye, lass," Euan said, his expression showing him to be touched by the sentiment. "I feel the same."

"And, of course, there's my other bestie, Mal."

Grace smiled. "I'm really glad you and Mal hit it off."

"Me too! It has been amazing to hang out with him and have it be platonic from the get-go. No awkwardness, no having him try to hit on me because he secretly wants to hook up. It has been a straightforward friendship."

"We'd be happy to have ye stay, Vanessa," Euan said. "I'm sure everyone else will be happy about it as well."

"See, that's the other thing. I may be moving away from my blood family, but I'm getting a family of choice and sometimes that's even better."

"I have absolutely found that to be true," Grace said.

"So, what do I do?"

"Meet with The Council, I assume," Euan said. "They

will tell ye what is required, what they will pay ye, all of that."

"How do I meet with them?"

"I'll tell them," Grace said, chuckling. "I'm sure they'll arrange a meeting quickly and Caia will come to take you to them."

"Would you go with me? The both of you?"

"If ye want us to, aye."

"It's still a bit scary going there."

"Ye get used to it," Euan replied, laughing. "As I'm sure ye will."

"I'm really excited about this now that I have finally decided and told you about it," Vanessa said. "This is such a huge change, but I think it's the best thing for me. It feels right in a way I can't explain. Logistics will be crazy though."

"They are," Grace replied. "But I'll help you with those. You'll still have to go home first and get everything in order. Unless you're planning on keeping your apartment, I'd just sell off everything you don't need. You can buy new things here, and I know The Council will give you extra for that."

"Then, as soon as I do that, I can come back."

"Pretty much. Take your time to say goodbye to people you may not see again, spend time with your family, go to some of your favorite places."

Vanessa nodded. "That will be the hard part."

"Aye, it will be," Euan said.

"Well, I'm definitely going to be back by summer. I don't want to miss it, and there's no way I'm missing the party Mal is planning."

"Ah, ye should nae." Euan grinned. "It will be amazing, I am sure."

"Even if you aren't ready to move, you can fly back for that," Grace added.

"I'm not going to drag it out longer than I need to. I don't think that will help anything."

"Give me a minute," Grace said as she stood and left the room.

"Where is she going?"

"To contact The Council."

"How do you do that, anyway?"

"It is a bit like meditation. Ye have to be focused, and ye often want quiet when ye do so if ye can manage it. She has likely gone to our room or the mission room to do it and will nae be long."

"Are you sure you don't mind this?"

"I am sure," Euan replied. "I think it will be a great help to Grace and to me. It will be good for her to have someone here who knows her as well as Caia and I do, someone she has known just as long. Just as I have Mal, she has ye."

"I don't think I know her anywhere near as well as you do, Euan. I don't even think Caia knows. There are parts of her only you've seen and things only you've been privy to."

"Ye know her in a different way. Ye have a past with her that I dinnae. Shared experiences. I know she loves ye, Vanessa. If she did nae, ye would nae be here, and she certainly would nae have wanted ye to remain. She may nae say it, but she does. If ye look beyond the words, she shows ye more than she tells."

"Those are very valid points," Vanessa said. "It's always hard to tell with her."

"Ye know why that is. Are ye really surprised by it?"

"Is she that way with you?"

"More at first than she is now. She did tell me the first night we were home together that she cared for me very much, but I was surprised she said it. At first, she would nae always confide in me and would withdraw. She does it less now, far less, but there are still times when she needs her distance and I respect that. I understand it because I am the same."

"If both of you are so guarded, how in the world did you ever get together?"

Euan's laugh was soft as he looked down for a moment. "By all rights we should nae have. There was just something about her. When I met her, I felt as though I had already met her somehow, that she had come back to me. There was no defense I could put up against that even though I tried.

From what she has told me, it was very much the same for her. I was already in her heart before she even met me, as she was already in mine."

"That is, possibly, the most romantic thing I've ever heard and not in the sappy way. It's genuine."

"Aye. I dinnae think there is anyone anywhere better suited for me than she is."

"And now you're always together."

"Aye, we are. Bound by the moment when she pulled me from one world into another, sealed with her death and her blood. Her sacrifice. I can feel her within me, and I know if she is well or nae. If she is nae, I can feel it, and she does nae need to say a word. It is a feeling hard to describe if ye have never felt it. In the end, we will leave this world together."

"Together?"

"Our bond means that if one of us dies, the other will follow. The link will be broken, and one cannae survive without the other. It is what makes all of this so serious. I had to agree to that and so did she. To be honest, I am glad of it. If she was nae here, I would nae wish to be. I could nae be."

"That's so sad!"

"That is why it is a relief to know it is never something I will face. It is how they tried to kill her. They tried to take me from her and give her nothing to live for."

Vanessa frowned. "Who? Is this the thing in France?"

Euan seemed to realize he'd said more than he'd meant to and looked slightly uncomfortable. "Aye. Did she tell ye about it?"

"Only that something went wrong. She didn't say what it was, just that something happened, and she became human enough to die."

"That she did. I will nae go into all of it, but I will say the things that made her human were able to attack her through her dreams. They stripped her memories until she could nae remember anything. The first time, she forgot everything before she met me."

"Everything? Even me and her family?"

"Aye, even that. Then she forgot everything after we had returned to California. She lost the months we had spent here, our wedding, all of it gone. Then, she forgot me before she went into a sort of coma. At the last, she remembered naught but the day she died. They used my image to lure her, to try to get her to accept death because she had naught else. They were nae counting on our bond and how it was different, and it was the only thing that saved her life."

"Oh my God," Vanessa whispered. That Grace should forget Euan was something unthinkable to her.

"I could feel her dying even though that feeling I had of her within me was gone. I could feel her slipping away because it was taking me with her." Euan shook his head. "My point is that what ye are taking on really *is* a big commitment. Ye know what we do, our secrets, everything."

"You don't have to worry about me spilling them."

"I know," he said. "I just want ye to realize how truly important ye will be to us."

"I do, and that's all the more reason for me to do it."

"The Council will see you in the morning," Grace announced as she came back downstairs and into the study.

"Cool! Better get some rest then. Night, guys," Vanessa said as she stood up and left.

***

Vanessa was up early the next morning, eager to move forward, and Caia came to collect them. When they arrived, they were right outside the doors to Council chambers, and the doors opened for them. Alice was now back to looking like Councilwoman Rochford and the difference startled Vanessa, but she smiled and put Vanessa at ease. That part, at least, was the same.

"Welcome, Miss Farron. Watcher and Companion Cameron, I trust you are enjoying your time away?" Rochford asked.

"Aye, thank ye. I think it was very much needed."

"I am sure it was and is. We miss having you, of course, but it will be much better for everyone if you return to us rested and better adjusted. We all know how tiring this job can be and how it can wear you down after a while."

"Do Watchers often take long breaks like this?" Grace asked.

"Indeed," Rochford replied. "Maybe not six months, but a few at a time are not unheard of, particularly when a Companion comes into play and there are children."

"That's good to know. It explains those long stretches I remember where my grandparents didn't go anywhere."

"Precisely. I assume you are here for Miss Farron?"

"Yes," Vanessa said, nodding resolutely. "I've decided to take you up on your offer."

"Excellent! I am very glad to hear it. The Keeper is always so valuable to a Watcher and their Companion."

"Whoa, it has a name?"

"It does. You are called that because it is what you do. You keep the secrets of the Watcher and her Companion. You keep everything in order so their lives run smoothly. You keep their children safe. More than anything, you keep them grounded to the present. You are their touchstone, the person they count on the most. You are a friend, a confidant, family, and the link to remind them who they are when they return."

"Wow, that sounds really heavy."

"It is, and it is one of the most important jobs you could have. Do you still wish to take it on?"

Vanessa looked at Grace and Euan, then back to Rochford. "Definitely."

"You will be assisted, of course." All three of them looked at her with curiosity and she chuckled. "Malcolm and Mal will be there to help when it comes to safety and for you not feeling so alone in all of it. As I told you before, there is a long history between the Cameron Watchers and their caretakers. It will be passed on and still exists. They still serve us and do so proudly, ensuring our safety. They are still family and always will be. Vanessa's grandchildren will take up her role as Keeper in the future and serve the same function for your grandchildren."

"Dude," Vanessa whispered. "Wait, so, you know my future people?"

"More than know them. One of them is *my* Keeper," Rochford said. "They're very good at what they do."

"Minding and working with the Cameron Watcher takes a special sort of patience and talent," one of the other council-women quipped, which made Rochford laugh.

"We are not that bad," she said.

"One has to be able to put up with a great deal of mischief, sarcasm, training, and the occasional draw of blood," the other said with a wry smile.

"Christ, why am I nae surprised?" Euan said.

"You shouldn't be," Grace and Rochford said at the same time, and he looked at them both with a bemused expression. Vanessa tried to stifle a giggle in her hand and shook her head.

"All of that being said, we welcome you, Miss Farron. Please come forward, would you? I assume this will be suffi-cient pay?" she asked, handing Vanessa a piece of paper.

Vanessa took it and looked at it, then looked up, eyes wide. "You're kidding, right?"

"Is it not enough?"

"No! I mean, yes, it is, but … wow. I just …"

"We always want to make sure those who assist us are well-paid. Doing so makes sure they do not fall prey to the desire to give us up for more money."

"People do that?!"

"They could, and we would rather not chance it. Do you accept?"

"Makes sense and yes."

"Very well. You will spend some time with us today to learn how to contact us when you need to, and once you return home, you will have the ability to do so at will. When you return to California to get things in order, there will be funds available to you for that purpose. Grace will show you how to set up your accounts so that you can access them after you return to Scotland. When you leave today, you will have the appropriate documentation allowing you to live there."

"Wait, so, I'll be an EU citizen?"

"Not yet," Rochford replied, a mischievous smile playing across her lips for a moment. "You will have what you need for now. Do you have any other requests?"

"Actually, yes." Vanessa looked at Euan and Grace, and then back to Rochford. "I want to see what happened to them."

"What?" Grace asked, shocked. "Vanessa —"

"Why would ye want to see that?" Euan asked.

"I want to understand."

"Ye dinnae need to see it for that!"

"I do. To really understand what made you what you are, I do."

Euan looked at Rochford. "Ye cannae mean to let her do this?"

"If it is what she wants ..."

"Vanessa, you really don't want to do this. Please," Grace pleaded. "Please don't do this to yourself."

"I want to. I know it's going to be awful, but I want to understand what happened. I want to understand the bond Euan talked about, really understand it. I want to understand what you went through to be together because that's what makes you what you are."

Euan sighed heavily and ran his hand through his hair. "We cannae come with ye, Vanessa. Ye understand that, right?"

"I know, and you shouldn't. I want Mal to come."

"Wait ... no," Euan said.

"Only if he wants to, but I have a feeling he will."

"Euan, when you took everyone through your Observation, you said that some people need to truly experience something to understand it. That's what you are facing here," Rochford explained. "Send someone for Mal, please."

Vanessa looked at Grace, now pale and crying, and walked back to her, taking her hand and squeezing it gently. "Gracie, this means you'll never have to tell me. I'll always understand without you saying anything at all. I need to understand you in a way I can't right now because you can't share it. I'll be okay, I promise. Like you told me, nothing there can hurt me."

"It isn't that, Van; it's that you'll have to see it at all! I don't want it to do to you what it did to me even if you can't be physically hurt."

"It won't. Please trust me. Grace, you *have* to trust me. If I'm going to do this job, you have to trust me."

The doors opened, and Mal walked in, looking surprised to be there at all. "Hello. Is everything all right?"

"Hello, Mr. Cameron. I am Councilwoman Rochford, the head of The Council. You are here because Vanessa has made a request to see something in Observation before she joins us, and she has asked that you accompany her."

Mal looked at Vanessa curiously. "What is it?"

"She wants to go to Culloden and see what happened to Euan and Grace."

"Vanessa, are ye sure about that?" Mal asked, dubious.

"Yes. I want you to come because you're my friend and you need to understand this as much as I do. I know you want to."

Mal looked conflicted but nodded his agreement. "All right, I'll go with ye."

Euan closed his eyes and turned away from them, and Grace followed him, placing a hand on his back. He pulled her around into a tight embrace, whispering something to her that none of the rest heard. It was clear they were both in tears.

"Caia, take them to Observation," Rochford said.

Vanessa and Mal followed Caia out, silent as she led them through the halls. Once they reached the Observation area, Vanessa's heart was pounding as they hooked her in. She needed to do this, but it didn't mean she wasn't nervous about it. She looked over at Mal, who seemed just as nervous, but when he looked back at her, he gave her a small nod.

"What you will see first are pieces of what came before. You don't want to go straight into it," the archivist said.

Vanessa and Mal both nodded and closed their eyes. As soon as they felt the change of atmosphere, they opened their eyes and found themselves in what had been Aileen and Euan's home.

"She has the mark, Euan!"

"A mark that could be faked!"

"If you think it is fake, try to rub it off."

They watched as Euan grabbed Grace's wrist and then pulled back as if she had burned him, stumbling back against the wall.

"Are you all right?"

"What did ye do to me?"

"Nothing."

"I heard … I heard things. I cannae think …"

"I have no idea what you mean. That is not something that happens."

"Perhaps it is yer own guilt," Aileen said.

"No. I dinnae want her here. Please, Mam, she has to leave. There is something nae right about any of this."

Vanessa winced as she saw the look on Grace's face, something neither Aileen nor Euan had seen. There was hurt there, the pain of rejection. "Oh Grace," she whispered.

The scene around them changed quickly, and they were standing at the loch.

"A king is a king no matter his name as far as I am concerned, all of them the same, but Lochiel believes in it and I am one of his officers. Where he directs me, I go. It is as simple as that."

"But why stay committed to something you do not believe in if you know it means your death?"

"Because that is my life. It was what I was born to and what I will die for if I must. I know ye dinnae understand that, but it is the truth of it. Ye can do yer best, but ye will nae sway me."

"Wait —" Grace said, grabbing his hand before she suddenly gasped and fell to her knees.

"Grace? Look at me, come on, lass, come on …" he said as he cupped her face in his hands and patted it gently. *"Grace."*

"No!" she cried out as she slapped his hands away from her and stumbled backward.

"Grace, what happened?"

"I saw you. I saw you dead and then I saw what you have if you stay. I do not understand!"

"Ye saw me dead? What do ye mean what I would have?"

"You have a life. Someone you love and a child. You are happy. I want that for you. Please, you have to stay."

"I may still have it, but that is up to ye," he said quietly as he turned and walked away from her.

"It happened to both of them," Mal said in a quiet voice. "They both saw something."

"Is that supposed to happen?"

"I don't think so."

The sudden sound of someone singing got them to turn around, and they saw Grace sitting on a boulder, feet in the water.

"Ye there! Dinnae move!"

Mal and Vanessa both jumped, and Grace turned around. "Those are Cameron men," Mal whispered to Vanessa.

"Who are ye, and what are ye doin' on Cameron land?"

"My name is Grace, and I —"

"She is English, look at her," one said angrily, cutting her off.

"No, I am not," Grace replied.

"What are ye doin' here? Are ye spyin' for the illegitimate king?"

"If I were, would I be out in the open?"

Mal and Vanessa both laughed.

"Shut yer mouth, woman! Tell me what ye are doin' here."

"You told me to shut my mouth."

The man then slapped Grace across the face so hard that her entire upper body turned with the blow. *"Answer my question and dinnae back talk me again."*

Both of them gasped.

"Christ, that was unnecessary!" Mal said.

"I am here to visit a friend."

"Who?"

"Me."

Mal and Vanessa watched Euan step out of the woods and saw the men look suddenly worried as they touched their hats in salute to a superior officer. The scene then jumped forward, and they watched as Euan took Grace's hand in his own. They heard the short conversation between them about his intervention and Grace's dislike of being talked down to. Euan slid onto the rock beside Grace, holding her hand and singing with her.

"The Grace I know would never have let anyone do that," Vanessa said.

"She already knew. They both did. That's the only explanation. Somehow they knew."

"He told me they felt as though they knew each other already."

Euan was so close to Grace now that Vanessa was sure something was going to happen before he pulled away from her and walked away, spurring the scene to change once again. They were now in the woods, Grace and Euan both on their knees. He held her as she cried into his shoulder.

"I am so sorry, Euan," she sobbed out.

"Sorry? For what? Grace, shh, it is all right."

Grace looked up at Euan when he said her name, and again, they were extraordinarily close. Vanessa had never seen Grace this way. He was far too close for the Grace she'd known then, and Vanessa gasped as he stroked her cheek and Grace closed her eyes, enjoying it.

"What?" Mal asked.

"Just shocking that she reacted that way. She never would with anyone else because she hated her face being touched. Anyone else would've been shoved away long before this."

"Please do not go," she whispered. *"Please."*

They heard Euan sigh softly as he rested his forehead against hers, closing his eyes. *"I must."*

"I cannot do this. Please. I cannot do this. Please choose someone

else, you have to choose someone else," they heard Grace whisper.

"Ach, she asked them to take her out, and they ignored her," Mal said, frowning.

"For a reason."

"Aye, but still."

"What do ye mean?"

"I mean the ones who sent me. They need to send someone else. It cannot be me. I want them to replace me."

"No. Please ..."

"Why?"

"I dinnae know, I just ... There is so little time left, and what time there is I want to spend with ye, nae some other. Please dinnae leave."

The scene changed again, this time putting them in the castle. Grace and Euan walked past them, Grace holding Euan's arm while following Lochiel. Mal watched with interest as Grace walked up to the map and studied it.

"Perhaps if you simply lined up here," she said as she moved some of the pieces, *"instead of here, you have a chance of avoiding being caught in the marshy ground I have heard is there. If you go through it, it will skew your line toward the wall you have marked here and could trap you under fire with no way out."*

"Oh my God," Mal said, incredulous.

"What?"

"She just told them how to change history. She is nae supposed to do that!"

"Are you serious?"

"Aye! That was one of the problems that trapped them under fire at the start!"

"Thank ye for trying to help, lass, but ye should leave the battle strategy to the men. We are where the prince and Lord Murray will wish us to be," Lochiel said.

"But, if you just —"

"Euan, ye should see the lass out to a glass of wine and return."

"Lochiel, what if —" Euan began, but stopped. *"Of course. Come, Grace,"* he said as he took her arm.

"Ye bloody idiot!" Mal shouted at Lochiel. "And ye Euan, ye knew it. Ye *knew* she was right, and ye backed down."

"Euan, wait, please!"

"What have ye done? Ye fool woman! What are ye about?"

"You told me the only way to stop you was to help you win. I just told you how. Why will you not listen to me?"

"Ye said ye could nae do such, and yet ye did. So, ye were either lying to me before or ye are up to something else."

"I have never lied to you. I do not want any of you to die."

"It is too late for that now."

"No, it is not. Please, just listen to me! The prince's forces, along with those of Murray, Stewart of Appin, Lochiel, and others, will try to mount a night attack at Nairn the day before the battle. It is not supposed to work, they get disoriented and turn back, they lose the element of surprise, but if you can just convince them to —"

"Grace, stop."

"You have to believe me! I am breaking every rule there is, and I am doing it for you! How do you not understand!"

"I am nae sure what I believe now."

"Christ! She did it again! What is wrong with ye fools!"

"How?"

"The army tried to launch a surprise attack on Cumberland and his men when they didn't engage them that first day as they'd expected. It fell apart because the men were exhausted and starving, some of them collapsing as they walked. They had to turn back, and these same men had to face Cumberland's men with no rest. She just tried to tell him what to do to make sure it didn't fail."

"Grace, what are you doing?"

But there was nothing else as the scene switched again. It was brief as Euan kissed Grace and she disappeared from his arms. He screamed her name and looked around for her but didn't find her. It switched again, and Euan lay beneath his plaid, singing.

"Oh, Jesus … it's tomorrow."

"The battle?"

"Aye. He is here. He knew he was going to die," Mal said, his voice tightening. "He knew he would die, and he came anyway out of loyalty. I cannae imagine what he feels right now."

"Not sure I want to."

"Nor I."

It suddenly became light, and they heard the boom of a cannon. Vanessa screamed and jumped, turning around to see the shot landing amongst the gathered men and killing several instantly because they were now stuck under fire as Grace had said they would be.

"No! You cannot! Euan, please!"

Both of them turned quickly, watching Grace grab Euan's arm and try to hold him back.

"Grace, please. Let me go."

"No!"

"Begone, ye wailin' woman! He has no need of yer distraction before battle," a man said before he shoved Grace hard away from Euan and caused her to fall. *"There ye go, lad. That is how ye handle such a pest."*

They both saw the rage build in Euan's face before he punched the man and sent him sprawling to the ground.

"Hell yeah, Euan!" Vanessa shouted.

"How dare ye lay a hand on her! Grace," Euan said as he knelt to help her up.

It was then they saw what his men hadn't when Grace pulled his dirk on him.

"Oh, shit," Vanessa whispered.

"I will not let you do this!"

"Dinnae make threats ye know ye cannae keep, Watcher. If ye kill me yerself, ye still fail." Euan took the dirk from her hand, re-sheathing it on his baldric. *"It is over,"* he said again before he cupped her cheek and placed a gentle kiss on her lips. *"Goodbye, Grace. Remember me as ye said ye would. Soon enough ye will be the only one alive who does."*

"No! Wait!"

"No, Euan!" Vanessa shouted as he gave the order to go forward.

Vanessa and Mal stood and surveyed the battlefield in awe and horror. There were already so many dead, piled on top of each other as those still standing ran over and around them to charge the enemy lines. Euan had been right: Nothing one could read could *ever* come close to the reality of it. Grace ran past them, and Mal grabbed Vanessa's hand as they ran after her. All around them, men screamed, died, and dropped to the ground as they were blown apart by cannonballs, hit by grape-shot, lead balls from muskets, or bayonets. Others screamed a war cry as they ran at the government lines and leapt into them, swinging their swords and catching more than a few victims before being killed themselves. The scent of sulfur and the metallic tang of blood was all around them, the smell of it clinging to their mouths and nostrils. Vanessa was sobbing in fear and horror, and Mal looked terrified, but they were here for a reason and at least *they* couldn't die or be hurt. They then saw something Grace hadn't, and that was Euan fighting with and killing government men. He didn't look like the man they'd just seen, the one who had so tenderly kissed Grace good-bye moments ago. He looked frightening, singularly focused on doing as much damage as he could, a man resigned to the death he knew was coming but determined to take as many of them with him as he could. Pulling his sword from a man's gut by kicking the body away from it, Euan ran forward.

"EUAN!"

Vanessa and Mal heard Grace scream out his name at the same time Euan slid to a stop in the face of a line of muskets pointed right at him. Grace grabbed him and moved in front of him just as the guns went off, and Vanessa's screams echoed Grace's as the musket balls meant for Euan tore through her body.

"Grace!"

Grace fell on top of Euan, who wasn't moving, her dress

rapidly reddening as she rolled away from him and onto the ground. She lay there, crying in pain and fear, and Mal was in tears himself. She'd known she would die here amongst these screaming men, in terror and horror. As Grace pushed herself up, she coughed up blood as she choked on it, which brought a small wail from Vanessa. Forcing herself forward, she grabbed Euan's arms to drag him away. Mal saw it coming first and screamed.

"NO!"

It was too late. The bayonet was shoved through Grace's back, stopping any movement she might've made, and the high-pitched scream it brought from Vanessa might've been heard even in Council Chambers. Grace looked down at it before it was pulled back, the movement turning her toward the man who'd done it. Her fingers went to her chest before she dropped to the ground. In the next moment, Euan and Grace were gone as if they had never been there, and no one seemed to notice in the heat of the battle.

"No! Get me out, get me out, get me out!" Vanessa shrieked.

The pull back was immediate, and Mal got himself unhooked and to Vanessa, who was now in the midst of a full-blown panic attack. He unhooked her as quickly as he could and pulled her into his arms as she screamed, though he was crying with her.

"Shh, ye are all right, Vanessa. It's all right. Ye are safe, and everyone is fine now."

"Grace," she sobbed.

"I know, I know. But ye know she's fine. She's here."

Vanessa's panic started to ease as Mal held her and reassured her, though it took quite a while. She didn't know what she'd been expecting, but it hadn't been that. When they had sufficient control of themselves, they were taken to a room to wash up as best they could before they were taken to Euan and Grace. When the door opened and Mal walked in with Vanessa, they looked up. Their faces were anxious and pained, but they stood up when the two entered.

When she saw them, standing there alive and whole, Vanessa burst into tears again and ran to Grace, who hugged her tightly. "Oh God, Grace, I had no idea! I don't … I can't …"

"I know," Grace whispered. "You see why I didn't want you to see it now."

"Yes, but I'm glad I did."

Grace squeezed her eyes closed and hugged Vanessa again. "Everything is all right now."

Euan cried in silence, and Mal put his hand on Euan's shoulder. Euan looked over at him before the two of them embraced, and he cried into Mal's shoulder. When everyone had calmed a bit, Grace, Euan, and Mal went home while Vanessa stayed to learn how to contact The Council. She was also sent to the Specialist, who helped her process what she'd seen.

By the time she returned home, she was herself again, though wiser in a way she'd never intended. Walking into the kitchen, the other three looked up from their cups of tea, their expressions questioning. With a smile, she held up her wrist to show them the mark it bore. She was one of them now.

CHAPTER 14

Over the remaining few days, Grace helped Vanessa set up what she needed as far as bank accounts in Scotland and the transfer of funds from her US accounts. Like Euan and Aileen, Vanessa had left The Council with needed documents: a work visa that allowed her to stay for five years, identification, and the offer letter in case she needed to prove it. For security, mail for occupants at the lodge was sent to a post office box in Edinburgh so as not to reveal their actual location or even be anywhere near it, and Caia would pick that mail up every other day and drop it off for them. Vanessa was added to the list for the box, and she filled out the online form for the US Post Office to begin forwarding all her mail.

They remained at the lodge, at her request, just spending time together as a family group. There'd been movie nights and days spent in conversation. They all soaked up the company of their new family, knowing it would be at least several weeks before they were all together again. There were hugs and kisses at the airport in Inverness, where she'd fly to London and then home, and even Mal came along to see her off. To him, she was as good as a sister now, and they'd shared an intense emotional experience that had deepened and cemented the bond they'd already formed. It was hard to let go of those final hugs, and they waved to her until she was out of sight.

It was a quiet couple of days once she'd left, and Grace had struggled to not withdraw from everyone. Someone she loved had left again, and Euan watched as she forced herself to remember that Vanessa was coming back, not letting it pull her down. Grace pushed through it and stayed with them, and Euan was extremely proud of her for it.

When everything settled back into a normal routine, Euan did as he'd promised and took Grace to the Isle of Skye for a camping trip. It was something they'd both very much looked forward to, and aside from the more modern tent and having food with them instead of hunting, Euan kept it as close to what he remembered as he could. Phones were shut off and left stored in the truck, and they kept their conversation away from deeper topics purposefully. This wasn't the place to discuss any of those things, and it would all be waiting for them when they got home. Euan took Grace to the Fairy Pools to marvel over the crystal blue of the waters, to the bay at Glen Brittle to look out onto the North Sea from what felt like the end of the world, as well as other places of natural beauty, which she'd loved every moment of. It made him happy that even though she'd gone everywhere in her work, there were still places she hadn't been and things she hadn't seen, things that could still fill her with wonder and awe with the magic they possessed. Long hikes ended with evenings snuggled up next to a fire with a dram or two of whisky as they stared up at the millions of stars visible without light pollution.

When they returned, they were relaxed and happy, full of stories and pictures of the things they'd seen, more at ease than anyone had ever seen them, the ever-present shadow within each of them having retreated a great deal. Mal and Malcolm came over to have supper with them and hear about their trip, only for Mal to make Euan swear to take him on the next one.

The pair resumed their training with each other and often took a long afternoon walk when they were done. It was on these walks that Euan forced himself to do what he'd never intended to do: speak to Grace of the battles he'd fought and the things he'd done. After he'd told her about Alexander, he'd been amazed at how much lighter he felt having spoken about it to someone other than the Specialist. It had been painful to do, but she'd helped him look at it in a different way that allowed him to banish it, to consign it to the past where it belonged instead of haunting his present. It was his hope that the other moments would follow that one into the darkness, and to his surprise, they did. Grace didn't press him for details he didn't want to give, but simply listened to the things he *did* want to say. There was discussion about why things were done or why he felt the way he did about them. These memories were harder to overcome, but he felt he made significant progress with them. He no longer saw himself as a villain in those stories, but instead as someone who'd fought to survive a war he hadn't chosen to be part of. While he feared that coming near them would bring back that man he'd been forced to become, it didn't happen. He recognized it for what it was now, a way of coping, of being able to say he wasn't the one who'd done any of it. In truth, he was both men, and he forced himself to accept it. Euan had done those things in battle for which he was not sorry, not someone else. It was Euan who'd devised tactics and strategies to help them to victory. While it troubled him that he wasn't sorry for the men whose lives he'd ended, they'd intended to kill him, like Alexander had, and wouldn't have been sorry for it either. It was his life or theirs, and he'd come out on top.

More than any of that was the relief of seeing that Grace didn't view him any differently despite his confessions. She didn't recoil from him or look at him in horror when he told her what he'd done. She loved him still, just the same as she had before he'd told her, and it was that reassurance he'd needed most of all. As they discussed each memory, each moment, she helped him reason them out and pack them away where they belonged. With each piece he faced and closed away with the help of both the Specialist and Grace, his soul and mind felt easier, and he felt closer to who he'd once been.

There was also time spent by himself to think about who he was and who he wanted to be. In the end, he realized he was everything Lochiel had told him he was, as well as what he'd been told he wasn't. He was a brilliant soldier, an intelligent young man who excelled at strategy and varying types of non-physical warfare. Euan very much had the ability for diplomacy, as he'd well proven in France, even though it was something Lochiel had always insisted he wasn't meant for. He was more than a soldier who was only good at killing; he was a leader, as Malcolm had told him that day in Edinburgh, with the ability to inspire people to follow him if he chose to use it and sometimes even if he didn't. He was the man who'd struck fear into the heart of others higher in command and social station than he was because of that ability, a man they'd all sought to control in order to use it for their own benefit. Aside from all of that, he was also someone who loved and felt deeply. He loved to make others happy, to make them laugh or even smile. Honor meant a great deal to him, coloring all his actions and the way he treated others. There was sarcasm and humor, as well as a passionate temper. Rebellion was in his blood, and he wouldn't deny it, though he could and did control it. Euan was a man who loved his family and his friends, who would do anything for them, and God help anyone who tried to hurt them.

In the end, Euan decided he was exactly what he wanted to be. Through perseverance, he'd become his own man despite Lochiel's best efforts, and he'd done it without the man knowing. He remembered what Lochiel had said to him in France, that he hadn't realized that what he'd created had become stronger than he was, and he used that in his work with Grace. Euan was proud of what he did for The Council, proud of the ways in which he helped his wife succeed. He was the husband to her he'd always meant to be one day, though to him that was easy because he loved her far too much to find it at all difficult.

It was at supper at the lodge in the first week of June

when what he'd expected to happen finally did. As they sat around the table, eating and laughing, Malcolm waited for a lull in the conversation before he spoke.

"Lads," he said.

Both Euan and Mal stopped and looked up from their plates with curious expressions.

"I need to ask ye about something."

The two young men looked at each other and then back to Malcolm.

"Did ye need to see us in the study?" Euan asked.

"No, it is nothing like that," he said with a small chuckle. "I would like to have the blessings of both of ye to marry Aileen."

Grace's eyes widened over the top of her wine glass, while Aileen beamed. Euan and Mal looked at each other once again, then both men shrugged and nodded in near perfect unison.

"Nae unexpected," Euan said. "Ye have it from me."

"Aye, I have been waiting for this for weeks. I am fine with it, too," Mal said.

"Really?" Aileen asked in surprise.

"Aye, Mam. Surprised it took this long, to be honest."

"I thought for certain ye would say it was too fast, Euan."

Euan set his fork down and looked at her with amusement. "Mam, I agreed to tie myself to Grace after I knew her a week, and I married her another two after that. Nae counting healing time because she was nae awake. Who am I to judge ye on fast?"

Grace laughed. "He has a point."

"A good one, too," Malcolm said, laughing. "Besides, we are nae getting younger, are we?"

"No, that is true," Aileen said.

"Ye are sure ye are fine with it, Mal?" Malcolm asked.

"Aye, absolutely fine. Actually, I'm thrilled. I want ye to be happy, Dad, and ye have mourned Mum long enough. Besides, I get more family out of this and probably the single coolest brother anyone has ever had. I am nae the least bit unhappy about that."

"When did ye want to do it?" Euan asked.

"I am fine with the register's office. I dinnae need anything big," Malcolm said.

"Nor I," Aileen agreed. "Whenever ye wish to go is fine by me."

"It will take some time; we cannae just go tomorrow," Malcolm said. "But I will get it all together. I think it is something like a ten-week wait so that they can look over documents."

"So long? Well, that is fine, I suppose. August is a fine month."

"And Vanessa will be back by then. I know she wouldn't want to miss it," Grace said.

"Aye, that is right! That will be even better," Aileen said, smiling. "In the meantime, maybe I should —"

"Move in with Dad?" Mal finished.

"I know it will be a bit cramped, Mal, so I will nae if ye are against it."

"No, it's fine. I can find a place of my own, and it will nae be a burden to me to have ye there."

"Like hell ye can," Euan said. "Ye can move here when Mam moves there."

"Ye would want me to?" Mal asked, surprised.

"Would I have said it otherwise?"

Grace smiled. "I'm fine with that, too, you know, just in case you felt the need to ask me."

"Oh, right, sorry about that, love," Euan said, his smile sheepish.

"If ye are sure, then aye, I would love to. Cannae think of better actually."

"Then it seems we are all settled," Malcolm said.

"Aye," Euan said, lifting his glass. "To the both of ye. All the blessings we can give for a long and happy marriage between ye."

Over the next week, Aileen's things were shifted to Malcolm's, while Mal moved his to take Aileen's old room at the lodge. They still all met for supper, though it was strange at first for Euan to not have his mother there. He was so used to her constant presence that it seemed a bit empty now. He adjusted to it, however, and enjoyed having a brother there in her place. Euan and Mal had, almost immediately, taken on the family references, and it seemed the most natural thing in the world.

When Grace and Aileen finished the replica uniform, it was given over to Malcolm and the museum, where it was placed in a glass case along with a replica broadsword Malcolm had commissioned and a copy of the bounty notice for Euan made from the one given to Malcolm. Beside it was a plaque that attributed the uniform to being a copy of the one worn by Captain Euan Cameron during the Jacobite rising of 1745, as well as some information about him.

At the unveiling ceremony, Euan stood in front of the case, looking at the contents with a sort of curious detachment. No one else had been allowed in yet, just the family, and Euan stood across from a former version of himself while dressed in an entirely different suit. This one was all black and tailored to fit him in ways the suit in the display never could've. He wore a silk necktie in Cameron tartan, the red and green a vibrant contrast to the dark fabric, and his hair was pulled back and tied at the base of his neck. The fact that he was wearing black at all would've stunned the young man who'd once worn that uniform, because black was an exceedingly expensive color that only the richest could afford, yet here he stood wearing the color head to toe. The silk, too, would've been a shock, though perhaps less so after his time in France. The display was lovely, but he felt strange about it. It was a tribute to a man who'd died, but that man was very much alive. He couldn't even say *that* version of him was dead because it wasn't.

"A shilling for your thoughts," Grace said, placing a gentle hand on his back as she stepped up beside him.

Euan smiled, some of his tension easing immediately the moment he knew she was there. "Ye should have a bag full, as I have many thoughts."

Grace chuckled. "That's true. Are you okay?"

"Fine," he said. "I was just thinking how odd it is to stand across from a display that says I'm dead even though I'm standing right here."

"I imagine it would be."

"I'm nae sure I remember him," Euan admitted quietly. "So much has changed in the last year, so much he never would have even dreamed was possible."

"Then perhaps he *is* dead after all."

"No, he is nae. He is still here, changed along with everything else, and I simply cannae remember what he was like before everything fell apart. I thought I had nae changed much between now and then, but I was wrong. I have. If he were here, I dinnae think he would recognize the man standing here now."

"Is that a good thing or a bad thing?"

"Good," Euan said, smiling. "He would nae recognize what it was like to be truly happy and how that changes ye, how it feels to live in peace for once, the confidence ye have when ye are yer own man and in control of yer life."

"If he were here, what would you tell him?"

"That even when things seem blackest, there is hope. Ye will always find yer way out of it with the help of the most beautiful woman ye will ever know. Ye are more, always more, than what ye believe. Ye are worth more, and worthy of more than ye are given. Seek it, bring it to ye in the way only *ye* can. Dinnae give up, dinnae despair, but fight with all ye are for yer future, for the one who is coming for ye, for yer own mind."

"All of that is very good advice."

"I wish I could give it, but then again perhaps it is a lesson that must be learned."

"Perhaps."

Euan turned to look at Grace, placing a gentle hand on her face and running his thumb softly across her cheek. "Ye look beautiful, in case I have nae told ye so."

"Thank you."

"I can most definitely say I would never have expected to

have a wife as beautiful as the one I have, in more ways than one."

"Why is that?"

"Well, for one, ye did nae exist then. Two, I never in my life saw a woman who looked like ye. Ye are the picture of health, and no one near me could have matched ye in that. Ye stood out when ye came here because of it. What I *do* know is that I am a lucky man to be able to call ye mine."

Grace smiled. "You are so very good at flattery."

"I am, but in this case, it is nae flattery; it is the truth," he said, laughing gently. "I do like to see the Cameron sash on ye and my badge," he said, running his fingertips across the Cameron badge that pinned the sash at her shoulder and had once pinned the feathers to his bonnet in another life.

"It seemed only fitting that someone should wear it. I'll put it back on your hat later."

"I love that ye made the choice, and it means a great deal to me that ye would want to wear this very one. It has seen much, and ye have brought it here to witness this moment as it has witnessed so many others."

Grace leaned up and kissed him. "If you feel uncomfortable, just say so, and we'll leave."

Euan gave her a small nod as Malcolm came into the room with Mal and Aileen. "Are ye ready, lad?"

"Aye, let us get this unveiling underway, shall we?"

"Go ahead!" Malcolm called back to the front desk.

The door to the museum was opened, and people filed in, led by the new Lochiel himself. There was a great mix of people present, from the local villagers to dignitaries from Inverness and Edinburgh, as well as curious folk from the surrounding area. Euan spied Moira, whom he'd invited personally, and gave her a smile and a small wave. Lochiel gave a brief speech about the former Euan and what they knew of him, about how the display had come to be and the contents within it. Last, he dedicated the display to the young man who'd gone out to fight for his chief and his clan but never came home again. The ribbon was cut, followed by applause before champagne was handed out.

***

Euan stayed by the display as Malcolm introduced him to those he knew and let them know that Euan had played an instrumental role in sourcing both the display materials and the history of his ancestor. Aileen and Grace chatted happily with Moira, who, now that she wasn't on duty, could have an uninterrupted conversation with someone. To Grace's surprise, she turned and found Euan in a lively discussion with some members of the Scottish Parliament who'd come up from Edinburgh. He seemed quite happy, holding his own in political conversation, and she shook her head with a small smile.

Making her way through the other exhibits, Grace studied the artifacts. A pair of boots worn by Sir Ewen, the grandfather of Euan's Lochiel. Dirks, ceremonial swords, buttons, badges, more modern uniform pieces. There were small boxes with pieces of cake from royal weddings, including the most recent one, the flower girl dress worn by the current Lochiel's daughter when she was part of the wedding of Lady Diana Spencer and Charles, Prince of Wales. She was fascinated by the entire section devoted to the commandos who'd trained at Achnacarry during the wars and the things left behind or donated to the museum. As she came around a corner, she stopped, finding herself face-to-face with a painting of Euan's Lochiel. She studied the man's face, no hint there of the man she'd seen or experienced through Euan's memories. He looked pleasant, and she wondered if, like Euan, he'd been a different person once before life and war changed him. Stepping away from it, she navigated through the section dedicated to the 1745 rising, a knot in her stomach. She recognized these things, recognized letters and the massive standard they'd carried into battle those nine months. She remembered seeing it that day, waving in the wind before Euan and the rest had charged forward. Grace shook her head and closed her eyes for a moment, shoving that away along with the anxiety it brought.

Moving forward, she stopped before a glass display case containing a waistcoat, lace cuffs, white handkerchief, and white cockade, all having belonged to the prince. Beside it was a prayer book that had belonged to Lochiel, all references to the Hanoverian monarchy inked out, and it made Grace laugh in spite of herself. There was also a ring with a hidden portrait of the prince, and it reminded Grace of the ring Queen Elizabeth had, with a portrait of herself and her mother hidden within. Moving to the next section, she looked up at the battle cry of the Camerons, one she'd heard shouted so many times in different ways. The sound around her seemed to fade and then come back again, and she hurried to make her way outside to get some air. Standing at the edge of the road, she breathed in deeply and then released it, closing her eyes and trying to tame the building anxiety.

"Are ye all right, Grace?"

The sound of Mal's voice made her open her eyes and turn around. "I'm not sure."

"Can I help?"

"I just … I'm feeling a bit anxious. Seeing some of the pieces in there reminded me of when I was here."

"Ah," he said with an understanding nod. "I can imagine that's a bit difficult."

"I'm surprised it doesn't seem to bother Euan."

"It was his life; none of it is out of the ordinary to him. To ye it was all compressed into this life-changing event. At the same time, he's had time to come to peace with it, where ye have nae."

"He's made himself go to the Specialist and face it. I haven't."

"Why nae?"

"I can't. Not yet. I know it's hard to understand, but there's so much more than that moment and I'm afraid of facing any of it. I'll have to someday but not yet."

Mal put his arm around her shoulders. "Ye are in two worlds right now, aren't ye? Living in what is while remembering so clearly what was. Ye can see it all around ye."

"Yes, but then I'm always living in two worlds."

"But nae quite like this. This one never goes away."

Grace gave a soft shake of her head. "Part of me wishes it would, but the rest of me doesn't want it to. I'm one of three people alive who know what it was like, what was here before. I walked in it, lived in it, spoke to the people who are now nothing more than names in a book, some of them not even having that much."

"I saw what ye did when ye were here. Ye tried so hard to save them all."

"I wish I could take credit for being so altruistic, but I can't. It was selfish because to save *them* meant to save *him*, and he was the only one I cared about."

"Ye wanted to save others, too, though. I know ye did. Malcolm, Duncan, Iain, and the rest. Ye wanted to save the people who meant something to him."

"Maybe," Grace said. "In the end, it doesn't matter."

"It matters to me that ye tried. He is alive because of ye, and that matters, too."

"Would you have done the same?"

"Tried to stop them? Aye, probably, but that's why ye do your job and I don't. I could nae let disaster happen when I could stop it even though it was what I was supposed to do."

"What do you think would've happened?"

"What do ye mean?"

"If I'd stopped them," she said, turning her head to look at him. "What do you think would have happened then?"

"Hard to say, really. Ye may have saved them from the battle, but ye could nae have saved them from everything else to follow. They'd already committed treason at that point; retribution would have been swift and hard even if they weren't there that day."

"But all those men would've lived. They would've had time to prepare, to flee, so that when Cornwallis and the Munro got here, they'd find no one to go after. They could've come back when it was safe."

"Perhaps, but that's assuming they'd want to do so and nae stay to defend their homes."

"I could've come here and taken over the army. We could've won."

"What?"

"I could've won that battle, Mal. I know I could've. I *did* win it."

"Grace, what are ye talking about?"

She turned to look at him. "I'm going to tell you something not even Euan knows. He knows I went to Nairn, but he doesn't know what I did there."

Mal raised an eyebrow. "Sure."

"The night attack was supposed to succeed that time, and it was my job to make sure it didn't. I forged a letter and took it to the Nairn encampment where I gave it to Cumberland myself. He left his tent to go handle things and left me by myself. He had the battle plan all set out, and I set out extra pieces against what he had there. Mal, I would've crushed him."

"Are ye serious?"

"Why would I lie?"

"Wow."

"Can you imagine it? What do you think would've happened?"

"I honestly have no idea. I mean, there are so many variables there. What would ye have done?"

"My orders would've been to take Cumberland alive. We could use him as a bargaining chip."

"For what?"

"For Scotland."

"I'm sorry?"

"I would've ransomed him back to England for Scottish independence."

Mal laughed. "Really?"

"You think I couldn't?"

"No, I know ye plenty well enough by now to know ye would've done just that. So, let's say that worked. Then what? Ye put the prince on the throne of Scotland?"

Grace scoffed. "Hell no. I would've sent him back to France. No, it would be someone else. Maybe Euan."

"Ye would make Euan king?" Mal asked in shock.

"Why not? He'd be as good as anyone else."

"There are several clans who had more claim to it than he ever would."

"They'd have to get through me first, wouldn't they? I control the army, I won the battle, I won the country back. I get to choose."

"I'm nae sure he would be good at it, or that he'd have the patience needed."

"Yes, he would. He may think he doesn't, but he does. He could do it."

"With your help, perhaps."

"Kings and queens always have advisors."

"Ye would be queen yerself if he was king."

"I'd refuse it."

"What!"

"I'd be happy to be his wife without all of that other stuff. The point is that part of me wishes I could do it just to see what would happen. I never would, of course, but I know I could've smashed him and I wish I could've done it."

"I'm sure The Council would've loved that."

Grace smiled and shook her head a bit. "Silly dreams, I know, but haven't you ever wondered what things would've been like if history had gone another way?"

"Of course. I dinnae know any historian of any sort who hasn't."

"But none of them actually have the ability to make it happen. I do."

"No, ye dinnae, because ye have rules to follow and they would never allow it. They would pull ye out the second they caught wind of what ye were about."

"There are things that could be done faster than they could pull me out."

"I'm nae sure I want to know what those might be."

"Probably a good call."

Mal laughed. "Ye really are the perfect woman for my brother. Ye are so alike it scares me."

"It should."

"See, that doesn't help."

"Wasn't meant to."

"Stop it, ye are creeping me out."

Grace laughed and then rested her head on his shoulder. "Sorry, just teasing you."

"Uh-huh."

"I'm glad you're here."

"So am I."

"It's nice to know what having a brother would feel like."

"Ach, well, I think that's the case all around, isn't it? Euan gets to have a brother; I get to know what it's like to have a brother and a sister-in-law. A sister-in-law I adore, by the way. Ye have fast become one of my favorite people."

"That's sweet, thank you. Likewise."

"Ye are also an absolutely amazing cook, which only adds to yer legendary status in my mind."

Grace snorted softly. "You two and food."

"Hey, we cannae help it if ye provide us with the best snacks. Speaking of, there are some inside, and I want a dram. Come back inside and stop fantasizing about annihilating the British army and ransoming Cumberland back to his father to strike a blow for Scotland."

"Can't we do both?"

"No," he replied, laughing. "Come on, ye."

CHAPTER 15

"**A**re ye sure?" Mal said into the phone. "There is nothing that can be done?"

Grace, sitting on the settee in the living room, glanced up from the report she was reading. Mal's agitation was obvious by his tone of voice alone, but his expression of irritation mixed with resignation certainly sealed the impression. She watched as he paced the floor, a call he'd not been expecting having pulled him from what he'd been studying with her. There was an artifact found on a dig, and he'd pulled her in for her history expertise in not only trying to figure out exactly what it was but why it was found where it was and when it might've been left there.

"Right, fine. Thank ye," he said as he hung up, clutching his phone tightly in his hand as he closed his eyes and sighed.

"Everything okay?" Grace asked, though she could tell it was otherwise.

"No," Mal replied. "Ye remember how I told ye we are having a conference next week about the recent digs we've been working on in London and the digs at some of the battlefields?"

Grace nodded.

"Well, our speaker for the major evening talk backed out."

Grace grimaced. "Oh, Mal, that's awful! I'm sorry."

"Aye, so now I have to find another speaker with a week's notice."

"What's the topic?"

Mal paused and looked over at her. "Um … well …"

"Well …?" she said, looking at him expectantly. "Go on."

Mal sighed, his posture shifting to discomfort. "It's about the recent finds at Culloden in the outer conservation area and what they might mean. Fragments of weapons found where they'd nae been expected, things like that. Also, a background on the rising itself and the varying reasons it happened."

"I see," Grace said before looking back down at the report in her hands. "I can do it if you want," she said after a moment, lifting her eyes again.

"What? Ye cannae be serious."

"Why not?"

"Well, for obvious reasons, really, but how would ye prepare the materials in less than a week?"

Grace gave him a bemused look. "You do realize I have a Master of Arts in History Ancient and Modern, right? With a joint honors in politics?"

"Do ye really? I mean, I knew ye went to Oxford and studied history but —"

"You didn't know what kind?"

"Aye."

"Well, now you know," Grace quipped, following it with a little chuckle. "I can do it."

"Are ye sure? I mean, it's —"

"Yes, I know. I'll be fine."

"Ach, ye are an absolute *legend*, Grace! Thank ye for saving my arse!"

"Saving it from what?" Euan asked as he walked into the room and dropped onto the settee beside Grace, where he nuzzled her cheek and then kissed it.

"From having to find someone to replace a speaker at the conference next week. Grace has said she'll do it for me."

"Oh," Euan replied, smiling. "Well, she would be yer lass, that is for certain. What is she supposed to speak about?"

"There have been some recent finds by archeologists at

Culloden," Grace said. "Mal needs someone who knows enough to talk about what it might mean to a group of people who are interested."

Euan looked startled. "Why would anyone want to talk about it? And why would ye, love?"

"History is always interesting, and it *is* history. There has been a recent surge in not only research on the Jacobites and the rising but also public interest on the subject. I'm not surprised they found things outside the area they expected," Grace explained. "As for me, I'm perfectly able to separate my own experiences from an academic presentation."

"If ye think ye can do it, I trust ye," Euan replied.

"I can," she reassured him.

"Actually, now that we are on the topic, there was something I wanted to ask ye about," Mal said.

"Oh?" Euan asked, his demeanor and expression becoming immediately guarded.

"I noticed something when I went with Vanessa. At the end," Mal began but stopped in order to choose his words very carefully, "when ye spoke of it, ye spoke of it as if she saved yer life, that ye were alive when ye went to The Council."

"I was," Euan said.

Mal shook his head. "No, ye were nae."

"What do ye mean? Of course I was. That is how it works. She had to give herself up to save me."

"She did. But ye were dead before ye hit the ground, Euan. I know what a dead body looks like, I've seen plenty of them, same as ye have."

"No … that … no, ye must nae have been able to see me clearly."

"I could see ye just fine. What is the last thing ye remember?"

"Grace screaming my name," Euan said, his voice strained.

"And nothing else?"

"No. I woke up at The Council; that is what I next remember."

"Ye just woke up?"

"Nae exactly, I —" But Euan stopped, his face going pale. "I took a deep breath because it felt like I had been holding it for a long time."

Grace looked over at him, her face registering the same shock.

"When ye woke up, love, did ye nae do the same?" Euan asked, clearly trying to seek some confirmation of what he'd always believed to be true.

"No," Grace replied in a whisper.

"Grace, what do ye last remember? Other than the pain, what do ye remember?" Mal queried.

Grace looked down, searching her memory for the things she'd tried so hard to block out. "We fell. He was unconscious from the moment I grabbed him. I was hurt, and I tried to —"

"Ye tried to drag him, aye, but ye could nae because he was too heavy. Ye knew ye were dying, but ye had to try anyway."

"Yes," Grace said, her voice still quiet. "But I couldn't move him, he was —"

"Dead weight," Mal said gently, finishing the thought for her.

Grace shook her head. "I don't … I don't understand."

"Euan was already dead. Something happened there and ye still managed to save him, but I have a feeling it was a much closer call than they want ye to believe."

Euan looked stricken, clearly trying to remember something, anything, but there was nothing there. Both men looked at Grace when she made a small sound and covered her mouth, her eyes filling with tears.

"Euan … Euan, he's right. He's … you were …" she stammered after collecting herself. "The Divergent, he knew it. That's why he kept saying we'd died there together. He knew what we didn't."

Euan looked like he might be sick. "There is only one person who can answer this. Get Caia here."

"Euan, maybe we should —"

"Get. Her. Here," he said, cutting Grace off. It was very clear to her that this was not a request.

Grace nodded and closed her eyes to call Caia.

"I'm sorry, Euan, I thought ye just did nae think of it that way."

"I did nae know, Mal. What we told ye was what we were told."

"Ye told me once that ye were different, ye and Grace. That there was something stronger between ye, something they did nae understand. I wonder if this is part of it. Ye died there together, on that field, and ye were both rescued from it."

Euan rubbed his face. "I cannae comprehend any of this."

"As ye said, there is one person who has the answers ye seek, though I am nae sure even she can say what is between ye or why."

"I dinnae know if it matters," he whispered almost to himself. "What is between us is ours, no matter what caused it. She is mine."

"She is," Mal said, doing his best to quell that thought in Euan's mind. "That is never in doubt, and I dinnae think anyone means to take her from ye."

Euan looked up at him. "Anyone who did would find themselves on the wrong side of my blade. That is a promise."

"As they should," Mal said, his voice calm.

Grace opened her eyes and looked over at Euan. She could see the anger in Euan's eyes at such a thought, and anyone who saw him in this moment would see that he meant what he'd said. Anyone trying to take her from him would find only the most brutal death he could accomplish at that moment waiting for them.

"It's all right, Euan. Try to relax. No matter what ye learn, ye are still here and alive. Ye are still married to Grace, and ye have kept her safe from anyone who might try to take her."

Caia came through the front door, looking extremely concerned. "What has happened?"

Euan looked at her. "I need ye to take us to The Council. We need to speak to the Councilwoman immediately."

"But —"

Euan stood, and Caia went quiet. The absolute change in

his demeanor and bearing was unmistakable, and even Mal seemed to feel as though he should either salute the man or run. "It was nae a request, Caia. Take us *now*."

The tone of his voice brought Grace to her feet, and she placed a hand on his chest. "Euan, don't. Whatever this is, Caia had nothing to do with it."

Euan closed his eyes and took a deep breath, releasing it as he opened his eyes. "My apologies, Caia. This has naught to do with ye, but I need ye to take us now, please."

"Of course, Euan. Apology accepted." Caia held out her hands to them, transporting them as soon as they touched her. "Let me see if they can see you."

Caia hadn't even moved before the doors opened; The Council clearly knew Euan and Grace were here. Euan wasted no time and walked in quickly, very much the officer and soldier he'd once been, Grace's hand in his so that she was at his side. It didn't go unnoticed, and several of the members sat back. The only one who didn't was Rochford.

"Was I dead?" he asked her.

"Euan —" she began.

"No, ye will answer the question. I dinnae want dissembling; it is an aye or no question, Councilwoman."

"It is not that simple."

"Aye, it is! Was I dead? Answer the bloody question," Euan replied, his voice raised just a small amount, but with a sort of authority he'd never used toward anyone here before.

Rochford sighed. "Yes."

"Christ, and ye did nae see the need to tell me, did ye?"

"Because it did not matter in the end. We managed to get to you in enough time to bring you back."

"Ye seem to do quite a bit of determining what matters to us and what does nae, Councilwoman."

She seemed taken aback by his words, faltering for a moment. "I do not mean it that way. What I meant is that there was no reason to traumatize you further by telling you a detail that, in the end, was irrelevant because you survived."

"Are ye so sure it is irrelevant?"

Rochford gave him a quizzical look. "What does that mean?"

"There is much ye dinnae know about us; ye are fully aware of that and so are we. How do ye know any detail is irrelevant when it comes to us? Ye dismiss them so easily."

"Are you telling us you know something?"

"No, I dinnae. I can only guess, like ye, but I have a right to know, Councilwoman. We both do! These are our lives, and ye are holding back details from us even now!"

"What is it you want to know?"

"Is there anything else about this ye are nae telling us? Things ye know but have decided to withhold for whatever reason?"

"There are things that are necessary to withhold per our rules, but —"

"If ye find something ye *can* tell us, do ye plan on hiding it?"

"No, as you clearly do not want that."

"Who would?"

"Many people are happy only knowing what they need to know and not all the small details. I forget you are not one of those."

"No, I am nae, and neither is Grace. Ye have nae forgotten; there is no way ye could."

"You told me that we had to sacrifice ourselves to get our Companions. You never said our Companions have to sacrifice themselves, too," Grace said, interceding before the exchange could get heated and Euan said something he shouldn't.

"Because they don't."

"What? Clearly that's not the case!"

"I told you that you were the first to gain a Companion in this way, and that was the truth. Every other time, the Watcher sacrificed themselves and the Companion lived. They were both brought here, but the Companion was always alive and always conscious."

"But not this time," Grace said.

"Not this time. Euan was dead the moment you touched

him, but it wasn't because of you. We had no idea what happened because it was not the way he was meant to die, so we were not prepared for it. While we thought you had stopped it by stepping in, there was something else. We weren't sure if we could save him, but thankfully we did. He was saved in enough time. Had your own death taken longer, then perhaps not."

Grace felt ill and grabbed Euan's arm, trying to steady herself. "How long?"

"I am not sure what you are asking."

Grace looked up, her eyes full of anger. "How long did it take? How long was he dead!"

"He was only dead on the field for a few minutes at most, as long as it took for you to try to help him before your own death. However, it took us a full week to get him healed here."

Euan's lips parted as though he might speak, but he said nothing. His hand tightened around Grace's as he struggled to process what he was hearing. "Was I breathing?" he asked, finally finding his voice.

"No, well, not when you arrived. We had something breathing for you. We took you off it when you were ready, and then you took that first deep breath on your own and were awake."

"But it was not the same for me," Grace said.

"No. You were much more complicated, and that is why it took so long. The damage to your heart and lungs was so devastating that you couldn't use them, not to mention the rest of your body. In those cases, we have ways to keep you alive even if your body is not while we repair it. I cannot go further into it than that."

"Then why were you afraid you couldn't bring Euan back?"

"In the end, he was still a normal human, Grace, and you were not. At least not entirely. There was still enough of the mission body present in you at that moment that you lived through what should have immediately killed you. Euan did not have that. The concern was that the shift in time would make it impossible, that he couldn't survive that transition, but he did. We were worried he had been down too long without help. Thankfully, we were wrong."

"How did ye nae know what would happen? Even I knew I would die in the war. Somehow, I knew. Turns out I was right."

"It is not that simple. As I said, it was not supposed to happen that way, so we were not prepared. War is unpredictable. Things change in an instant, something with which you are quite familiar."

"If I was supposed to save him, then how did it work if he was dead before I did?" Grace asked.

Rochford offered a sad smile. "You still sacrificed yourself, Grace. That alone was the requirement. You chose *him* over yourself. You cared enough for him that you made your choice, you were more than willing to die for him, and I am thankful it was not in vain."

"How did I die? What killed me?" Euan asked.

"You were shot in the back. The ball hit your heart, which is why your death was instantaneous."

"Shot in the back? What sort of coward would do that?" Euan said, his temper rising again.

"You know very well who your enemies were, Euan."

"There were so many there that day. Enemies does nae narrow it down."

"They have always been your enemies."

As Euan realized what she was saying, his anger turned to quiet rage. "Ye are saying I was shot in the back by a Campbell?"

Rochford nodded gently. "Someone in the Argyll militia. The same ones who fired from behind a wall at your retreating clansmen. The same ones who killed Grace."

The last sentence seemed to suck all the air out of the room, and everything went still.

"What did ye just say ..."

"The government troops shot her. She would have died from that, but she was trying to help you. A Cameron. An ancient enemy. One of the Argyll militia made sure she no longer could."

Grace paled, knowing exactly what that information would mean to him. "Euan —"

"Those treacherous sons of mongrel whores," he hissed through clenched teeth. "Nae bad enough to shoot a man in the back, but content to bayonet a woman in the back, too."

"Not that it matters now," Rochford said. "All of that has gone, and they were laid as low by the government policies as anyone else."

"It matters to *me*," Euan said, his voice calm but with a deadly and frightening edge to it. "It will *always* matter to me. I have hated them all my life, as I was born and taught to do. That would nae have changed no matter where ye put me, but this? This makes sure I will curse their names until I die and beyond. If I were home in my own time, I would exact revenge on them as bloody as I desire. I would hunt them down and kill them all, and I would *relish* bathing in their blood. Nae vengeance for what happened to me, but for her. No one harms her and goes unpunished, especially nae them."

There was a stunned silence at his words, all the members of The Council staring at him with a mix of surprise and horror. The only one whose face didn't wear that expression was his wife. Grace understood perfectly well what he felt and why. She knew this man now, the one whose rage was so strong he shook with it. His oldest enemies had brought harm to what he loved most, exactly what he'd told her would happen during a blood feud. The only proper response for that was to make them pay with their own blood, and he'd more than happily slaughter any and all he could find if he were allowed to do so and set loose.

Grace reached out and touched his arm. "Euan," she said, her voice calm and even. "Love, it's all right. Come back to me."

He looked over at her, but she didn't flinch at what she saw in his eyes. "It is nae. They killed ye, Grace. They all deserve to die for it and die as painfully as I can make it."

"No," she continued as she turned him toward her and

placed a hand on his cheek. "I was already dead, Euan; it didn't matter. It was a horrible act by a coward, but he wasn't the sole cause. In the end, we won; we are alive. They couldn't kill us. We are alive, and they are dead," she paused and stroked his cheek. "They are already dead," she whispered.

Euan closed his eyes, and she knew he saw the sense in her words. Those who'd done this were long dead. They may have even died later in the battle when the Camerons fought back against the Campbells who shot at a retreating force. Those men were all dead while he and Grace lived on.

"Aye," he whispered in return as he covered her hand with one of his own. "We did win."

Grace leaned up and pressed her forehead to his. "The how and why makes no difference," she whispered to him in Gaelic. "We died together on that moor, and the strength of what we felt in the end was what mattered. No one can part us now, and they won't. If the Divergents couldn't do it, then the Campbells sure as hell can't."

"I swear to ye, if anyone tries it, they will find themselves dying painfully."

"I know," she said with a knowing smile. "You will always protect me, fight for me, and I am safe with you. Nothing will stop you from getting to me, not even the devil himself, just as you said."

"Ye are damned right naught will."

"Come on, it's time to leave this behind us, to leave it where it ended. Dead with the former versions of us."

"Aye, ye are right. I am ready to be rid of it."

"No more fear. It will be a day like any other."

Euan opened his eyes and smiled at her. "No, it will nae. Instead of what it was, it will be the day we earned each other."

"Earned?"

"Aye. The day we did what we had to do to be together, no matter the pain or the cost, even if we did nae know it yet."

"That's a much better way to think of things."

"I agree," he said as he kissed her forehead.

Euan looked over at The Council, who were watching them in confusion because they hadn't understood a word the two of them had said.

"Thank ye for the explanation," he said to them, switching back to English. "We are done here."

CHAPTER 16

Euan filled Mal in privately on what they'd learned once they'd gotten back, and unsurprisingly, Mal was just as angry about who the perpetrators had been and the way in which it had been done. Mal hadn't noticed in the chaos who'd bayoneted Grace, and to have it be confirmed that Euan *had* actually died upset both men. At the end of it, Euan sobbed, unable to hold back the anger and the sadness that information stoked in him any longer. There was something about it, something about someone else having seen it, that allowed him to finally, truly feel it. There were times when he'd first come that he'd cried, of course, but he'd been too busy trying to adjust to a new life and worrying about Grace. When they'd visited the battlefield, his tears had been tears of mourning for the loss of all those he'd held so dear, but this was different. This was for himself, for Grace, for the fear and the horror and the blood. For the death that had brought them here and the love that had saved him. Mal hadn't said a word, holding Euan in a hug for a long while and allowing him to get it out, just as a true brother would.

Grace buried herself in preparation for the conference, though it hadn't been all that difficult. She was already well-versed in the subject matter even without her firsthand knowledge but took great care with her wording, constantly verifying she wasn't saying something she shouldn't, things she and Euan knew as facts even if no one else did. Euan assisted her in the only way he could: making sure she took breaks and ate, refreshing her tea, and being silent company in the study while she worked. More than once they'd gotten a good laugh when she'd turned to him after she'd read something to ask if he knew about it, only to stop halfway through her question because of course he knew.

Euan decided to make the trip to London with Mal and Grace, as he had no desire to stay home alone for several days. There were a few talks Grace wanted to attend as well as the one she was giving, and with Mal there too, the lodge would've been empty. Such a situation sounded horribly boring to him, so there was no question as to what his choice ought to be. They'd taken the short flight from Inverness to Heathrow, where they parted company with Mal. He was staying with friends at the hotel where all the participants were staying, while Grace and Euan were once again staying at the Savoy.

Once they settled in, Euan was happy to discover Grace had no intention of looking at her presentation and instead wanted to spend some time talking with him. They lay on the bed together, her head on his chest while he stroked her hair, and he caught her up on the week's news, the conversations he'd had with Mal and Aileen, and how he'd helped Malcolm with some of the caretaking work just to be outdoors and working again. They met up with Mal again for a nice dinner, meeting some of his colleagues, and then retired to get a good night's rest.

Over the following couple of days, he attended the talks Grace went to for her own education. He found them interesting, though he didn't always understand the terms they used, but Grace always quietly explained them and he appreciated that. There were discussions on the new digs at Vindolanda, the wall Euan had always known about but not thought much of. Another was on the new discoveries about the Norse invaders, how they may have spread farther than originally believed, as well as the possibility that half of their warriors were women. That last part really intrigued him, though it didn't surprise him either. Women could be fierce fighters when they wished to be and, if trained, could be just as, if not more, deadly than a man.

When the day finally came for Grace's presentation, they went back to their room after the afternoon sessions to change clothes and return. Grace emerged from the dressing area in a simple black skirt suit and heels, hair pulled back and fastened into a bun, with a triple strand necklace of black pearls around her neck. It was a manner of dress he wasn't used to seeing — she'd not looked this formal when they'd met the solicitors about the scholarship fund at Oxford — but it looked good on her. He'd changed into a suit while she was dressing, and Grace smiled when she saw him.

"Well, don't you look handsome. Not that you don't always."

"I could nae very well show up on yer arm looking like I just walked in off the street, could I?"

"No, of course not," Grace said as she chuckled, "and I would expect nothing less from you. I'm just saying you look particularly handsome right now."

"Aye? Are ye sure ye need to go right now? They cannae start without ye," he replied, the smile he gave her saying all it needed to.

"Stop it. Yes, I do."

"That is a shame. I think I would quite enjoy making ye look nae so serious and professional. Or sound it either."

"Euan!"

He laughed and then stepped forward to give her a tender kiss. "I know, I know, I am the worst. Of course ye need to go. Ye have worked hard on this all week, and I would nae stop ye now."

"Good. Not that you could, anyway."

"Is that so?"

"It is. Your charms are powerless at the moment."

"I have other ways if I wish to employ them."

"So do I."

"Mmm, true. We are at a stalemate then."

"Only temporary," she said with a wink.

"Shall we?" he asked, offering her his arm.

Grace accepted it, picking up the leather case containing her laptop and notes on the way out. There was a cab waiting for them out front, with Grace taking the opportunity to check her notes and presentation one final time during the drive. Mal was there to greet them when they arrived, looking relieved to see them, as if he'd somehow thought Grace would back out.

"Ye look amazing," Mal said to her as he kissed her cheek after helping her out of the cab. "But I think ye are missing something."

"Am I?" Grace asked, looking concerned.

From his pocket, Mal pulled a thin length of Cameron tartan, draping it around her neck and tucking it in behind her collar so it lay flat. The red was bold against the black as it made a small band around the narrow lapels of Grace's jacket.

"There, that's better. For luck," he said, grinning. "Are ye ready?"

Grace chuckled. "Marking me as your own, are you? And yes."

"Marking ye as a Cameron," Euan said. "As ye should be."

Grace rolled her eyes, and both men laughed before she joined them in it. "Let's go."

They followed Mal inside to a massive lecture hall, the seats rising like they would in a stadium. Mal took Grace's laptop and hooked it up to the projector, while Euan studied the crowd. It was larger than Euan had expected, filled with varying sorts of people of all ages.

"Euan," Grace called out as he started to move toward the back of the room to find a seat.

There was a note of panic in her voice, small but clear to him, and he immediately returned to her side. "Are ye all right?"

"Yes," she whispered. "Please sit close, so I can see you. It will help me not think of —"

"Shh," he said, placing a finger against her lips. "No need to say the words, I understand ye. Ye can do this; I know ye can and so do ye. Dinnae doubt yerself now. The battle has begun, and it is too late to falter or turn back. Courage is all ye have," he whispered back to her in Gaelic. "Show them all what a Cameron scholar can do."

Grace took a deep breath and nodded, taking her seat at the front of the room, facing the audience. Euan winked at her, and Mal directed him toward the seats reserved for family and guests of the speakers before making his way to the lectern.

"Good evening, and welcome to this year's showcased presentation. As ye are aware, our previously scheduled speaker could nae be here," Mal began after the room had gone quiet. "However, as your programs note, we've brought an equally brilliant replacement who will still be able to cover the evening's topic of the recent archaeological finds nae only at Culloden battlefield but also at others as well. She holds a Master of Arts in History Ancient and Modern with the joint honors course of Politics from the University of Oxford. Please welcome our speaker tonight, Grace Evans Cameron."

The introduction brought a raised eyebrow from Euan. He knew, of course, that Grace had gone to Oxford, but he hadn't been aware of the exact level of her education or even what she'd studied beyond history. At the same time, that she should've studied such a breadth of history was not that surprising, given what he knew of her and the preparation that had gone into getting her ready to one day assume her duties as a Watcher. That she was introduced with her former name included sounded strange to him even though he'd known it was coming. It was a name he'd never really heard used in connection with her, as she'd been Grace Cameron to him since the moment she'd woken up at The Council. Her degree and accomplishments, however, were under that name and thus allowed anyone to verify her credentials if they wanted to do so.

There was applause as Grace rose, smiled, and took her place behind the lectern. "Thank you, and good evening," Grace began. "Tapadh leat agus feasgar math."

Euan smiled to himself at the ripple that went through the room at Grace greeting them in both English and Scots Gaelic.

"It's good to see so many people interested in listening to an American talk about Scottish history," she continued, which generated laughter. "However, having gone to school here in England and then marrying a Highland Scot before moving to the Highlands myself, I feel much more Scottish even though I don't sound like it."

There was more laughter at that, and Grace's smile widened. "Those are not, of course, my actual qualifications, as Mr. Cameron ever so kindly listed for you, and I'm very happy the scheduling worked out and allowed me to be here tonight. I've prepared the presentation with notes in both English and Scots Gaelic, so anyone may follow along in the language of their choice. Let's begin with a bit of background as to what previous digs have led us to believe."

It was fascinating for Euan to see her this way, looking so comfortable and confident in her knowledge and ability. Normally she hated to be the center of attention, and he'd seen her in many situations where she'd eschewed any such focus on herself, but never in an academic setting like this. Here, she was an entirely different person. *This* Grace was clearly used to speaking publicly, to proving herself and backing up what she was saying, as well as keeping people interested in what she had to say.

What he'd not expected was that he, too, would be learning things tonight on a topic he thought he knew all about. He listened intently as Grace not only discussed the historical nature of the recent digs, what they'd found, and what it could mean, but also wove in the politics of the rising. The political and religious factions that had fought for supremacy and doomed it from the start. The splits and divisions that had only grown the longer it had gone on, while those in power sought to control the prince for their own ends. The way it was, in a sense, an extension of the war that had been raging on the

Continent at the time, though it had been presented to those waging it as being otherwise, all things the men fighting those battles alongside him hadn't known or even considered. For them, the reasons had been entirely different, and the overarching reasons completely irrelevant. Politics and religion had very little to do with it, and for most of them, it had none at all. They trusted what their chiefs told them, trusted in them to make the right decision, and if his decision was to fight for whom he felt was the true king, well, so be it. It wasn't their place to question it because the chief knew and understood all the politics and other reasons, so they didn't need to. Not to mention that it was their *duty* to be there, not a choice. Part of their tenancy on clan land required them to be available for the chief to call up and raise the clan forces if need be. Not doing so would see them branded as cowards; it could cost them their homes and their land, or worse, their lives.

It was when she turned the discussion to precisely the reasons the common men had, and what that truly meant about what they were finding, that Euan sat up. She'd know those reasons better than anyone here could possibly understand. She'd met those men, spoken to them, listened to them talk. She was married to one of them. That she was able to keep her actual knowledge away from some of those topics impressed him because she knew more than she could say about many of these discoveries, and he couldn't imagine how difficult a line that must be to walk.

After she finished the presentation, there were questions asked and very capably answered, even ones that, to Euan, seemed to be designed to catch her out or poke holes in her statements. Grace didn't flinch or even seem bothered, answering those questions with an unwavering surety that clearly showed she knew exactly what she was talking about. When there were no more questions, her talk was concluded, and there was applause that was more than polite. Euan found himself unbelievably proud of her, knowing he would *never* have been able to do what she'd just done, and he'd lived it.

He stood back as others approached her afterward and thanked her or complimented her on the presentation, and as the room finally cleared, Mal turned to her with a grin. "Ye were absolutely brilliant. That was more than I had even expected of ye. Thank ye *so* much for filling in."

"You're welcome," Grace replied. "It was a bit like being back at school, debating in tutorial. I'm happy I could help."

"With a degree like that, I am nae surprised ye were able to step in on such short notice," Euan said as he placed a hand on her back. "I am so proud of ye, love. I thought it was fascinating, and I learned something myself."

"Did you?"

"Aye. The politics of it were nae something I had dealt with before."

"Yes, well, I am not sure you needed to for what was expected of you."

"If I had possessed such knowledge, my choices may have been different."

"I think that's true for pretty much anything, but it's bold of you to think you even *had* a choice."

"Ye are nae wrong there."

"I owe ye a drink, if ye are up for it," Mal said.

"That sounds grand," Grace replied.

"I know just the place."

"I'm really happy it all worked out," Grace said as they started the short walk to the pub.

"Aye, me, too. Honestly, I think ye may have been better than our original booking. How hard was it for ye to hold back on what ye know?"

"Very. Though I imagine it's now just as difficult for you."

"Aye," Mal replied, laughing. "It changes yer perspective a bit, does it nae?"

"When you have been to all the places I have? Yes."

The pub was active but not crowded, and they secured a table while Euan excused himself to use the restroom. As he was returning, he saw a young woman with an angry expression stand up from a table across the room and stalk over to where Mal sat having an animated conversation with Grace, the two of them smiling and laughing. Her body language caused Euan to slow his steps so that he could take stock of what was happening.

"So, is this who you dumped me for, Mal?"

The sudden interruption of their pleasant conversation was jarring, and Grace looked over at the young woman standing there, her expression both angry and hurt. "Sorry? I don't thi —"

"I'm not talking to you!" she snapped at Grace.

Grace raised an eyebrow and sat back, while Mal frowned at her. "Mara, what are ye doing?"

"I came to have a drink and you show up here with some strange woman! This was *our* place, Mal!"

"Mara —"

"No! You told me the breakup was because I wouldn't come and live up in Scotland with you and you felt we had grown apart. Clearly you had other reasons, and not only that, but you bring this little blonde bimbo into our place!"

Grace rolled her eyes, and Mal stood up. "Mara, what in the hell are ye on about? I'm nae dating her! This is my *sister-in-law*, Grace."

Mara looked taken aback at the revelation, her eyes shifting between the two of them. "Oh."

"This, however, is part of the reason. This right here," Mal continued. "Ye and the jealousy issues. I was tired of it, and ye have just proved me right. Grace came and gave a talk tonight at the UCL archeology conference, so I thought I would buy her a drink."

"Wait, since when do you have a brother?" Mara asked as she dodged Mal's insinuation.

"As of about two weeks ago," Euan replied, making his presence known and fully returning to the table.

"Mara, this is my stepbrother, Euan. Grace's husband."

Mara stared at Euan for a long moment before she shook her head. Grace folded her arms across her chest and fixed Mara with a look of irritation that said everything her mouth currently wouldn't, though it was clear she wasn't impressed.

"But I thought —"

"Ye thought what ye always did, though ye have no right to now since we are nae together and have nae been for several months. It was all the reasons I told ye, and just so ye know, I'm happy where I am."

"Bu chòir dhut innse dhi gun do chaidil thu le Vanessa agus faicinn dè a chanas i ri sin," Grace said. *You should tell her you slept with Vanessa and see what she says to that.*

Euan didn't even bother trying to hide the laugh her words brought forth. It was, of course, a lie, but it was funny all the same. "Aye, Mal, ye should."

Mal laughed, too, he couldn't help it, but he shook his head. "No!"

"If you're going to talk about me, at least have the courtesy to do it in English," Mara huffed.

"Ifrinn," Euan muttered. *Hell.* This wasn't going to be good, and even Mal took a slight step back in order to be out of range of the daggers Grace was being invited to throw.

Grace's smile was cold. "Are you sure that's what you want? I'll be happy to oblige you."

When Mara just glared at her, Grace shrugged.

"All right, then. Do you really think this kind of behavior will win him back? Because it won't. Not him, not anyone, and they'll all run from it sooner or later. You could be the best shag in London, and they'd *still* get tired of it. Every move, every word, stinks of desperation and your rank insecurity, your fear of being alone. Jealousy, possessiveness, and stalker-ish behavior is such an ugly look on anyone, and good sex can only hide the crazy for so long. Why would Mal need you and your drama when he could have someone who doesn't bring him any? Someone who understands him much better than you seem to, who is happy to be part of his home life and his family, and who would be welcomed by that family warmly, something I can guarantee will *never* happen to you as far as *this* family is concerned."

The eyes of both men widened, and Grace continued to fix Mara with a look so cold that Euan was sure at least seven generations of Mara's ancestors could feel the chill. Mara looked momentarily stunned before she returned to glaring at Grace, though that seemed far less powerful than before as she struggled against Grace's withering expression.

"Whatever, you bitch."

"At least a bitch still gets laid, and often, which is more than I can say for you."

Euan didn't laugh this time, but he did smile in satisfaction. He loved to bear witness to his wife's way with words when it came to putting someone in their place, something she only did when necessary, like now. "Is that yer best defense? Calling her a bitch? The truth hurts, does it nae, Mara?"

"I want ye to leave, Mara, and let me enjoy a drink with my family," Mal said.

Mara huffed and stormed off to rejoin her friends, all of them looking angrily in their direction before Mal shook his head and sat down as their drinks were brought to the table.

"I need this more now than I did when I got here," Mal muttered.

"I ordered some food for us to split, love," Grace said in a bright tone as though nothing had happened, and she hadn't just verbally shredded Mal's former girlfriend.

"Thank ye, I am starving," Euan said, smiling as he sat down beside her. She passed him the glass of whisky she'd ordered for him, and he sniffed it before giving a happy sigh. "There is so much to be said for a wife that knows ye as well as she does herself."

Grace gave him a wry smile but snuggled into his side all

the same, resting her head on his shoulder. Euan kissed the top of her head and then took a drink.

"You are well shot of that, Mal," she said, flicking her gaze briefly in the direction of Mara and her friends.

"Aye, I am, and I dinnae know why I let it go on so long. Certainly was nae the sex," he groused as he shot her a wink over the top of his glass before taking a sip of his pint.

Grace laughed. "That's unfortunate. You didn't even get anything good out of it for all of your suffering."

"Ach, ye are sharp tonight, love," Euan said even as he laughed.

Grace shrugged. "Women like that just irritate me, and what does it even matter if we *were* dating? You're not with her anymore. I should've just grabbed you and kissed you to really make her mad."

Both men looked at Grace in surprise.

"Ye would nae dare," Euan said.

"Well, not now I wouldn't."

"Damned right ye would nae now," Euan said, though he was clearly amused. "Just because I have a brother does nae mean ye get us both."

"I mean, she *could*," Mal said with a small shrug.

Euan mock-glared at him. "I will kill ye. We have nae been brothers that long."

"It could be a contest," Mal said, trying not to laugh. "She could try us both and see which is better."

"Would nae be a contest," Euan said with a smug smile.

"Ach, see, ye dinnae know that."

"She married me for a reason."

"What!" Grace exclaimed, sitting up.

"Well, ye did."

"Not for that reason!"

"Ohh! And the truth outs!" Mal said, laughing now. "Nae as good as ye thought, brother."

"Oh no," Grace said, pointing at Mal. "It wasn't the reason, but it certainly didn't hurt his cause."

"Thank ye for at least giving me *that* much, Christ," Euan muttered playfully before taking a drink.

"Shut up, you. You know perfectly well that in bed with you is my preferred way to spend a day," Grace said before a mischievous smile appeared on her lips. "Fine. There's only one way to settle this: a contest. Should we invite Mara to watch and judge?"

Mal nearly spit his drink out, and Grace laughed. "Jesus, woman!" Mal exclaimed, coughing.

Euan let his head fall back, laughing so hard he was nearly crying.

"We could give her scorecards," Grace continued. "Bunny Boiler, the English judge, gives Mal's form on that position a seven."

It was a pop culture reference Euan didn't understand, but Mal definitely did, resting his forehead on the table and laughing hysterically. Grace, too, was laughing too hard to continue speaking. When Mal looked up and tried to stop laughing, he started again as soon as he looked at Grace, which only made the other two laugh all over again. It was a moment Euan wouldn't trade for anything in the world right now. He felt like he hadn't laughed this way in years, and perhaps he hadn't. He couldn't remember anymore. All he knew was that what had come before was becoming an ever more distant memory and, right now, he felt the most complete sense of happiness he could remember in a long time. This was what was worth fighting for and always would be. Lochiel had told him to always remember who he was fighting for, and he would never forget. He was fighting for them. For the two people at this table, for those at home. He was fighting for his family.

CHAPTER 17

Vanessa felt a palpable sense of relief when the plane touched down in Inverness. She closed her eyes, sighed, and smiled: She was home. It might be her *new* home, but it already felt like returning to where she belonged. A couple of days before she'd left, she'd gotten a call from Grace saying they wouldn't be able to pick her up because they had a meeting, but they'd have a car waiting for her to bring her to the lodge. Though she'd been a little disappointed by it, she also knew they wouldn't have done it this way if there was any chance for them to do otherwise.

"Happy to be on the ground, dear?" the elderly woman next to her asked. "Afraid of flying?"

"Oh no, not afraid at all. I'm just glad to be home."

"Home? But ye are —"

"American, I know. I apologize," she said, smiling. "I work here, so this is home for me now."

"Oh, well, that is good for ye then. Always good to come home after a journey."

"Very. I can't wait to get back to the lodge."

"Where is that?"

"It's what we call the house. It's at Achnacarry, near Fort William."

"Ach, lovely country there but a bit remote. What is it ye do for work?"

"I'm an assistant for a business run out of my boss' home."

Vanessa recited the decided cover story without even a stumble. She was, by now, very polished with it because she had to be. If she wasn't, it would put everyone in danger, and she'd practiced it with everyone she'd bid farewell to in Los Angeles.

"A good job if ye can get it?"

"Definitely," she replied as the plane reached the gate. She was grateful to be in first class because it meant she got off the plane sooner, and after so much travel, it was all she wanted.

Vanessa picked up her cabin bag once they were given leave to do so and pulled her seatmate's bag down from the overhead bin for her before filing out with the others. Bidding goodbye to the kind lady who'd sat beside her, she headed for the entrance to the terminal. There was no customs to go through, she'd already done that at Heathrow, and there were no bags to collect either. Everything she was bringing here was shipped ahead to the lodge and was already waiting for her. After she found her driver, she was helped into a black SUV, sending a text to Grace to let her know she'd landed safely and settling in for the short trip south. Vanessa was too excited to take a nap, eager to see everyone again, and found she couldn't stop smiling, the anticipation of being with them again setting her heart racing. She'd had video calls with them at least weekly, often more, getting filled in on all the news. She knew about Aileen and Malcolm, that Aileen lived with him now and Mal lived at the lodge, about the hilarity at the conference, all of it. It had only served to make her all the more eager to get back to her new family.

It had been bittersweet to go home, to say goodbye to people and places she'd always known. She was well aware that, though many promised to stay in touch, they likely wouldn't. Her true friends, however, would. Her parents had been sad about it at first but then saw it as a good opportunity for her and relaxed. Her little sister Katie, however, was devastated by the news and refused to speak to her for several days. Eventually she'd relented when Vanessa promised her as much time together as they could squeeze in, and Vanessa had cherished every moment of that time. Of anyone she was going to miss Katie the most, the two of them close despite their age difference.

There were family cookouts and visits so people could wish her well. Trips to her favorite restaurants with friends, to her favorite outdoor locations, hikes in the rugged beauty of the Santa Monica mountains and time on the beach. The experience of selling nearly everything she owned had been strange but freeing at the same time, and it was interesting to see what she'd deemed necessary when she was limited as to what she could take.

When they came closer to the road that went past the castle and museum, Vanessa sat up. "Can we stop for a minute please?"

"Aye, where?"

"The museum. There's something I want to see."

The driver nodded and took the road to the left, following it down and then pulling into the parking lot.

"Be right back," she said as she opened the door and hopped out.

Walking inside the small space, she looked around her. There was a gift shop filled with varying things from candles to books, to jewelry, and engraved silver pieces. Cameron tartan items sat on shelves against one wall, purses, local soaps, and all manner of fun things lined wooden shelves on another. She hadn't been here yet and she'd need to come back to see the rest, but there was only one thing she wanted to see right now. Vanessa handed over the donation requested for entry to the woman behind the counter.

"I heard you recently added something to your collection?"

"Aye! News of it has made it all the way to America, has it? Back there," the woman said, pointing.

"Thanks!"

Easing her way through the other items of the exhibit, she found what she was looking for, stepping up to the glass case and smiling at the contents. There was the bounty notice, which brought a tiny laugh from her as she thought about the story of how Euan had earned it. The true centerpiece, however, was the uniform. The work Aileen and Grace had done was beautiful, and it was just as she'd remembered seeing it on Euan during her Observation with Grace. There was a surge of satisfaction in knowing she'd had a hand in making the uniform.

Vanessa found it nice that they didn't have the uniform on a mannequin, instead hanging it on a clear plexi frame shaped like a person. It was made to match the dimensions of the uniform and fill it out as the young man who'd once worn it would've done, but they'd stayed away from giving him a face. Vanessa knew why.

"Is it nae lovely?" the woman from the front asked as she joined Vanessa.

"It really is," she replied. "You can only imagine how they all looked when they were together."

"Oh, aye, can ye nae? I'm sure they made a striking bunch. This one, though, I would *love* to know what he looked like. He sounds like he was quite the rebel and held a high position here; I bet he was one of those yer father warned ye about," she said with a wink.

It took all Vanessa had not to start laughing. *You have no idea how right you are*, Vanessa thought before she nodded. "Maybe."

"Though," the docent said, lowering her voice just a bit. "When we put this in, Malcolm's family came as part of the unveiling ceremony. He's the caretaker and helps Lochiel with the records, and he's the one who sourced this uniform. I think he said his wife-to-be Aileen made it. Anyway, his son Mal came and so did his new stepson, who shares a name with this lad here," she said, gesturing to the case. "That one? Woo." She fanned herself with a smile. "I like to think that's what our old lad looked like."

"Sounds like a solid choice," Vanessa said, suppressing her smile.

"Shame for all the lasses he's married, though."

"Aren't they always?"

"Aye, sure ye are right, lass," she replied, laughing. "But his wife is a beauty, too, as ye would expect. American, like ye."

Vanessa checked her watch and then gasped. "I'm running late, but I'm absolutely coming back to see the rest," she said as she turned to make her way up to the front. "But before I go, I want to buy all of those tweed purses and the matching wallets."

"All of them!"

"They'll make great gifts for me to send home to my family," Vanessa said.

"As ye say!" the woman said as Vanessa started gathering them up.

Once she'd paid, Vanessa jogged back to the waiting car, putting her bags in and then climbing in herself. Once she shut the door, they pulled out again, turning around to go back the way they'd come, and Vanessa felt free to indulge in the laughter she'd been holding in at the museum.

Her sense of excitement peaked as they pulled into the drive and the lodge came into view. She was finally here, and the happiness it gave her brought tears to her eyes. She couldn't explain why she was so emotional about it now. Perhaps it was the weeks of anticipation or being so excited that her body didn't know any other reaction. What she did know was that she immediately felt within her soul that she'd made the right decision. Thanking the driver as he opened the door for her, she grabbed her bags and stepped out of the car. The house seemed dark from the front, but that wasn't unusual if everyone was at the back of the house in the study or the kitchen. Walking to the front door as the driver pulled away, she heard it unlock to let her inside as the security keys Grace had given her before she'd left deactivated the system for her.

"Hey! Guys! I'm here!" she called out as she stepped inside and shut the door, but there was no response. "Guys?"

Vanessa left the bags by the door and walked back to the

kitchen, finding no one, then crossed to the study, which was also empty. Hurrying up the stairs, she found it to be quiet and empty there as well, and Vanessa came back down, a frown on her face as she pulled out her phone. This wasn't right, and it worried her. Someone was always here, and she knew they wouldn't forget she was coming today. As she got to the bottom of the stairs and into the living room, a light flipped on.

"Surprise!"

Vanessa screamed and jumped but then started laughing. Standing there, laughing with her, were all the people she'd been looking for. "You guys suck!"

Her shock, however, didn't stop her from hurrying to them for the welcome she wanted. She got to Grace first, giving her a long hug and a kiss on the cheek.

"Welcome home, Van! It's good to see you!"

"I don't forgive you," she said with a wry smile that made Grace laugh. "Okay, yes I do," she said as she hugged Grace again.

"Sorry for nae picking ye up, lass, but this seemed more fun," Euan said as she got to him and let him wrap her in one of the big hugs he was so good at giving.

"You guys had me freaking out! Did you actually have something else to do?"

"No, we just wanted to throw ye a party."

Vanessa rolled her eyes and playfully jabbed him in the stomach. "Jerk."

Euan laughed in response as Vanessa hugged both Aileen and Malcolm. "Congrats, you guys! I'm so happy for you!"

"Ach, it is good to see ye, love," Aileen said.

"Aye, it is," Malcolm agreed. "Ye have the look of someone who knows they're home."

"I definitely feel that," she agreed before she looked at Mal, whom she'd purposely saved for last, and smiled at him. "Hey."

"Hello. No tackle this time? Ye are slacking."

Vanessa grinned and hurried over to give him the biggest hug she could. He laughed and hugged her back just as tightly, and they held that for a long moment. They might just have been friends, but there was already a deep affection and tight bond there.

"It's really good to see you," she whispered. "I missed you."

"And ye," he whispered back.

When they released each other, Aileen brought out a cake that was hidden in the kitchen, and they all sat down to eat and catch up, with Vanessa regaling them with stories from her time at home, during her flight, and how she'd confused the poor elderly woman flying beside her.

"Oh, but then," Vanessa said, "when we came to the road by the castle, I remembered what you said about the display, so I asked the driver to take me down there so that I could stop and see it. The lady there is hilarious."

"Why do ye say that?" Malcolm asked.

"So, I was looking at the display, right? It really is beautifully done. Anyway, she comes up beside me and we're talking a little bit about it and then she says she wished she knew what he looked like."

"Oh no," Grace said, laughing.

"Oh yes," Vanessa said with a grin before she continued. "She said he sounded like quite the rebel and was probably one of the types a father would warn his daughter about."

All of the others paused before they acknowledged the truth of it with a small nod.

"Then, she said that she'd seen Euan when he came in for the unveiling with all of you, and she fanned herself and said she likes to think the old Euan looked like that."

Euan laughed loudly, thoroughly amused by the entire situation. "Little does she know," he said.

"Right? So, then she says it's a shame for all the ladies that you're married, but that your wife was as pretty as anyone would expect."

"I should talk to her about that," Malcolm said.

"No, you totally shouldn't. It was fantastic and gives a kind of humanity to all of it. I think she only said it because I was the only one there and went right to that display," she said and then gasped, looking at Euan. "Oh my God, you should totally wear your real uniform in there and just freak everyone out."

"Ye only say that because ye want to see me in it," he replied.

"That'd be a bonus."

"He will do," Mal said. "At the gathering he's going to wear it as part of a sort of informal history talk we're doing."

"Nice! Did you pick a date?"

"Aye," Euan said, looking at Mal. "When did ye choose? Ye never did tell me."

"Nineteenth August," he said, his lips spreading into a mischievous smile.

Euan's eyes widened. "Did ye —"

"Do it on purpose? Aye. Perfect date for all of us to come back together, dinnae ye think? Nae to overthrow a government but to recognize our own history."

"No Jacobite standards raised?" Euan asked, mirroring his smile.

"Christ, no."

"Good, or I would have to wonder about ye as well as decline yer invitation."

Mal laughed and shook his head. "I may believe in the cause, but that belief stops with the death of Charles. No need to worry."

"There's always a need, just not about this," Vanessa said, taking another bite of cake.

"What! Ye are supposed to be my friend!" Mal countered.

"I am! Just acknowledging the facts," she replied, grinning and leaning back against the couch.

"Ye traitor. I will be watching ye," Mal said with a mock glare before he laughed along with everyone else.

Once Vanessa settled back into the time change, she went into Inverness with Grace to pick out new bedroom furniture and a bed, as well as any other things she wanted for her room like linens, pictures, and lighting. When it was delivered and set up, she unpacked and made the room her own. She switched her phone over to a UK number — though she was keeping her old number for a while and having the calls to it forwarded — and picked up a new phone that was built for primary use on European networks. She'd sent a message to everyone in her contacts list to update them on her new contact information before she turned the old phone off and put it in a drawer. Sliding it closed, she felt as though she were putting away the last piece of her former life.

She joined the other three on their planned hike of Ben Nevis, and the views were stunning, though she was shocked to find snow still at the peak and the view from there obscured by clouds. Both Mal and Euan assured her she'd arrived back just in time to enjoy the best parts of a Highland summer, and she certainly agreed. The weather was mild, and there was more sun than clouds, the previous months of rain and snow leaving everything green and lush. The air was fresh, and the waters of the lochs and rivers shimmered and sparkled like diamonds in the sunlight. The water beckoned the unsuspecting with the promise of a lovely swim, only to greet its victim with the shock of the icy cold temperature even in the summer months.

July slipped slowly by, filled with long walks in the woods and around the loch, as Vanessa got acquainted with the land. It felt like a strangely beautiful dream, this new life, and it was exactly as she'd hoped it would be and more. The slow pace, the quiet, really drove home that this was a different world she lived in now, and it was a world perfect for truly finding herself. When she felt she knew her way around enough to go walking alone, she'd often find a quiet place to sit and think, or to lie on a blanket in tall grass or beneath a tree to do the same, and it surprised her how little she missed life back home. It had been so busy, so frantic, but she'd never realized it until now because it had been all she'd ever known. Even when escaping to some of the wilderness areas, she'd found it hard to forget the sprawl of the city and the constant pace living in it required.

Vanessa was glad Euan and Grace had this time off as well. It gave her time to adjust to life here with them, but both of them seemed to be in a much better place now than they'd been in even when she'd left. The things that used to shadow them seemed mostly gone now, and the darkness that always bubbled just under Euan's surface appeared to have retreated to where it belonged, to be used only when necessary. To Vanessa, he seemed an entirely different person in some ways, and none of them were bad. He laughed more, smiled freely, talked about almost anything anyone wished him to. No longer so guarded and closed off, he was seen as he truly was. He loved to please people, to make them happy by doing things for them or giving small gifts, like bringing back their favorite candy or a coffee if he went into town.

Even Grace seemed different. She was lighter, more open, and back to the way Vanessa remembered her from before that mission where she'd met Euan. Always ready with a joke or something witty to say, able to make others laugh at themselves, and no longer avoiding affection with those closest to her. Instead, she was more willing to let them in, to take the chance of being hurt in order to reap the benefits of that closeness. In that new openness, other people could see what Euan, Vanessa, and Caia had always known: how kind and caring Grace truly was beneath everything. Grace never wanted anyone around her to suffer, and she was driven to do whatever she could to make it right if they had, something that applied to missions *and* home life.

Vanessa's new job hadn't technically begun, but she started familiarizing herself with their routines, bills, and protocol. She sat down with them and found out which vendors they'd used in the past for repairs, and if there wasn't one, it would be left up to her discretion. Who was their solicitor? Who were the emergency contacts? What happened before, during, and after missions? How should she communicate with Caia if she needed to? What things did they need to have ready when the pair came back? She made lists of preferred foods and toiletries, what stores to shop at, and varying other practical matters. Once they started working through things, only then did Vanessa truly realize how important her job really was in their lives and recognize the massive scope of what the two of them did each time they went out on a mission. It was the same realization everyone who knew the truth came to, the same sense everyone had of working for something greater than themselves, of protecting the world even though the world had no idea they were doing anything at all. She'd already felt a strong sense of duty when she'd left with that mark on her wrist, but it deepened once she'd closed up her former life and turned herself toward starting a new one. It was a life of service, of putting herself and her needs second, though she knew Euan and Grace would never ask her to do such a thing. To do so was her choice, her sacrifice, and it was something she was honored to do. She was the first Cameron Keeper, and she wasn't about to let anyone down.

***

On the first Saturday of August, Malcolm stood nervously in his own garden in a dress kilt and jacket, waiting for Aileen while Mal tried to calm his nerves. Inside, Vanessa and Grace fussed over the last bits of Aileen's outfit, tucking flowers into her hair after they'd pinned it up, adjusting the small veil she wore, attaching the jewelry given as a gift by Grace and Euan especially for this day. A gentle knock sounded at the door before Euan walked in. He stopped when he saw his mother and smiled. She looked so blissfully happy, and it made him just as happy to see it.

"May I have a minute, lasses?"

Vanessa and Grace smiled at him and then left the room, shutting the door behind them.

"Is everything all right, Son?" Aileen asked, trying not to seem concerned but failing.

"Aye," he said in a soft voice. "Ye look beautiful, Mam."

His compliment brought a blush to her cheeks, and she smiled, though there was a sadness in it. "Thank ye, love. Ye look handsome yerself and so much like yer father. Are ye sure ye are fine with this?"

"I am, I promise," he said as he took her hands. "I could nae have asked for better for ye. When I brought ye here, I had no idea what that would mean for ye, and I am glad it was this. Ye have a life that once was denied ye, ye have found another to love, and he is a good man. Ye are here with me, I still have ye in my life, and that is more important than ye know."

Aileen pulled a hand back to dab at her eyes with a handkerchief. "Ye have always been a good lad, Euan. I was blessed with the most loving boy anyone could ask for, and ye have always been the light of my life. I am glad ye are still here, that I have my son in my life, snatched from Death's claws and given safety. I cannae say how many times I thought ye never would be with me again and I know I came close more times than I want to think about, but ye survived and now ye are thriving as ye always should have. Ye are becoming freer by the day, free of all of it; I can see that. Free of all that was done to ye by those ye wanted to believe loved ye, free of the torment of what the war did to ye. I have my son back."

Euan squeezed her hand gently and then opened his own, holding it up to show her what rested in his palm: the wedding ring his father had given her. "Ye gave me this once, for luck, to always remember who I was."

Aileen gasped and looked at him, eyes full of tears.

"I think ye should have it back now," he said, slipping the ring onto the ring finger of her right hand before he kissed it. "Are ye ready?"

"Aye, I am. More than."

Euan held out his arm with a smile and she took it, walking her out to the garden with the two young women behind her. Malcolm tried not to get teary when he saw her but failed, and Mal patted his shoulder while pressing a handkerchief into his hand. The officiant smiled, and Euan passed Aileen's arm to Malcolm before he kissed her cheek and joined Mal. Malcolm grinned and patted her hand where it rested on his arm. The ceremony was short but sweet, and Grace and Vanessa threw flower petals at them when Malcolm kissed Aileen, making everyone laugh. There were hugs all around, but everything stopped when it became clear that Euan and Mal were up to something. Malcolm and Aileen looked at them with curiosity as Mal stood before Aileen and Euan before Malcolm. The two young men looked at each other and then knelt before them, bowing their heads. Aileen burst into tears and Malcolm became emotional as the two adopted an attitude of submission, each requesting the honor of a blessing and acceptance by his new parent. It was a custom no longer done in the present, but one which meant a great deal to Euan, and Mal had happily agreed to join him in it.

Aileen reached out a trembling hand and placed it on Mal's head. "The Lord bless and keep ye, my son."

Mal reached out and took her hand when she pulled it back and kissed it gently. "And all my love to ye, Mum," he said as he stood up and embraced her.

Malcolm placed a hand on Euan's head now. "I've loved ye as though ye were my own from the start, but now ye are truly my own and always will be."

Both Vanessa and Grace were in tears as the young man who'd always sought a father to love him now found one, and it wasn't a pretended love to manipulate him, no strings or conditions attached to it. It was the true love a father would have for his son.

Euan stood and embraced Malcolm tightly. "Thank ye, Father." It was all he could say before his own emotions overwhelmed him. Malcolm understood and simply held the embrace, with Aileen and Mal joining it.

"Wow, this is just —" Vanessa began.

"Perfect," Grace whispered. "It's perfect."

CHAPTER 18

The following day, Grace and Euan took Malcolm and Aileen to Inverness where they were catching a flight to London, Los Angeles, and then Hawaii, courtesy of their son and daughter-in-law as a wedding gift. There were protests at first, but Mal and Euan insisted they'd keep up with the caretaking work while Malcolm was gone, and the pair should go enjoy themselves. Because Aileen had always wanted to go since she'd seen it in pictures and films, Malcolm accepted it and headed off on his first real holiday in who knew how long.

While they were away, Mal and Euan kept busy, both with covering Malcolm's work and working on the approaching gathering. The two of them often returned in the evenings tired, sweaty, and grimy, but they couldn't have looked happier about it. They were getting done some of the bigger and more physical projects Malcolm had wanted to do but lacked the labor for. For Euan, he was glad to be out in the sun and working on the land again, something he'd always done before, and which felt calmingly familiar. Between training and other duties, there'd always been this sort of work to do, and that work fell to the young men in service. Vanessa and Grace made sure supper was ready when the two came in and would join them for lunch in the afternoons to force them to take a break. By the time they finished eating supper and showered, they were so exhausted they collapsed into bed. Euan was usually so deeply asleep that he didn't even feel Grace get into bed beside him when she finally came in, and he was almost always gone before she woke in the morning.

By the time Malcolm and Aileen returned, Euan and Mal had gotten done most of what they'd set out to do. Malcolm was touched by how hard they'd worked and for their thinking to do the things he'd needed younger bodies for. They brought all sorts of gifts back — the chocolate-covered macadamia nuts nearly started a play brawl between the sons — as well as pictures and stories. Aileen had loved it there and loved to wade in the warm seas, but it had also reminded her of home with all of its lush greenery, making her miss all of her "bairns" back in Scotland.

The following morning, Malcolm was out with Euan and Mal, helping to set up the canvas tents. Those clans attending would bring their own, but the Cameron contingent set up a replica officer's tent, a few larger pavilions — one of which was a replica of a command tent — where everyone could meet for the varying activities, and smaller tents for people to sleep in. Long tables were set out for sitting and chatting or eating, a pit for a cooking fire was dug out and the spit set up with hooks to hang the varying pots to be used. Aileen was cooking a stew for everyone in the old style, with Vanessa and Grace drafted to help with the prep work. Mal and Malcolm followed Euan's directions on the setup of the officer's tent and the command tent because he knew better than any of them where things would've been located and how they would've been arranged. The cots themselves were easy enough, and a few had been ordered to use for this purpose. There was enough space for Euan, Grace, Mal, Malcolm, Aileen, and Vanessa to all fit inside, just as it had been when he'd had to share the same space with the other men while out on campaign.

When the day finally came, people started arriving early to set up. Through Mal's work there were at least a few representatives from nearly every surviving Jacobite clan in attendance. The Frasers of Lovat, Glengarry, MacPherson, Mackenzie,

Gordon, Murray, MacDonald and its many branches, Chattan, Stewart, and others. While there were some older members like Malcolm, most of them were the same age as Euan and Mal, young men and women interested in their histories and proud of where they'd come from, all eager to learn and spend time in what was essentially a re-created Jacobite camp. There was no shame now, not as there used to be, and young Scots all over the country were actively researching and reconnecting with their history and culture. The surge in the same age group of those learning to speak Gaelic — if they didn't already — was astounding to some, but for Euan it wasn't a surprise. For two centuries they'd been pushed away from it, taught to be more English, and the language was deemed antiquated and unnecessary. It had all begun to change, slowly at first, and growing daily as the interest in Scottish independence resurfaced. The evidence was all around them in the sheer amount of Gaelic spoken between attendees.

The Frasers were the first to arrive and were greeted as the old friends they were. They were followed by MacDonalds, Mackenzies, and MacPhersons. Mal introduced Euan to the present members of those clans if he hadn't yet met them, though Euan often caught himself looking for the men he knew who'd once borne those same names. Once everyone arrived and set up, Mal welcomed them and let them know what the plans were. They were welcome to attend some of the historical talks or not as they pleased. There was great interest when it was mentioned that Euan would be discussing the military tactics and strategies used during the rising, as well as what the life of a typical officer was like. The officer's tent and the command tent were quite a draw, and people found them fascinating. Within an hour, most of the young men had either changed into kilts — with the ladies wearing skirts, dresses, or sashes of their clan tartan — or wore their clan badge to let everyone know who they were affiliated with.

Euan ducked into the officer's tent and closed it up so that he could change into his uniform, intending to be in it for the majority of the day. He felt as though his talks might be more effective if they could *see* what an officer looked like, not just hear about it. Looking at himself in the mirror, he found his reflection strange. It was strange to be wearing this again, strange to see the young man he remembered in a place he shouldn't be. It had barely been a year, yet here he was back in uniform, back at Achnacarry, but changed in so many ways. Though he might outwardly look the same as he had that day when he'd marched off to war, inwardly he was anything but. The man standing here was a better man. Euan reached out to touch his reflection in the mirror before he closed his eyes and sighed, suddenly very much missing those who'd once stood beside him wearing these same colors. He could hear their laughter, their voices, hear the jokes they'd once told, and the quiet confessions made in the darkness of a tent just like this one on the eve of a battle.

"It's been a long time since I've seen you in that."

Euan opened his eyes and turned around to see Grace standing there, holding his baldric.

"Nae that long. Ye went to Observation."

"Not the same," she said as she walked up to him. "I mean since I *really* saw you wear this. You still look as beautiful in it now as you did then."

Euan smiled and shook his head. "I'm nae sure about beautiful."

"You are. To me."

Euan stroked her cheek gently with his fingertips. "It is odd to wear it in such a setting again, on this day."

"I know. It makes you miss them so much, doesn't it?"

"Aye," he whispered. "I cannae help but feel as though they should be here with me, as though they are. I keep waiting for them to come in and jokingly give me grief for something. This had been such a promising day then. Ye saw it."

"I did, and they *are* here. Maybe not in body, but they're

here. They're here because we remember them, you and I, and your mother."

"I had nae thought of it that way, but, aye, ye are right. I dinnae recognize that young man anymore, the one who left here at dawn over 200 years ago."

"Because he's changed. He would've never stayed the same, no matter what happened; he would always change. I also know that while it was promising for others, it never was for you. It was always a disaster in the making to you. You knew better."

Euan made a small sound of amusement. "I sometimes forget how well ye know me."

Grace smiled and slipped the baldric over his head and across his body, adjusting it so it sat properly and smoothing out his coat beneath it. "You mean how well I *remember* you," she said as she picked up his bonnet and handed it to him.

"That too," he said as he put the bonnet on and adjusted it, happy to see that she'd even got the placement of the feathers and badge right when she'd returned it after the museum unveiling.

Grace quite suddenly grabbed hold of the front of his coat and used it to pull him into a kiss that made him wish he didn't have to leave at that moment. He wrapped his arms around her and kissed her until she pulled back, and he could tell she was suddenly wishing he didn't have to go either.

"What was that for?" he whispered.

"For all the times I wanted to do that when you were wearing this and I couldn't. For being ridiculously handsome in that uniform," she said.

"Ach, ye are a cruel woman, ye know that, right?"

"Yep, I do. You love it."

"God help me, ye know I do, and that is why ye do it."

Grace chuckled. "Now, go on with you. Show those people what a Cameron officer looks like. Show them what he can do and what he did."

Euan grinned, kissed her again, and walked out. Grace took

a moment and then stepped out in enough time to see the reactions to him from the others, who all stood in stunned silence. The moment he'd stepped out, he immediately became the officer he once was, the officer he *still* was. He still looked large and intimidating, still a presence that couldn't be missed. It was easy to see why Lochiel had kept Euan close when she saw him this way. Grace saw Aileen smile and then shake her head, and Grace knew she once again saw that young man who'd left for war and took 275 years to come home again.

"It's honestly unfair how damned good he looks in that," Vanessa muttered as she stepped up beside Grace.

"And he is all mine."

"Hell yes he is. Seriously though, he looks amazing. It's easy to see now why he was as respected as he was and why that guy used Euan as his number one security."

"I certainly wouldn't want to see him across from me in a fight."

"Yeah, me either. I think I'd just run."

Grace laughed. "Come on, I want to see this."

As Euan launched into his presentation, he was cool and collected. Because he was talking about what he knew so well, there was no hesitation, no need to think about it. Grace and Vanessa sat in the back of the command tent, watching Euan speak to a rapt audience. Starting with the organization of the army and the regiments themselves, he talked through the way decisions were made, the movements of the army from Glenfinnan to Culloden, and details of the battles themselves. Regiment placement, pride of place, strategy, things that worked and things that didn't, all attributed to information from his "ancestor." Afterward, a great many people came to talk to him, to get a better look at his uniform, or simply look at *him*.

The other activities went well, too. After his presentation, Euan had taken to horseback, running people through the same drills he once used to train their forebears. This time, however, there were no life-or-death stakes, and mistakes were met with laughter instead of consternation. Grace watched him as Euan tried to remain as stern and serious as he'd started out, as he'd been when he'd done this for real, but it eventually became impossible, and he was laughing just as much as everyone else. There was a family research station as well, with many people having brought pieces of their own history or records to share with the rest of the participants. Malcolm and Mal were on hand to help tie pieces together, sometimes with Euan's help, while Grace reprised her presentation from the UCL conference, which went down just as well at this gathering as it had at the conference.

When a spirited game of shinty broke out, everyone stopped to watch, with Malcolm explaining it to Vanessa and Grace. Grace quickly realized Euan was checking himself to keep from hurting anyone, as the rules had changed since he'd last played. When they took a break between matches, Euan made his way to Grace, who held water for him.

Euan took a long drink before leaning forward with a sly smile and looking at Vanessa. "Turns out I know more than a few of the new Frasers," he whispered.

"What?" she said, looking at him in confusion.

Euan stood up and laughed before he turned around. "Drew!"

One of the young men standing in a group wearing the same tartan turned around to look at Euan before he excused himself and walked toward them with a smile. Like Euan, he was tall, but his hair was a lighter brown. His eyes were hazel, though tending more toward the green, and his build clearly showed that he didn't sit around all day doing nothing.

"I want ye to meet my wife, Grace," Euan said as Drew reached them. "Grace, my love, meet Andrew James Fraser."

Drew looked at Euan curiously for using his full name — not seeing Vanessa's face at hearing James and Fraser in the same sentence — but shook it off and smiled at Grace. "Ah, the infamous Grace at last! Great to finally meet ye. I have heard a lot about ye from Mal and Euan."

"Is that so?" Grace asked with a small smile. "All good I hope."

"Oh, aye. Ye are a bit of a legend, to be honest."

Grace laughed. "I'll take that."

"Drew, this is our friend, Vanessa," Euan said.

Drew held out a hand and shook hers when she accepted it. "The one who just moved from America, right? Nice to meet ye."

It took Vanessa a second, but she smiled at him and nodded. "Vanessa Farron."

"Euan tells me ye are working for them?"

"Yes. They travel so much that it gets hard to stay on top of things, and that's where I come in."

"I cannae imagine traveling so much. It sounds exhausting."

"Only if ye dinnae like what ye do," Euan countered. "I happen to love my job."

"How about you?" Vanessa asked Drew.

"I work at the hospital in Inverness."

"Oh? Doing what?"

Drew smiled. "I'm a doctor in emergency medicine."

"Wow! That's really cool!"

"I think so, aye," he replied with a gentle laugh. "And, like Euan, I love my job."

"I'm sure you see some crazy stuff in the ER."

"I have definitely seen my fair share of crazy in A&E, aye," Drew said.

"Oh! Right! I keep forgetting it's called something different here, still learning, you know? I'm surprised you got the day off; that's pretty tough for a doctor, isn't it?"

"Sometimes, but Mal told me about this months ago, so I put in as soon as I heard."

"Oh, you're a friend of Mal's, too?"

"Known him since we were kids. I heard about ye from him, actually. I saw him a couple of weeks ago, and he told me how his friend from America had come back. He'd mentioned ye before when ye first came to visit and he brought Euan to a Fraser meetup in Inverness."

"That was nice of him," Vanessa replied.

"Mal is a pretty nice guy. He actually suggested I meet ye, so thanks for that, Euan."

"Nae a problem," Euan replied, winking at Vanessa over Drew's shoulder. "Ye know, love, could ye come help me? I cannae find that spare shirt. I swear to ye I packed it, but now I dinnae know where it went."

Grace raised an eyebrow but then understood and got up. "It's probably staring you right in the face," she said. "You owe me a drink if I find it."

"I owe ye more than that," he said with a grin as Grace rolled her eyes and walked off with him.

Drew laughed. "Ah, the discussion of couples everywhere: 'Where did I leave it' and 'What's for dinner.'"

Vanessa laughed with him. "Except with them it's some-times some next-level stuff, and honestly, he probably hid it on purpose."

"Really?"

"Almost guaranteed with the smile he's sporting."

"Nice," Drew said, laughing harder. "How are ye liking it here so far?"

"Oh, I love it. It's why I agreed to take the job and come back."

"What did ye do before?"

"I worked in production for one of the television and movie studios."

Drew's eyes widened for just a moment. "Did ye really? That sounds fascinating; why would ye want to leave that to come here?"

"It gets a bit old after a while. Really hectic, never knowing if the show you're working on is around for another year, ri-diculously long hours. This is a lot better."

"May I?" he asked, gesturing to the chair beside her that Grace had vacated.

"Of course!"

"I suppose I can see that," Drew said, smiling as he sat down beside her. "Things getting stale is nae a problem I really have to fight because work is always interesting, always changing. I can sympathize with the ridiculously long hours though."

"I'm sure you felt that way during your training, right? When you were just starting out and you got the boring stuff?"

"Ach, aye, that's true."

"Are you a trainee?"

"No, nae anymore. Fully qualified."

"That's awesome! What a massive achievement. I'm sure your wife is super happy that at least you're not working the crazy training hours anymore."

Drew smiled and looked down for a second. "I would nae know since I dinnae have one. And I still work crazy hours. Always will, I suspect."

"Oh. Girlfriend?"

"Nope."

"Too busy?"

"That's some of it, aye."

"Well, if some girl dumped you for that, then she's an idiot."

Drew couldn't help but laugh. "Thank ye for the compliment; I appreciate that."

"You're welcome, just calling it like I see it."

They both sat there quietly for a moment before Drew spoke again. "This is a bit of an odd place to really sit and get to know someone. Would ye be interested in getting dinner with me the next time ye are in Inverness?"

"I'd like that a lot. That doesn't mean you get to ignore me the rest of the night, though."

"I would nae dream of it," he replied with an amused expression.

"Andrew James, hm?"

"Aye, but I dinnae know why Euan used my whole name," Drew said, chuckling. "*I* dinnae even use it."

"Oh, I'm pretty sure I know why."

"Aye? Do tell."

"He likes to give me grief about the Frasers."

"Why?"

"When I first met him, I got over-excited and asked him if he knew Jamie Fraser," Vanessa replied with a wry smile.

Drew stared at her for a moment before laughing. "Ah, I see. Came to Scotland to hunt red-headed Fraser men, did ye?"

"No!" Vanessa said, though she was laughing. "I do like the show but no. So, you see why he used your name now?"

"I do," Drew said, still laughing. "Sorry to disappoint, but I'm nae that one. Jamie is a pretty popular name, though, so I'm sure it would nae be all that hard to find one."

"I wouldn't want you to be that one, all good."

"No? I think a good many lasses would disagree with ye."

"Nope. You're here, and he isn't. If you were him, then you wouldn't be here now, and we wouldn't be having this fun conversation," Vanessa offered with a gentle smile.

"I appreciate that. Would nae want to be him either; he had a bit of hard luck, no?"

"You could say that."

Drew grinned. "Tell me more about what making movies and television is like."

***

As the sun set and a great day turned into a lovely night, everyone gathered around the tables to eat the stew Aileen had cooked, and it was so popular there was none left. Afterward, the group gathered around a bonfire to relax. It had cooled considerably, which immediately necessitated the bringing out of coats, blankets, plaids, or whatever else people brought for the occasion. They all lived here and knew well what the night could be like, so there was no way any of them came unprepared. Euan sat back to simply observe while laughter and conversation swirled around him. He remembered nights like these, before war had come and stolen them forever, always a good way to pass a summer evening during fine weather. There were others like it, times with just the men, and he'd loved both. It was always fun to have the women join them, however. They added something with their presence that was hard to describe.

Grace sat in front of him, leaning back against his chest, the back of her head against his shoulder as she watched the fire dance before her. He was wrapped warmly in his plaid, and she had the arasaid she always used. No one else here, save the family, would know that the pieces these two carried with them were from a time when such gatherings were common, from a time when Euan had used it on nights like this one, just as everyone else had. He felt at peace, happy, thankful, and it had been a long time since he'd truly felt any of those in their entirety. There were pieces of each at varying times, but the past was always there to shadow them. Tonight, however, that seemed to be gone. His arms tightened around Grace for a moment, and he said a silent prayer of thanks for her being here. She'd changed his life entirely, in more ways than he ever could have dreamed, and he couldn't imagine a life without her. There was the obvious, of course, she'd saved his life and brought him here, but it was more than that. With her help he'd taken his life back, his identity, his self-worth. She gave him the strength and the courage to do what he had to do in order to make those things possible, as well as coming to terms with all that had happened. With her love and support, he was able to discover who he truly was underneath all the conditioning of 20 years in service, who he was without someone else telling him what that was.

He'd helped her, too, helped her to step away from her own past and the pain in it. It had been interesting to watch her change when she realized she wasn't alone in anything anymore. He was there with her and for her, he'd always be there, and he'd always protect her. With that comfort, she'd welcomed people into her heart and her life without thinking, without worrying if they'd hurt her somehow, something she'd never done before. Euan kissed her cheek and smiled at the scent of her hair and her perfume, those things which would always remind him of her no matter where he was.

"Have I told ye today that I love ye?" he whispered.

She smiled, her gaze distant as she continued to watch the fire in front of them. "You have, but I will never get tired of hearing it."

"Good, because I will never get tired of saying it."

"You seem so relaxed."

"I am. I needed something like this more than I could have realized."

"We should do it again, then."

"It has been a massive success, so I am sure Mal would be happy to do so."

"Does it remind you of before?"

"Oh, aye, but it does nae bring me pain. They are all happy memories for me, and it is good to remember that there was happiness before. It was such a short time in my life, but it casts such a long, dark pall over everything."

"Of course it does. It changed you and everything you knew. It changed everyone."

"Aye, that is the truth, but I want to remember life before all of it. All the fun we had, the laughter, and the life we celebrated whenever we could."

"Then you should. Whenever those other memories appear, try to counter them with one of those happy ones. Like a parry."

Euan laughed. "It is nae that easy, but I do get yer point."

"I know it isn't."

"I know ye do. I could nae have done any of this without ye, ye know that? I dinnae mean being here at all, but everything else. Without ye I could nae be the man I am now."

"You mean the man I always knew you were?"

"Just."

Grace smiled. "I'm glad of it, but you did the work yourself and you're still doing it."

"Aye, I am and will be, but I feel as though this time we have had has been what I needed. I needed a rest from everything so that I could get my bearings, and so did ye. We went from one war to another and never had time to truly come to rights with any of it. Now we have and we are better for it."

"You're right."

"Ye seem better, too. Better than ye were."

"I feel better. I feel more grounded, steadier, and it'll only help us now that we're both working with clear heads."

"Indeed. The past does nae know what is coming for it."

Grace laughed, and he smiled.

"Though, I do wish I could go into the future."

"Why?"

"I want to help catch whatever they are. I would love to be in the same room with the one who hurt ye, so I could beat him until they could nae recognize him. And then beat him some more."

Grace shook her head and laughed. "Oh, I love you."

"Sometimes violence is the only way!" he protested.

"I know; I don't disagree," she said, still laughing.

"Ye know what this is missing?" one of the Frasers called out. "Music!"

There was a rousing cheer of agreement before several people immediately left the fireside only to return with instruments, and it wasn't long before the sounds of singing, drums, and laughter filled the space where conversation had once been. There were, of course, the happy and silly songs, the dirty drinking songs Euan once sung to her, though they were different now. Euan sang a few of those on his own, much to the delight of the others who laughed until they cried. It was in the silence between songs that Grace did something that surprised him. She started to sing the same song she'd sung here so long ago, his favorite, and the entire party went silent listening to her. At the next verse, the other women joined her because they knew it; it was an ancient song to them now. Euan closed his eyes and listened, the sound of the women's voices blending into a beautiful harmony. None of the men dared intrude upon it, though they knew the song, too, for it was far more moving to leave it to the women. It stirred so many things in Euan, things he couldn't describe. This song would always touch something deep within him; it held too much meaning and too many powerful memories for it to be otherwise, but to hear it this way was something else entirely. There were tears in his eyes as he opened them again, and as he looked across the fire, he saw them in the eyes of the other men, too. There was something so incredibly extraordinary about this moment, and he knew he'd never forget it; it was burned into his memory forever. When they finished, it hung in the air for a few long moments before the men applauded them.

"Well done, ladies," Mal said. "That was beautiful."

"Aye," replied a bunch of the others.

"Euan, what do ye say to a few of the old ones, eh?"

Euan smiled at Mal. "Which ones? More drinking songs?"

"No, ye know which ones. It just seems the right time for it."

"It does, does it nae? Go on then," he said with a nod to Mal, who had one of the drums.

Euan grinned when Mal started up with the song Euan remembered from that night at Glenfinnan about victorious warriors. As Mal started singing it, a cheer came from the men. They knew these songs well, too, though they'd never had the chance to hear them in the context Euan had. These words, these melodies, they were in the very blood and bones of the young men and women who sat here. They immediately joined in, right where they should, and it made Euan happier than he could say. This was perfection, and it was exactly what needed to happen.

When it finished, Mal pointed at him. "This one is ye."

Euan looked at him with curiosity until he heard the beat, and then he understood. The song they'd sung going into Glenfinnan on this same day over two centuries ago. He started the song and heard everyone go quiet before they all joined him in what had become a Jacobite standard, one sung in their families even though that cause was long gone. Still in his arms, Grace sang along. Euan very much wished at that moment that he could take all of them to that point in time. To let them see it as Mal and Malcolm had, to hear those proud voices singing loudly at the start of what so many of them had been sure would be a new future.

When it finished, he stood up and immediately moved into what he felt he should: the song from the English crossing, from his burial in another time. As soon as Mal heard the first words, he knew and began the drumbeat. When the others joined him in song, it sent something sweeping through him, a collision of his past and present, and he closed his eyes. To hear the women's voices in this was incredible to him, and it added a power to the moment that was surprising. He felt Grace's hand slide into his, heard her voice as she sang with all the rest and the other drummers picked up the beat. There was, quite suddenly, a dramatic increase in the sound and the number of the voices singing, and he opened his eyes in confusion. From the woods across the field, he saw his past walking out toward him, singing with him. Instead of stopping, he kept hold of Grace's hand and walked to meet them. These were not the Divergents to be feared, they were something else, and it seemed both of them knew it. They were the souls and the imprints of the men who'd once lived on this same land, forever attached to the place they held so dear. He knew none of the others could see these men, and he could hear them singing behind him still.

Euan stopped, a space of only 20 or so yards between him and the men he'd known, the new and the old connected by a young man and a song that spanned centuries. Euan recognized so many of those faces, but it didn't hurt him to see them this time. They were still here and always would be, he knew that, and he'd always felt them, but they were visible now. It felt as though they were letting him know they were still with him and were well. It was only then that he noticed the past was not made up only of his own clan, but the clans of those here with him tonight. The past saluted its future even though they wouldn't see it. As they touched their hats, Euan saluted them back. Through those gathered here tonight, the blood and the spirit of these men lived on despite all the attempts to erase them from existence. They had endured, survived, and they were here before their ancestors as living proof of it. They would carry on forever. The soul and the spirit were immortal, things death, enemies, and governments could never touch.

From the crowd stepped four familiar figures, and the sight of them almost made Euan want to weep with the joy of seeing them again. Malcolm, Iain, Findlay, and Duncan stood before him, all four smiling at their old friend. Together, they each placed a fist against their opposite shoulders, their arms flat across their chests. It was a silent salute to brothers of the heart, and it was a gesture Euan returned before the four of them stepped back into the group. Just as quickly as they'd appeared, they were gone, fading into the night along with the final notes of the song, leaving Euan and Grace standing there alone.

Euan smiled at the place where they'd been. "Goodbye, lads," he whispered.

CHAPTER 19

After all their guests were seen off the following day, Euan told his family what he and Grace had seen, but they weren't as surprised as he'd thought they'd be.

"What did ye expect?" Aileen asked. "It was a full moon out, ye had a fire going, ye gathered all the same clans on the same day as ye once gathered them to rise against the government, ye sang those songs, and somehow ye are surprised the veil thinned enough for ye to see them again?"

"She has a point," Mal said between bites of toast. "I'm sad I didn't see it though."

"Me, too!" Vanessa said.

"Ye saw them well enough before, Mal," Malcolm said before he looked at Euan. "They are always with ye as long as ye remember them."

"They are always here because their souls live within the land here. This was their home, and it will remain so forever," Euan replied.

"It's both," Grace said. "Though you were the link, Euan. As you said, it was your present coming together with your past at that moment."

"It was what I needed to see, another piece to help close the book on that life forever. Perhaps they knew that."

"Aye, perhaps they did," Aileen said, patting his cheek gently. "And perhaps they knew ye needed to know they were all right so that ye could let them go."

"It really was a huge success, Mal," Grace said, smiling as she changed the subject. "And so much fun!"

"Yeah! You should totally do it again next year," Vanessa added.

"Ye think so?" Mal asked.

"Aye, I agree," Euan said. "We have a whole year to plan what activities we want to do at the next one, though I have a feeling once word gets out, there will be a great deal more people next year."

"I'm glad ye all enjoyed it so much. I think we can definitely start planning for it if everyone is on board."

"Count me in," Grace said.

"Aye, me as well," Euan said.

"Me!" Vanessa chirped.

"Looks like ye have a consensus, Son," Malcolm said, laughing. "Ye can count me in as well, of course."

"Someone has to feed an army," Aileen said as a way of volunteering her services, which made everyone laugh.

"Soooo … Vanessa," Mal said, a sly smile on his face. "Ye seemed awfully cozy with Drew Fraser last night."

Malcolm raised an eyebrow. "Yer friend from Inverness, Mal?"

"Aye, the very same. He did nae leave her side after the shinty match."

"He's very easy to be cozy with," Vanessa retorted.

"Easy on some other things, too," Grace muttered into her teacup.

"Excuse ye?" Euan said, watching Grace's lips curve into a playful smile.

"You're totally right, Gracie. Thanks for the introduction, Euan. He's a really nice guy."

"Aye, I thought so," Euan said. "Yer welcome."

"Drew is a really good lad," Mal said. "I've known him most of my life, and he's one of the best doctors at Raigmore."

"Is he?" Vanessa asked.

"Aye, but he would nae be one to brag about it and never has been. Humble as they come. But he really is one of the best, and if I were unfortunate enough to need emergency care, he'd be the one I'd want to have working on me. I know a couple of nurses there, and they both told me that everyone respects him, including the other doctors. There are sometimes squabbles amongst them as to who gets to work with him."

"Squabbles?"

"They all want the shift assignment, but there are only so many spots," Mal explained with a chuckle. "And it is nae because he's a pretty face. He treats the staff well, and they told me that everyone thinks he'll be running the department eventually."

"Wow. Well, we're having dinner next week," she said, her smile bright.

"How wonderful for ye, lass!" Aileen said.

"I think that's fantastic, Van," Grace said with a smile. "Where are you going?"

"Don't know yet. He said he'd check his schedule just to make sure they didn't have him scheduled for anything crazy since he's working days this week, which would allow us to go to dinner instead of breakfast."

"I think a breakfast date would be awesome," Grace said. "A great compromise when the scheduling is weird."

"When we are working, ye and I have most of our meetings late at night or early in the morning," Euan said. "Though it is nae quite the same."

"True, but not always. If we're working apart, there isn't any of that."

"Dinnae remind me," he groused, which made Grace laugh.

"I meant to ask you, Euan; did you really misplace a shirt?" Vanessa asked.

"No," Euan said, laughing. "It was just an excuse to leave the pair of ye alone to talk."

"I thought so. Also, an excuse to get Grace alone."

"Also that, aye. Speaking of which, I would very much

like to return to bed with her if no one minds because I am exhausted."

"Aww, love," Grace said, reaching out and running her fingers through his hair. "You worked hard this weekend, so I'm not surprised."

Euan caught her hand and kissed the inside of her wrist. "Aye, and last night was a bit draining as well, if I am honest. Come to bed?"

"Of course. I'm actually pretty tired myself."

"Off with the pair of ye," Mal said. "We have it all under control here."

"Thank ye, Mal," Euan said, standing up and taking Grace's hand when she joined him.

They walked upstairs together, kicking off their slippers and then climbing back into bed. They hadn't changed out of their pajamas for breakfast, making returning to bed simple. Euan drew Grace back against him, feeling her snuggle into him before she sighed and kissed his arm. It seemed as though, within a moment, she was asleep again. The safety she found in his arms always warmed his heart, and it pleased him that he was able to be that peace and safety for her. For so long she'd found only pain from the touch of men, but he'd banished that, and it was his goal to never let her experience such a thing again. Taking in the soft scent of her, he closed his eyes and joined her in sleep.

***

Over the next two weeks, life returned to their version of normal. Vanessa went on a few dates with Drew with no signs of it stopping, and it pleased everyone to see her so happy. Euan and Grace took their leisure time, slept late and, more than once, hadn't gotten up at all. Instead, they'd spent it in bed, reading, watching television or movies, and napping.

On the first day of September, as the four of them sat around the table having breakfast, Mal and Vanessa watched both Grace and Euan pause. Euan stopped before he could take a bite of the toast in his hand, and Grace had her coffee cup close to her lips before they looked at each other and smiled.

"Looks like our holiday is over," Euan said. "Are ye ready to get back to work, lass?"

"Grace! Euan! I am here!" they all heard Caia call out.

Mal and Vanessa looked at each other.

Grace nodded and set her cup down. "More than. Let's do it."

"Queens and Spies,"
Book 5 of the Watchers Series
coming in May 2022!

ABOUT THE AUTHOR

A California native, Eilidh Miller, FSAScot, has a BA in English and studied history as an undeclared minor to better inform her literature studies. A Fellow with the Society of Antiquaries of Scotland, Eilidh is very active within Southern California's Scottish community, spending a great deal of time volunteering with the charitable organization St. Andrew's Society of Los Angeles.

A long-time historical reenactor, Eilidh loves research and educating the general public about historical events, as well as entertaining them with tidbits no one would believe if they weren't documented. She extends this same energy to her work, extensively researching the historical periods she includes in her writing to ensure that the information she presents is correct, even going so far as to travel internationally to access archives and scout locations.

She resides in Southern California with her husband, daughter, and her feisty Shiba Inu sidekick.

You can keep up with Eilidh on Twitter, Instagram, Tik-Tok, or her website www.eilidhmiller.com. You can also join her reader group on Facebook, Eilidh Miller's Reading Lodge, to keep up to date on the next release, get exclusive content, teasers, and enter contests!

OTHER BOOKS BY THE AUTHOR

THE WATCHERS
THE WATCHERS SERIES: BOOK 1

ENEMIES OF THE MIND
THE WATCHERS SERIES: BOOK 2

ECHOES OF THE RISING
THE WATCHERS SERIES: BOOK 3

CAPTAIN MERRICK

HER FATHER'S DAUGHTER

www.ingramcontent.com/pod-product-compliance
Lightning Source LLC
Chambersburg PA
CBHW060920190726

48286CB00002B/571